SEARCHING FOR EDGAR'S FIVE DANCERS

EFREN O'BRIEN

ISBN 978-1-54396-727-2
ISBN eBook 978-1-54396-728-9

To Cindy; thanks for putting up with me, telling me the truth and always being there for me. I love you...you're the best.

PROLOGUE

In April of 1937 Germany's Reichsminister of Propaganda Joseph Goebbels and Hildebrand Gurlitt, a well-known art dealer in Nazi Germany, stared at one another across the desk in Goebbels' office at the Reich Chancelry in Berlin. Gurlitt had Jewish blood in his lineage, and otherwise would have been excluded from any significant role in Germany's fascist government, but Goebbels knew the Nazi regime needed his expertise. The regime needed help smuggling art they had stolen from Jews, and artwork they had designated "Degenerate Art," out of Germany. As an art dealer, Gurlitt had contacts he had fostered all over the world that could be beneficial to Nazi Germany.

"Herr Gurlitt, please have a seat," said Goebbels in German. He continued, "Can I offer you Cognac or a cigarette?"

"The honor is mine to speak with you today, Reichsminister. No, thank you, but I am eager to learn how I may be of service to you, our Fuhrer, and our Fatherland," replied Gurlitt.

"As you know, Herr Gurlitt, at the present time our nation is contaminated with art that does not reflect the pure values of our culture. I am ashamed to say that some of this art has been created by disloyal Germans themselves. These include our own countrymen, such as Max Liebermann, Otto Dix, and Heinz Kirchner. Not to worry though, Herr Gurlitt, I will take care of these disloyal artists personally. There are also foreign artists who are despicable. These are Bolsheviks like Pablo Picasso, Chagall, Toulouse-Lautrec, Wassily Kandinsky, and that French idiot Renoir. Their art is an insult to Germany and flies in the face of our Fuhrer's message of wholesomeness, simplicity, loyalty, and decency. We must first remove these blights from our museums and other venues that house them. We must then rid ourselves in Germany of such filth wherever it may be on display, forever! I need your help in purifying our art and our culture. And, as repugnant as the thought is to me…there are collectors in other parts of the world that will pay for these godforsaken paintings and sculptures. You will represent the Reich as an art dealer officially authorized to travel to Paris, New York, Switzerland, or anywhere else necessary to sell these disgusting works of art. You will be an agent acting on behalf of our government and nation."

"I offer my services to the Reich in any way possible to achieve our national objectives, Minister Goebbels," said Gurlitt.

"Good, that is wonderful news, then you will be one of four art dealers who will assist in collecting this unwanted offensive art, and you will sell this art internationally. And we are always grateful, Herr Gurlitt, to our most loyal citizens who contribute to the national cause. So don't worry, you will receive a liberal stipend in the form of a commission from every sale you make. This obscene and perverse art must be expunged from Germany for good!" proclaimed Goebbels. "We are going to sponsor an exhibit here in Berlin later on this year, exposing many of these loathsome paintings and sculptures. I expect there to be many foreign buyers at this exhibit, and with your help we can start to cleanse Germany of these disgusting blights from our walls, minds, and hearts. "Do you know Herr Curt Valentin?"

"I have heard of Curt Valentin before, Reichsminister, but I've never met him," replied Gurlitt.

"Well, he may be of considerable assistance to you. He has supposedly opened an art gallery in New York and a large number of this degenerate art has found its way to his gallery there," said Goebbels. "He will be a good point of contact and perhaps even a buyer. I want this art out of Germany, but I think the Reich should be paid for it just the same. You may have to travel to New York, but contact Curt Valentin and try to work with his contacts in the art world. Get whatever money you can for this obscene work mistakenly referred to as art. Wassily Kandinsky! Can any educated German really appreciate that Russian Bolshevik's work? To expect a self respecting citizen of our nation to even glance at those disgusting paintings is an insult to our culture!"

The exhibit opened in Munich, Germany, on July 19, 1937. It was named, "The Degenerate Art Exhibition" and was moved to other German cities after display in Munich until November 30, 1937. The exhibit was not meant to be taken seriously, but was a satirical spoof the Nazi's conjured up that mocked modern art and the world's great artists who created it. Over 650 works of art were displayed in a manner meant to degrade and slander the artwork and humiliate the artists who were the creators. Goebbels was directly involved in choosing the stolen artwork that he claimed, "insult German feeling, or destroy or confuse natural form or simply reveal an absence of adequate manual and artistic skill." Despite the negative press, the Nazi government's attempt to condemn and minimize the importance of this artwork backfired. Over one million visitors attended the exhibition within the first six weeks of its opening. Over four million German citizens would attend "The Degenerate Art Exhibition" before it finally closed several months later.

But this was just the beginning. Before their purge was over, the Nazis would confiscate hundreds of thousands of paintings and other works of art from all over Europe. A small amount of the art confiscated was destroyed, but most of it was looted and sold for profit or simply hidden away. Several of the higher-ranking Nazis such as Joachim von Ribbentrop and Reichsmarschall Hermann Goering actually diverted millions of dollars' worth of the looted art to their own collections, hiding the artwork in various mines and other hidden locations throughout the war. The artists whose works were targeted suffered sanctions ranging from being fired from their teaching posts at universities, to being forbidden to ever create art again. Several well-known artists such as Ernst Ludwig Kirchner were so depressed after being forbidden to create art during the time of the Nazis, they committed suicide.

While in the late 1930s Europe was experiencing prelude to war and an assault on creative thought and expression, America was coming out of a tremendous Depression. Things though were not as repressive politically in America. Nearly a year later, in May 1938, the American painters Emil Bisttram, Agnes Pelton, and Raymond Jonson sat on the patio of Bisttram's casita-style home in Taos, New Mexico, discussing their artwork. Taos was a small pueblo town in the northern Jemez Mountains of New Mexico with small adobe buildings and homes. The town was part of the Taos Indian Pueblo, and had a pronounced Spanish influence as well, as the Spanish and Pueblo Indians had occupied and lived there for centuries; though not always peacefully. Taos was an artists' hangout, like Santa Fe, only smaller and about 70 miles to the north. The three painters gathered, each holding a favorite drink, as they stared at the New Mexico sunset with its naturally mixed shades of purple, red, and orange. It was a Thursday in May, and a slight breeze slowly swayed the bushes and trees. "These sunsets have made New Mexico famous.…I should paint this," said Bisttram. "You won't find a more peaceful and beautiful setting than this."

Agnes Pelton then said, "But that's not what our group is about, Emil. We've discussed this many times. We're going to do something different. We're like the Impressionists and Expressionists of the last century who went against the convention of the Academie des Beaux-Arts in Paris, and went on to modernize art. It is abstract imagery, thought, and interpretation we're interested in," she said.

"I'm not sure the public's ready for what we have in mind," said Jonson. "I mean…how far do we want to take the abstract themes in our painting?" he said.

"As far as we dare to, Raymond. Our whole purpose is to encourage spiritual discovery through the abstract. Every individual will interpret and discovers their own spirituality—not shown them or preached to them. We will follow the works of Wassily Kandinsky, and Transcendental Philosophy," said Pelton.

"When do we begin?" said Bisttram.

"Oh, we'll have opportunity soon," said Jonson. "First we need to create our charter," he said.

"Our charter, what do you mean?" asked Pelton.

"Well, for example, what are we going to call this group of progressive artists…? The 'Gang of Seven' is taken already," he said.

"What should we call ourselves?"

"How about, 'The Taos Painters,'" said Pelton. "We've all come from the East Coast and migrated to the West for different reasons," she said. "This name shows we're Western artists now."

"Yeah, that's true," said Bisttram, "but it doesn't say any more about us than that. What will make us stand out…why will we be different? Will we be like other Western artists who paint nature scenes, animals, mountains, and pueblos?"

"We're going to follow the Transcendental teachings and philosophy. Kandinsky and Blavatsky will be our role models," said Jonson. "We're going to focus on the abstract, but attempt to relate it to the real world. How about naming our group 'The Transcendentalist Group of Western Artists'?"

"Too complicated and too long," replied Pelton. "How about, 'The Transcendental Artist Group'? Or even better yet…'The Transcendental Painting Group'? We could even use the initials, TPG."

"Now that has a great ring to it," said Bisttram.

"Actually that does sound interesting," said Pelton.

"I still say right now the public's not ready for such abstract and conceptual art," said Jonson. "We've got war as a real possibility in Europe… and we've got Communists and anti-Semites in this country. Do you know we wouldn't even be able to paint this way in Germany right now? They've declared a moratorium and have restrictions on any type of modern art. They refer to it as '*Entartete Kunst,*' or Degenerate Art. They recently publicly burned over 5,000 paintings, some of them from well-established artists. It's real fascist stuff! We would most likely be jailed over there for even meeting and discussing this type of art. In America we're just coming out of our worst Depression ever, and there's a real possibility this country could be at war in a very short time. Who will appreciate and support this type of artwork here?"

Agnes Pelton then spoke. "As artists, we paint and create what we feel and where our imaginations take us. We can't base our work on who might or might not appreciate it! We also can't base our work on world events happening at any particular time. There has always been appreciation for our work before, and there will be in the future. There are several large exhibits I know we can show at next year including the World's Fair in New York," she said.

"Ask yourselves what the Nazis fear the most?" said Bisttram. "The imagination and free thinking is what scares them more than anything…. Their entire society is built on blind obedience to the propaganda, and conforming to their skewed philosophy. The way a select few view history, art, morality, political thought, and current events…and everyone gets in line and follows, or else. Abstract art and modern art require use of the imagination and critical thinking. That's why this art is being collected and destroyed over there. It's a real threat to them. The last thing they want to do is encourage free thinking."

CHAPTER 1

"Boom!" was the sound of the gavel the auctioneer smashed against his podium in the elegant room at the Grand Hotel National, in Lucerne, Switzerland. It was late June of 1939 and Hildebrand Gurlitt and the other Nazi art dealers were trying to sell the "Entartete Kunst" (Degenerate Art) that Goebbels had identified. Works from Pablo Picasso, Otto Dix, Lautrec, Matisse, Kirchner, Cezanne, Gauguin, Chagall, Van Gogh...and many more. There were hundreds of paintings for sale at this auction.

"This fine painting is sold to the gentleman in the third row!!" the auctioneer yelled. There was a mixture of the usual wealthy buyers who frequented these high-priced auctions in European circles...and a good number of whom appeared to be less sophisticated attendees. All that really mattered on this day was that the prospective buyers had money to spend, and they could be induced to buy artwork that would support the Third Reich.

The Nazis thought it an important enough occasion to hire the famous Theodor Fischer as auctioneer for this Degenerate Art Auction...."What a rare and incredible piece for the discriminating collector! Ladies and Gentlemen, the bidding for this one-of-a-kind self-portrait of Vincent van Gogh—one of the great Expressionist artists recognized today—will begin at $20,000 Swiss Francs." Fischer's assistant held up the self-portrait of Van

Gogh for the assembled crowd. Who will place the first bid on this beautiful and unique Expressionist's self-portrait?" said Fischer.

And the prospective buyers were there ready to purchase. The City of Liege, Belgium, sent a delegation on behalf of the city with five million Belgian Francs. The delegation spent this money on nine paintings which still hang in their municipal buildings to this day on display. Such were the kind of purchases made at the Lucerne auction—enriching the Nazi coffers by millions prior to the start of World War II only several months later.

This was the art that Adolf Hitler and Joseph Goebbels had identified as "lacking true artistic merit," and as "impure." The Nazis had been confiscating art that was too abstract and "modern" for their taste and propaganda since the 1920s. Much of this artwork was stolen from Jews in Poland, France, Holland, and other Nazi-occupied countries from all over Europe. The overall objective was to move the art away from Germany while making profits for the Nazi regime. In this international game of big money art dealing, however, many hands would reach into the "profit cookie jar" long before any money ever made it back home. And sadly, the majority of original Jewish owners would never live to see their prized works of art ever again.

When it began in 1937, the "Degenerate Art Exhibit" was held in the Institute of Archeology building in Munich. At that time, about 650 works of modern art were displayed that the Nazis claimed were degenerate, products of Jews, Communists, and Bolsheviks and unfit for the German general population. Adolf Ziegler, head of the Reich Chamber of Culture and Hitler's favorite artist, commented on the exhibition:

> Our patience with all those who have not been able to fall in
> line is at an end.... What you are seeing here are the crippled

products of madness, impertinence, and lack of talent...I
would need several freight trains to clear our galleries of this
rubbish... This will happen soon.

Hitler's restrictions on permissible and impermissible art nearly dec-
imated all artistic creativity in Germany from 1933 to 1945. Hitler's atti-
tudes towards art were consistent with fascist propaganda itself: "Firmly
believing that culture is the cornerstone of any enduring society." Hitler
recognized that art must play a major role in building the German nation
based on his ideals. He articulated the goals of what he considered true
German art: "It must develop from the collective soul of the people and
express its identity; it must be national, not international; it must be com-
prehensive to the people; it must not be a passing fad, but strive to be eter-
nal; it must be positive, not critical of society; it must be elevating, and
represent the good, the beautiful, and the healthy."

CHAPTER II

"Herr Diebner and Herr Heisenberg, what do you have that I can take to the Fuhrer?" said Erich Schumann in August 1939. Schumann was a General in the Wehrmacht and was appointed to lead the German Nuclear Research program by Hitler himself. Kurt Diebner was in charge of *Kernforschungsrat* (Nuclear Research Council) and was a military officer. Werner Heisenberg was a top scientist in Germany's nuclear development and a Nobel Prize winner in Physics in 1932. Heisenberg was credited for developing the theory for quantum mechanics, and now in 1939, he led the *Uranverein,* or Uranium Club for Germany.

Both men stared at Schumann. "We are making progress, Herr General," Heisenberg finally said.

"You are making progress on the blackboard, Werner. Our Fuhrer and our nation expect results…tangible results. Something we can see or measure soon!" said Schumann.

"Yes, Herr General. Right now our research is theoretical, but in time—"

Schumann interrupted him. " In time…" Schumann paused. "That's the problem, Werner, we don't have much time. And from our reports, the English and Americans have begun their research programs in this area," said Schumann. "We need results, Professor. I can't stand before the Fuhrer month after month reporting that we're continuing to work on theory. He'll cut off funding of your research altogether! I believe that this research is essential to our success, but the Fuhrer is a practical man and interested in what he can see. Right now we are winning the war. Our armies are marching through our enemies like a knife through butter. So with the Army having so much success, regular and conventional weapons are proving to be all we need to achieve our goals. There doesn't appear to be a reason right now to spend money on research and development of this new theory that could lead to an imagined superweapon. So unless we can show something…I'm afraid our funding will be eliminated."

"We have made progress, Herr General. There are several small obstacles we must overcome. Without going into much detail, my research team believes the source of incredible bursts of energy lies in the development of enriched uranium or even plutonium. For this, it will be necessary to build a sizeable reactor to house these nuclear explosions. And as you know, these reactions must be controlled as we perform our research. This is where the water from Norway comes in. We use the heavy water in our reactors to modify and even slow the fission reactions down. If we didn't have use of the heavy water, these reactions would be out of our control. But if we learn how to harness this massive power, we will someday be able to provide cheap energy in many forms for our people and cities," replied Heisenberg.

"May I remind you, Professor, that it is the Ministry of War that is supporting your research!"

"Yes, I know, Herr General. If we can break through with our research, the potential for tremendous unleashed amounts of energy will have no bounds. There would be no challenge to the Reich's power and dominance then," said Heisenberg.

"Werner, we have faith in you and your colleagues and therefore will deliver you the water from Norway you have requested from the Norsk Hydro plant in Vemork. We may also be able to aid your research in other ways," said Schumann. "So we will meet every three weeks, here at my office from now on, Professor…and you will provide me with specific updates on your progress in practical terms I can explain to the Fuhrer. I must be able to convince him that your research is not just theory and years away from development—that your research will result in the kind of power the military and the Reich can use!"

"Herr General, we are so grateful to you and our Fuhrer for your continued support, and let me say again that my team and I are close to a breakthrough in this science, which will provide a magnitude of unharnessed energy never before even imagined in this world."

"Werner, you have made Germany so proud of you before with your other scientific achievements. We are counting on you now for another great breakthrough and discovery. Do not let us down…please!"

Also in August 1939, another physicist helped set into motion the events to develop and use theoretical physics to create a superweapon… an atomic bomb. Dr. Albert Einstein, the Jewish scientist who had defected from Germany, wrote a letter to President Franklin D. Roosevelt warning the President of the incredible potential power of enriched uranium. Einstein also warned President Roosevelt that Nazi Germany was aggressively moving to research and develop its atomic program. Einstein's letter convinced Roosevelt of formally declaring America's intentions of developing atomic energy in October of 1941…two months before the Japanese attack on Pearl Harbor and America's entry into World War II.

CHAPTER III

It was a warm and sunny morning when Edmond and Julia Ballon from Toulouse, France, woke up in March 1941 to the pounding on their front door. Edmond Ballon, head of the family, was a Jewish doctor who had lived his entire life there. He had amassed money from his medical practice and investing in the shipping industry. He was a respected doctor and his family was well-known in the local community. "Monsieur Ballon, open up now!" yelled the ranking French policeman.

The Ballon family had also acquired a significant art collection. They had paintings from Renoir, Monet, Chagall, and Gauguin. They were French-Jews, and the entire family had to register with the prefect of police and obtain special documents and new passports after the Nazis invaded in July of 1940. Since the Nazis had invaded, Ballon and his family were restricted step by step, from living their normal lives and being part of the citizenry of France. This was due to a series of ordinances proclaimed by the Germans and Vichy French. First, the Ballon's had to turn over their radios, and then their telephones were disconnected. They were forbidden from patronizing local French businesses and entertainment venues. This included going to certain movie houses, libraries, theatres, and public swimming pools. Then came the ordinance that forbade them to move from one residence to another. After that came curfews that restricted them to their homes during specific times of the day and night.

When Ballon opened the door that day, he saw eight policemen staring at him...several had their guns drawn. "Monsieur Ballon," stated the tall Frenchman, "I have a warrant signed by our Prefect to search your house for illegal material. Stand aside, please, and allow us in."

Ballon had no choice but to comply. These unannounced searches of Jewish families were becoming more and more frequent. And most of the time valuable property of the party being searched was confiscated, eventually ending up with the Germans. Many of France's Jewish population had fled prior to the German invasion in the summer of 1940. Ballon's children had been smuggled out of France with fake passports with their uncle to Canada only weeks before—but Ballon and his wife remained in the hopes of keeping their house and belongings intact through the German occupation.

Unfortunately, Edmond Ballon would find out that he and his wife had made a big mistake. He had heard rumors about the harsh and unfair treatment of Jews in Poland since September 1939, but he didn't believe the same could happen in France. After all, he was well known and was a respected doctor. He had owned property here for many years.

The French police and Germans scoured his residence, which was his father's and one of the nicest examples of red brick classic Toulouse architecture in the village. They caught him off guard. When they were done, they loaded up several boxes of items from his home, including two paintings by the French painter Marc Chagall, that he had displayed. Anything in his home was ripe for the taking. "Monsieur Ballon, thank you for your cooperation," said the policeman in charge. "Please be advised that we will be conducting a complete census of all citizens in the near future. You will be advised when to have all family members present here at your home for the census count. Obviously, this means that neither you nor any family members may leave the local area without express permission from the prefect office."

There was little civility or emotion shown at all by the police in this visit except at the end. The tall lead policeman displayed a slight show of guilt as he couldn't look Ballon in the eye, and instead diverted his look down while saying, "Thank you for your cooperation, Monsieur." This was as his officers loaded their truck outside with the Ballon family artwork and other valuable property they had confiscated.

The Ballon family wasn't the only one to lose their belongings. Before it was all over, hundreds of thousands of works of some of the world's great artists would be stolen or sold off, never to be returned to the rightful owners. If the Nazis could hide or make the stolen art disappear, and if the owners of the art disappeared as well, then it might be possible to conceal that crimes were never committed against these people on such a massive scale in the first place.

CHAPTER IV

At 5:30 in the morning two months to the day after his home had first been raided, Edmond and Julia were awakened by the screeching of tires and shouting outside in the front courtyard. Next they heard yelling and pounding on their front door again. "Monsieur Ballon, your house is surrounded. By order of The Prefect of Police, I have a warrant for your arrest and that of your family," said the same tall French gendarme from two months before.

Ballon answered the front door. "Is your entire family at home now?" the policeman asked.

"No, my children have not yet returned from abroad," Ballon answered.

"You and your wife have thirty minutes to collect your personal belongings and report to the front of your residence. You may take the following items with you: the clothes you are wearing, one normal-sized suitcase and one suit for men and one dress for women. You must be able to lift and carry all items yourself, Monsieur," the gendarme said.

"Where are you taking us?" Ballon asked.

A German officer answered him. "Everything will be explained in the due course of time, Monsieur. Now please hurry, Monsieur and Madame, as we have a schedule to keep," said the well-groomed and impeccably uniformed German officer who spoke perfect French, even to the extent of using the local dialect.

Thirty minutes later the Ballons were ushered outside, leaving their front door wide open. Their house and its belongings would be searched and confiscated by the authorities. Eventually, a German SS officer and his family would end up living in Ballon's home.

Edmond and Julia Ballon were placed in the back of a German Army truck with a canopy. It was summertime and nearly one hundred degrees inside. Their luggage was thrown into another truck in the convoy. They were transported with the others to an internment camp near Toulouse. Saint-Sulpice-la-Pointe was a French internment camp that had been established several years earlier and had housed political prisoners, gypsies, Russian prisoners of war, and now in 1941, French Jews. This was a holding camp meant to house prisoners for a short period of time. For most of the Jewish detainees housed at Saint-Sulpice-la-Pointe, their eventual destination would be Auschwitz or Buchenwald.

From the Nazis' point of view, Edmond Ballon and his wife were doomed, as were the other Jews in France when the Germans occupied their country. Those who foresaw this tragedy and made efforts to get out before the Germans arrived may have been lucky enough to make it to a free country that would accept them, but that wasn't easy or guaranteed. From 1940 to 1945, most countries turned away Jewish refugees; including the United States of America. Many refugees who left by ocean liners could not find a safe harbor that would allow the ships to dock. Many refugees on large ships that could not dock or unload returned to where they had departed from in Nazi-occupied Europe. For these refugees, this meant immediate arrest, transport, and imprisonment in a concentration camp, and, in many cases, death.

For Edmond Ballon and his wife…the outcome would be different only because of Ballon's wealth and notoriety. The Ballon's were known to be well off financially. They had stashed plenty of jewelry and cash away before their arrest, and had smuggled some jewelry and cash with them into the camp. They therefore had a way to pay for better treatment at the camp and eventually a way out. They were still forced to wear the dirty, disease-infested prisoner black-and-white striped dungarees with the yellow star, and "Juis" plainly written inside; and they both were forced to work at the camp. But Ballon could buy and barter for extra food and privileges that more unfortunate Jewish victims couldn't buy. Eventually, Ballon bribed a camp official to arrange their escape from Saint-Sulpice-la-Pointe. A guard looked the other way, and Mr. and Mrs. Ballon jumped into the back of a laundry truck and stowed away as the truck rolled out of camp. Eventually they made their way to the coast and stowed away again on a ship to Lisbon. From there, they paid off another official and procured safe passage to New York where they were allowed to stay. This came only two weeks before they were scheduled for deportation to one of the notorious concentration camps in Poland, where in all likelihood they would have perished.

CHAPTER V

While in the early months of 1941 many people in Europe were coming to grips with the occupation of the Nazis, several thousand miles away and across an ocean Quinn Chase contemplated his static life at a bar in Albuquerque, New Mexico. It was a cold winter's night. Quinn slowly sipped his bourbon and soda. Quinn loved Old Forester Kentucky Bourbon, and was enjoying some that night. Quinn was 40 years of age, slightly overweight but still with a full head of sandy blond hair and light blue eyes. That night the jukebox was playing a Glenn Miller band tune as airmen from the nearby Kirtland Army Airfield laughed and slammed their mugs of beer on the table in an attempt to impress their dates. Quinn sat quietly at the bar and peered at his drink in the glass in front of him. He wasn't concerned with impressing anyone that evening. The ice in his glass shifted on its own and made a clinking noise. Quinn wasn't an alcoholic by definition…well, that depended on how the term *alcoholic* was defined. But in the winter and grey days of early 1941, drinking, smoking, and a monthly poker game occupied most of his attention. Work…well, work was just a place where Quinn would spend his days. He had learned to tolerate work. Once again he had been demoted by the Albuquerque Police Department. So his work had now become boring; a real chore. But he found solace at the bar.

Hell, no one at the department seemed to notice. As long as Quinn was there during normal hours, and didn't show signs of being intoxicated… everything was fine. He was a veteran police officer of over 14 years and a pretty good detective in his day. Quinn had even solved some serious crimes. He had reached the rank of lieutenant and was doing what he did best—solving crimes on the streets—only to find himself demoted back to sergeant and doing desk work after several accusations of excessive force by Quinn with suspects. Those accusations had never been proven. Nonetheless, it was obvious to Quinn he had progressed as far as he would ever go with the Albuquerque PD. Now as an administrative supervisor, he had a desk job handling citizen complaints. His daily workload normally consisted of minor thefts or property damage, complaints about barking dogs and other neighborhood disturbances.

The bar that Quinn frequented was appropriately named The 9:15. The bar got its name due to the train that left from the main Albuquerque station at 9:15 every Wednesday and Friday night for the three-day trip to Chicago, by way of Kansas City. Because the station was only a block away, The 9:15 was a welcome shelter for train travelers who didn't want to wait outside in the cold during winter months along the tracks. The bar provided a warm break for travelers in cold weather, so the Union-Pacific paid for the bar's sign outside and on the waiting platform of the train station. Quinn just looked forward to when he could leave work early and slip away to his retreat. At The 9:15, Quinn felt comfortable and was part of the scene. There was always good drink, and friendly conversation came most of the time. He was known by name, and always greeted with a smile. And in the overall scheme of things at that time in his life…that's all that mattered to Quinn.

The general attitude of the public at large in early 1941 was that America was headed for war. The Germans had ramped up their aggression…they had marched into Poland, Czechoslovakia, and Holland, and had annexed neighboring Austria without firing a shot. In the summer of 1940, within a two-week period they had attacked and conquered France, and inflicted heavy casualties on the British Expeditionary Force, while the British soldiers barely escaped from Dunkirk making it across the English Channel. The Japanese were showing aggression in parts of China, and in other parts of Southwest Asia. Their army was now over two million strong, and the Japanese were building a massive modern naval fleet.

It was obvious Nazi Germany wouldn't be satisfied with the status quo. Hitler seemed to be stirring the pot and always demanding more. In Central Europe, Adolf Hitler was an icon and a demagogue. Two hundred thousand cheering and starstruck Austrians in Vienna knocked barricades down and struggled with security police just to get a closer glimpse of their new Fuhrer as Hitler made a short speech and waved to the throngs of people in the city square from the balcony of a building in Vienna. The Austrians in attendance that day went crazy with enthusiasm. Hitler was more popular over there than any entertainer or public figure in America at the time. A million people lined the streets of Berlin and threw rose petals as his motorcade returned from Austria. They idolized and cheered for their Fuhrer like the Romans idolized Caesar. That was the way it was in early 1941.

So Quinn sat at the bar that night, sipped his drink and contemplated his mundane life at the Albuquerque Police Department. He couldn't help divert his attention from the loud conversation emanating from the third booth down. One soldier was becoming increasingly obnoxious in an argument with a young lady. The soldier was visibly upset. "You two-timin' hussy!" yelled the soldier as he stood up from his chair. "Find your own way home tonight…!"

The blond girl said nothing, obviously embarrassed, and just stared down. Quinn thought for a moment about intervening as a cop, but he was content on being by himself that evening. He didn't want to get involved. His days of jumping into other people's domestic disputes were over, unless things got completely out of hand. The soldier did an about-face and stormed out of the establishment, flinging the door open with such force that it swung repeatedly back and forth on its hinges. Everyone in the bar was silent. Quinn returned to his original purpose at The 9:15 that evening. He ordered another drink.

It was his third that hour…and the bourbon was goin' down smooth. About 20 minutes after the angry soldier left, the young blond woman got up and made a quiet exit out of the front as well. The Andrews Sisters were singing a lazy ballad on the jukebox as she walked out, and the whole place had a melancholy feel to it. Everyone was either engrossed with their partners or the drinks they consumed. The young woman was visibly upset, but Quinn knew there was nothing he could do at the time other than take note of the incident and feel a little sorry for her.

He stayed at the bar for another 15 minutes after the woman walked out. He didn't keep time, but it must have been about 8:20 when he finished his last one. He said goodnight to the staff behind the bar and put on his overcoat and Fedora in preparation to depart. As he stood up he became slightly unsteady on his feet. Such were the effects of six fairly strong drinks within a short amount of time. But Quinn had learned to handle his liquor…being husky, six feet in height, and weighing about 200 pounds. Quinn was an alcoholic who could mitigate the effects of liquor and reasonably function well. He composed himself, paid off his tab, and walked to the main door. The place was filling up now with train travelers and more soldiers from Kirtland Army Airfield and their dates. Quinn was beginning to feel the headache coming on. A good night's sleep would solve his immediate problems. He just had to get home and things would be alright.

What Quinn didn't plan on was what happened next. As he had experienced over the years, encounters leading to romance with the opposite sex for him were mostly random and unexpected. Quinn was shy and had given up on women for the time-being. And he had no way of knowing this, but—not only would the next few minutes be significant for him—he would remember this night for the rest of his life.

As he walked out of the bar, he saw the young blond woman from earlier with her back against the building wall not far from the bar's multicolored neon sign in green with red lettering that blinked "9:15" off and on. The woman, dressed in winter clothes and wearing a Betty Cloche hat, leaned against the wall, cigarette in hand. The cigarette smoke, highlighted by the pulsating light, curled and twisted upwards through the night like a slow-moving snake. The young lady's tears streamed down her face. She looked down the street, as if waiting for someone. Quinn had no choice but to pass by her on the way to his car, a 1937 black Packard "120" four-door sedan. The car was not a luxury auto for that time period, but it was in style and had a powerful eight-cylinder engine.

He stopped momentarily as he walked. The snow and ice crushed beneath his feet made a distinctive noise as he walked on the frozen sidewalk. This, along with a nearby auto's honking horn, added to the cacophony of Albuquerque's sounds on that cold night. Quinn lit a cigarette before proceeding. He felt inside what was about to happen…he felt it as he walked in the woman's direction.

"You alright, Ma'am?" Quinn asked.

"I'm okay…thanks," she replied.

Even though it was night, there was enough light out that Quinn could see she had large blue eyes. "Excuse me for intruding, but you don't seem okay," he said.

"I just had an argument with my boyfriend…"

"I know, I couldn't help overhearing that inside," said Quinn. "Do you need a ride somewhere?" he asked.

"A bus stops at eight fifty at the corner…I'm waiting for it," replied the woman.

"Where are you going?" asked Quinn.

"8th and University Avenue," replied the woman.

"I can drive you there…," said Quinn.

"Why would I want a ride from a total stranger? No, thank you!" she said.

"I've had alcohol tonight, but I'm fine to drive," Quinn replied. "I'm a cop with the Albuquerque PD," he said as he showed his badge. "You'll be safe."

The woman stared at him and paused for about 30 seconds before responding. "Alright, that's nice of you. Thank you…it's embarrassing standing here crying in public…people stare as they walk by," she said.

They turned to walk to Quinn's car. "You are okay to drive?" she asked.

"I'm okay," he responded. "What's your name?"

"Katrina Finebaum," she replied. "I'm German, but I've been in America for ten years. We moved here from the East Coast."

"Oh…," he replied. "Well, my name's Quinn Franklin Chase, and I've lived here in New Mexico pretty much my whole life. Call me Quinn please."

The trip to Katrina's flat was uneventful except that, after being told by Quinn she could smoke, she lit a cigarette and rolled the passenger window down. He tried to continue the conversation to get to know the young lady during the drive, but she seemed tense and remained silent for the most part. She still had occasional tears roll down her cheeks. Upon reaching the corner of 8th and University Avenue, the attractive blonde uttered a quick, "Thank You, that was so nice of you. I go to the 9:15 every now and then. Maybe I'll see you there sometime," she said as she jumped out of Quinn's car. Quinn watched her disappear into the adjoining brick building using a side entrance. *Damn, there goes a looker… Hope she'll be ok,* he thought to himself as he drove away.

CHAPTER VI

It was the first week of May, 1941. This year was proceeding just like any other. Katrina had not been seen at The 9:15 since Quinn had driven her home. And he had his work routine down at the police department. Quinn would come in late around 9:30 in the morning; see the status report of call and walk-in citizen complaints; and then forward those complaints to the sergeant on duty that day. The sergeant on duty would then farm the complaints out to beat officers or detectives for more in-depth, follow-up investigation. Quinn would leave about 4:30 in the afternoon every day. Several times during the week he'd go straight to the bar. He still carried his .32 caliber service revolver in its holster, but he saw no use for it. He couldn't see a reason why he'd ever need to remove the weapon from its holster again. This was his daily routine at the PD, and he figured he'd continue marking time at his boring job until he retired in a few years.

It was a Tuesday afternoon in early May, when Dan Sparks, a bald and serious looking detective, showed up in front of Quinn's desk. Quinn had worked with Sparks before on a homicide case several years ago. "Quinn, the Chief wants to see you. You got time now, or shall I tell him you'll speak with him later?" asked Sparks.

"You know what this is about, Dan?" asked Quinn.

"No, no idea. I was just told to let you know," said Sparks.

"Allright, I'll be right there," Quinn said.

Captain Brock Garrett's office was on the top floor of the three-story police department building in Albuquerque. It was a climb for a 40 year old who drank and smoked too much and wasn't in the best of shape. But Quinn huffed, puffed and lugged his way to the top floor. Quinn walked into the waiting room area and noticed the Chief's secretary was not at her desk. He then knocked on the door, the top half of which had the captain's name stenciled into glass. When Quinn knocked, he heard the voice of Chief Garrett. Brock Garrett seemed to always be laughing and smiling. *Hell,* thought Quinn, *maybe that's the secret for making captain—laugh and be jolly all the time!*

"Come on in, Quinn, and have a seat. Would you like some coffee or tea? I've got somethin' I need to discuss with you." Garrett was a tall, heavy-set man with a distinct crewcut who had been on the force for nearly 30 years. He wore his shoulder holster with his weapon displayed. Quinn had once idolized the captain, but he ceased being a role model when Garrett had busted Quinn down to sergeant two years ago. This was based on lead detective Daniel Reece's recommendation. It didn't take long after that before Quinn was sent to work in admin.

"Quinn, I've got to tell you…it has bothered me ever since I had to take you out of the detective division and move you downstairs. I didn't want to do it. I didn't think it was fair at that time, but my hands were tied. You solved some important crimes and did some great detective work."

"Thank you Chief, I really miss the live action on the streets and solving crimes," said Quinn. "That's where I belong and can do the department the most good. I never was meant to be a desk jockey."

"Well, I've got a job for you if you want it," said Garrett. "It isn't exactly street action, but it's a chance to redeem your reputation, in a manner of speaking. It's high profile, and …what I am going to tell you is top secret. Whether you take the job or not, you will sign a confidentiality agreement before you leave my office today. This is important, and I need someone I can trust," said Garrett.

Quinn gave Garrett his full attention.

"Here's what's going on, Quinn. I don't know how closely you've been paying attention or not, but this country's gearing up for war with Nazi Germany, and probably Japan, too. It probably won't happen for a year or two, but the way things are heading, it's inevitable—it's going to happen. There's secret research going on here in Albuquerque and another project rumored to be starting somewhere in northern New Mexico. I don't know a thing about it. But the military's bringing in scientists from foreign countries, so it's pretty important. The Army's flying in a scientist who's a German-Jew. We're asking you to keep him secluded and protected for two days and then hand him over to the Army. Then they'll bring him to one of their labs. Are you interested in playing police babysitter for a few days? Before you give me an answer, you might want to know why I'm asking you…and why the military isn't providing their own security for Professor Ariel Eisenbach."

"I'm asking you for two reasons. First, I can't afford to take one of my active detectives off the beat right now. But secondly…it's high profile, and I want to give you a crack at this one. The Army wants to sneak the professor in incognito, traveling as a civilian. They believe there are Nazi spies in the area and an attempt may be made on Eisenbach's life. The Nazi's are expelling Jews from Germany right and left, but Professor Eisenbach is too well known and valuable to their side.

"The decision has been made to fly him into the West Mesa Airport. He'll be in disguise, and you'll safeguard him till you hand him over to the Army. We think this will confuse the enemy. I need someone I can trust for this job, and someone I think will successfully keep the professor safe for a few days. I think that person is you, Quinn. What do you say?"

"Captain, I appreciate you selecting me, but there are others who would probably fight for this opportunity," replied Quinn. "Why me? I've been out of the loop for a while now."

"I've had my eye on you lately, and I think you deserve another chance… and I don't have any doubt that you can do the job. This is a good way for you to gain some recognition. Quite frankly, this shouldn't be much more than official babysitting that takes up one of your weekends. I wanted to give you first crack at it," said Garrett. "Success here might lead to your being considered for a detective slot again. Maybe even a promotion to lieutenant. But if you don't want it—"

"I'm happy to do it, but will I be by myself?" Quinn asked.

"No, we'll partner you up with someone we think you'll work well with, but you'll be the one in charge and responsible. I want you to get the credit on this one, big guy!" said Chief Garrett. "I want to see you as a detective again, Quinn."

"Well, thank you, sir…that's what I want more than anything too. Thanks for the opportunity,…I won't let you down."

CHAPTER VII

Two days later Quinn was summoned to Captain Garrett's office again. A red-haired Army Colonel was there in his dress greens with two other men when Quinn arrived.

"Quinn, come in, come on in…," said the police chief. "Colonel Hariman, this is Quinn Chase. He's an experienced detective, one of our best quite frankly. He'll protect the professor and deliver him safely on the designated date and time. He's going to partner up with Ethan Clark here… they're two of my best men and they'll get the job done."

"Nice to meet you, son," said the Army colonel as he extended his hand to Quinn. "We're counting on you to keep our new scientist out of the way and safe for a while. You're doing a great service to your country and government, whether you know it or not," said the Army colonel.

Quinn shook hands and nodded. "Thank you Sir," Quinn responded. "We'll make sure the professor arrives safely at the designated place and time."

"So here's the basic plan," said Colonel Hariman. "Professor Eisenbach will fly into West Mesa Airport on Saturday, May 31st, in the morning. He'll be in disguise, but you'll recognize him by the red scarf he'll be wearing. He'll also carry a white cloth bag in his left hand. Here's a picture of him clean-shaven," said Colonel Hariman as he handed Quinn a black and white photograph. It was of a short bald man who appeared to be about 50 years old.

"I'm told he has a beard and mustache now, and hair on his head," said Hariman. "He wears a tupee."

"He'll be expecting you, so he shouldn't be surprised when you approach, " said the police chief. "Take him to the Grand Marquee Hotel, make sure he doesn't venture out on his own and guard him. Keep him safe until the following Monday. You'll then bring him to the exchange point and hand him over to the military. Colonel Hariman will be there as well. You'll have a code phrase, which Eisenbach will respond to." He paused to chuckle. "This is big time spy stuff! What do you say, Quinn? And, it's a top-secret mission. Colonel Hariman looked over your service record and finds you suitable for the job. No one is to know about this, not even your own mother. Any mention of this to anyone will compromise your mission—and obviously would have extreme negative consequences for you, if you get what I'm saying. Clark, the same goes for you," Garrett said as he looked at Ethan Clark.

"With all due respect," said Quinn, "I'm still curious as to why the Army isn't just handling this on their own? Wouldn't he be more secure and safe with the military? Flying him into Kirtland Army Airfield and keeping him under military guard and on the base the entire time?" said Quinn.

"Believe it or not, we don't think he would be safer at Kirtland. We want a complete deception," said Colonel Hariman. "Nazi operatives are here in New Mexico, and we have reason to believe they have contacts on the base. They're trying like hell to find out every secret we have, and we've had trouble spotting and arresting them. Specifically, the secret stuff going on up north. They know Professor Eisenbach has defected, and so they're desperate to prevent him from helping our side. Even though Eisenbach is Jewish and the Germans were ready to expel him, his defection to the US is a real embarrassment for them. He'll be safer with you for a couple of days completely under cover until we can transport him up north," said the colonel. "They won't suspect him flying in on a civilian airplane, and if we can deceive them and throw them off…this will all go much more smoothly."

"Colonel, we'll pick him up and deliver him to you without a scratch," said Quinn.

CHAPTER VIII

The preparations were made ahead of time. The hotel room on the third floor was rented and paid for under a false name. For this operation both Quinn and Ethan were given fake IDs. The room was carefully chosen because it was in a semi-concealed part of the Grand Marquee Hotel and in a corner. It was close to a staircase where Quinn and Ethan could move the professor down and outside quickly if need be.

May 31 came, and was an unusually cold day with a cloudy sky in Albuquerque. There was a strong breeze in the morning. Quinn and Ethan Clark had accepted this mission, and were in the terminal watching as planes arrived and departed. A man who appeared to be around 50 years of age got off a four-engine, propeller-driven Boeing 307 Stratoliner at 10:35. He was a short man of average build wearing a tan overcoat and brown fedora. Around his neck and hanging down over the coat was a red scarf. The man had a beard. He carried a white cloth bag by the handle in his left hand. This was Ariel Eisenbach, Professor of Quantum Mechanics from the Friedrich-Wilhelm Universitat in Berlin, or at least Quinn assumed that's who it was. Quinn and Ethan waited until the man started walking to retrieve his baggage, and then the two detectives approached him.

"Hey buddy," said Quinn. "The Yankees will win the pennant this year. What do you say?"

The man looked at Quinn and responded. "The Tigers will win this year—not the Yankees!"

Quinn then whispered, "Professor Eisenbach?"

The man did not verbally reply but nodded quickly.

"I'm glad you're here, Sir...let's get your luggage and walk out to my car. We're both members of the Albuquerque Police Department," Quinn said as both he and Ethan quickly flashed their badges. "You're quite a popular man these days, Professor," said Quinn.

"That's not always such a good thing," said Eisenbach.

They collected Eisenbach's luggage and carried it out to Quinn's car. "Throw my luggage anywhere. There's nothing fragile in there," said the professor.

They all got into Quinn's 1937 black Packard sedan. It wasn't until they were inside Quinn's car that he formally introduced himself and his partner. "My name is Quinn Chase, and this is my partner, Ethan Clark."

The professor was seated in the back.

"We're both detectives on the force, sir."

"I forgot to let my daughter know I was coming here to Albuquerque. Will I be able to make a phone call sometime and let her know I'm here?" asked Eisenbach.

"Well, Professor, probably not for some time...this visit of yours is supposed to be secret. No one is supposed to know you're here right now. Those were my orders. At the soonest available time I will request that you be allowed to use the phone. But as for now and this weekend...I don't think so," said Quinn.

The three men loaded up and drove Quinn's Packard to the Grand Marquee Hotel, a five-story building in the center of the city where the top two floors had been converted to apartments. All was going well without a hitch. They arrived and checked into the room that had been reserved for them, one of the Marquee's larger rooms.

For the next two days the three men hid out in the hotel. Every now and then one of the police officers would leave the room briefly to smoke outside and surveil the hotel and surrounding area. Quinn had his whiskey bottle with him, pulled it out of his breast pocket to sneak a drink whenever he could without being noticed. Professor Eisenbach repeatedly asked to use the phone or smoke outside in the hotel's back parking lot. Quinn denied Eisenbach's request and explained time and again for security reasons the professor could not show his face outside. Quinn also ordered Eisenbach to stay away from the windows. Quinn knew that even allowing Eisenbach to speak on the phone for a moment to anyone was risky and might endanger all of their lives. And Quinn had his orders.

CHAPTER IX

The two days passed without anything out of the ordinary happening. Quinn was tired and slept most of the time in the adjoining room. Ethan, Quinn's partner for this mission, went out and brought food back for the three of them to eat. Quinn carefully concealed his bottle of bourbon at all times. It was Quinn's relief from stress as drinking had become an integral part of his life. Even still, he was careful when he took out the bottle for a quick nip. They left instructions at the front desk that they would forgo maid service, so there wasn't even a knock on the door while they were there. The phone didn't ring, and all was quiet over the weekend. So why did Quinn have an uneasy feeling? With all the effort put into this, things were going according to plan. But were things going too smoothly?

They had their instructions. They would leave the room Monday morning at 10:10. Quinn thought this was an odd time, but the idea was to not cause or draw attention to their behavior. The three men would drive Quinn's Packard over to a wide-open space with one hangar, which was used as a private airport (and several years later would actually be named Cutter-Car Airport) in southeast Albuquerque. Quinn had his driving route in an envelope, which he would open only moments before they left the hotel. The drive would take about 15 minutes. Everything appeared to proceed according to plan that Monday morning as they were ready to leave.

They quietly exited the room, loaded their luggage into the back of Quinn's car in the parking area behind the hotel, and prepared to leave in the Packard. There was nobody outside other than the occasional car passing by. There was little foot traffic on the street. Quinn took the driver's seat, Ethan Clark the passenger seat, and Professor Eisenbach sat in the back. Quinn pulled out from the parking area and turned the corner onto the adjoining street, Lomas Boulevard. None of them saw or heard the oncoming large truck approaching from their left a block or so away. The large white truck had no license plates.

The trio in Quinn's Packard approached the first intersection and came to a stop. It wasn't until Quinn moved into the intersection of Lomas and Central that he noticed out of the corner of his eye, the large white mass approaching from his left side. Quinn didn't even get the chance to turn his head…the Packard was struck directly on the driver's side by the large, quickly accelerating truck. The truck with no markings had reached 24 miles per hour upon impact. It hit the Packard with such force that it pushed Quinn's car through the intersection and compressed it against the streetlight on the far side. The initial impact caused all three men to strike their heads against glass or on some part of the metal interior of the vehicle. All three men were thrown from side to side in the car. Quinn smashed his forehead on the front dashboard, opening a large bloody gash. He also suffered a severe concussion. Most of Quinn's ribs were broken, and the impact snapped his collarbone.

All three men were unconscious and bleeding; unaware of each other's fate that day. Quinn was hunched over the steering wheel motionless, fading in and out of consciousness. He thought he heard the sound of voices, but he had lost a lot of blood and passed out again.

CHAPTER X

Hospital food has generally been pretty much the same the world over…it's always had nutritional value and has been filling, but is generally tasteless and devoid of appeal. Quinn had his opportunity to experience a fair amount of hospital food daily at Parkside General Hospital in Albuquerque. He was their guest for nearly two months as he remained in a coma for seven days, and rehabbed the remainder of his time there. When he woke up, he tried to speak but had trouble remembering how to form words into a sentence. "Ahh…," he moaned as he opened his eyes. "Wha…?" he barely muttered.

The attending nurse walked in and noticed Quinn slowly waking up. "You've been unconscious for a few days," she told him. "You still need a lot of rest and recovery. Do you remember anything that happened?" she asked him. When he didn't answer, she continued. "You were in a very bad car accident."

Quinn struggled, but finally found the words. "How long have I been here?"

"This will be your eighth day," she stated. "Don't try to get up…I'll get Dr. Reynolds. You still have a bad head injury."

"The others with me…what happened? The older man?" asked Quinn.

"I don't know," replied the nurse. "I'll try and find out what I can, but I don't know any details. I don't even know if the others involved are here. You have a significant amount of healing to do before you go anywhere," she stated.

Quinn tried to move his left leg, but the pain was excruciating. "Ahhh…!" he yelled out. He also became aware of the tubes from the intravenous drip and the catheter attached to him.

"Don't try and move now. You haven't had any physical activity for a full week…it will be painful for you to move at all for a while. Your rehabilitation will take time. You're going to have to be very patient," the nurse said.

So, he spent the next six weeks in rehabilitation and recovery at Parkside General Hospital. He couldn't walk for another two weeks, and when he did get out of bed he wasn't able to keep his balance. He fell down again and again. He couldn't speak coherently for another two weeks. Even when it was time for Quinn's discharge, he still had head bandages and needed to use a cane. He would need the use of a cane off and on for the next few years. Quinn's automobile, the 1937 Packard was completely demolished as a result of the accident.

He was told his partner for this mission Ethan Clark was alive but severely injured with a head injury. Clark had lost his spleen as a result of the accident. He was at the other large hospital, University Hospital in Albuquerque, in traction, and his recovery would be even longer than Quinn's. After asking several times, Quinn was finally told Professor Eisenbach died at the scene of the crash. Quinn wasn't given any other details except that the professor's daughter had come to Albuquerque to claim the body and no official statement was issued by any hospital or the police department regarding the professor. When Quinn pressed the hospital personnel for more information, he was told they had divulged all they knew about Professor Eisenbach.

Finally came the day when Quinn would be released. He had recovered enough to get around on his own. He still felt pain at times in his leg that had been partially shattered, and when he turned his head at all he felt pain running from his neck down his back. But with great effort it appeared that Quinn would be able to walk, talk, and eventually live a normal life without medical assistance.

The accident consumed his thoughts and attention. All he thought about day to day was getting out of the hospital so he could begin his own investigation into what happened on that tragic day…and discover who caused it. Once released from the hospital, he was placed on medical leave by the police department for another month to convalesce…so as long as he could get around, he would investigate. And amazingly, no one from the PD told him not to do so. He knew the only way he'd ever make it to the top floors would be through the use of an elevator. Would he ever resume his duties as a police officer again? At this point, that concern was the last thing on his mind. He was again told that Professor Eisenbach had died at the scene; that the driver of the truck had run away without being pursued or caught. The truck had no license plates and the police couldn't trace it. The incident appeared to have no explanation as no one claimed responsibility. Most concerning to Quinn was that no real investigation had been initiated by the department in over two months since the accident. It seemed as if the event had already been forgotten. Quinn was determined, however, to find out everything he could.

When he was released he could barely walk, and had no use of a car. Quinn was forced to take taxis everywhere for the time-being. The cab dropped him off at the Grand Marquee. It hurt him to walk ten feet, but to Quinn this pain was bearable. With the use of his cane he hobbled into the hotel lobby and quickly got into the elevator. He took it up to the fifth floor. Quinn struggled to shuffle out, and down the hallway. He began knocking on doors. The first door on the side overlooking the street opened, and an elderly man answered.

"Sir, I'm a detective with the Albuquerque Police Department," Quinn stated as he held his badge up for the man to inspect. "I'm sorry to interrupt your day, but a bad accident occurred outside several months ago and I'm investigating."

The man studied the badge intently, taking out his glasses from a shirt pocket.

Quinn said, "Can you provide me with any information? Do you remember what happened out front at that time? Were you here on the morning of Monday, June 2?" Quinn held his notebook in his left hand and pen at the ready in his right hand.

The elderly man told Quinn that he was having breakfast when he first heard the commotion of the crash outside. He stated when he looked out of his window, he didn't see anyone at first, but then a young man exited the cab of the truck and ran in the opposite direction down the street. "That's what first caught my attention…a guy got out and ran the other way. Then the people from downstairs in the hotel came running out," he said. "Mr. Garvin from 535—three doors down—he actually went down there right after to help. I saw him outside with the others, by the black car pressed up against the streetlight," the elderly man said. "It was a bad accident…there was glass and metal from the car all around. I went down later after the police came. At that time there wasn't much I could do to help at all. I just stood around," he said.

Quinn went to apartment 535 to speak to the owner. A man answered the door. He had greased black hair neatly combed back, appeared to be in his 40s, and was wearing gold-wire-rimmed glasses. Quinn presented his badge. "Please, sir, can I speak with you for a moment about the auto accident that took place about three months ago in front of the hotel?"

"What do you want to know?" asked Leland Garvin. "I was only there for a few minutes...the hotel clerks moved everyone back to the sidewalk from the street. "I could see I wouldn't be of any use, so I left and came back upstairs."

"What, and who, did you see?" asked Quinn.

"Well, I was up here when I heard the loud crash. The car's horn went off and sounded loud for ten minutes. I looked out the window. I saw a man get out of a large white truck. He sprinted in the opposite direction down Central," said Garvin.

"What do you remember about him?" asked Quinn.

"Not that much," said Garvin. "I remember he wore a dark knit cap... like a dockworker's cap, and he appeared to be young and agile from the way he jumped out of the truck and sprinted away down the street. He didn't hesitate for a second. He got out of that truck cab and made a run for it. His other clothes were dark colored. I couldn't see his face. I wish I could tell you more, but I wouldn't recognize that guy today if I passed him on the street. And Sergeant, I've been asking myself... what happened to the truck?"

"What do you mean?" asked Quinn.

"Well I looked out again about an hour later, and the truck had been removed. The three men in the car were unconscious, and I didn't get a good look at anybody in the car," Garvin stated. "The way that white truck was banged up…I just don't know how it was gone so soon after and I never heard a thing."

"I was one of those men in that smashed Packard sedan, Mr. Garvin," said Quinn.

"I apologize…I had no way of knowing…I wish you a full and complete recovery, Sergeant," said Garvin. "We did everything we could to contact the police and hospital and get an ambulance here as soon as possible," said Garvin.

"Is there anything else you can tell me…?" asked Quinn.

"No, like I said I wasn't there very long…and I had no authority to do much to help," said Garvin. "You should ask Velma Price if she remembers anything. She was at the scene right after me and stayed longer…I think she may have even talked to the police. She's four doors down the hallway. Number 543. Good luck to you Sergeant, on your recovery," said Garvin as he shook Quinn's hand. Garvin then began to shut his door.

Quinn then went to speak with Ms. Velma Price, further down the hallway. Ms. Price was a woman seemingly in her 40s, with a thin face, and brown hair tied behind her head in a bun. She also wore reading glasses. By all appearances she was a studious person…like a librarian. "I tried to help the injured men inside the car, but there wasn't much I could do," she said. "The driver and the man in the backseat were unconscious and bleeding from their wounds," she said. "The man in the front passenger seat appeared to be unconscious, but every now and again he would mumble something," she said.

"And what was it he said?" asked Quinn.

"I couldn't make his speech out," she replied. "He was bleeding badly too. It was a terrible accident. The black car was pressed up and against the lamppost on the corner down below by the white truck. I brought down two blankets and used them to cover the men in the driver's and front passenger seats, and I brought down some water and towels. That's about all I could do before others took over."

"How long did you stay at the scene?" asked Quinn.

"Oh, I was there for a good forty-five minutes, but things seemed to happen so quickly. I was there when the police and ambulance arrived," she said. "There is something else…before the police arrived, a man and woman showed up and pulled the injured man from the backseat, and moved him across to the other side of Lomas. Several people tried to stop them and told them to leave the man alone, but they brought the man out and across the street very quickly. It was the strangest thing. They just appeared out of nowhere. They laid him down on the sidewalk across the way, and then not long afterward they disappeared."

"Did you watch what transpired between the three of them?" asked Quinn.

"They must have helped him because the ambulance personnel were attending to him when I went back inside," she said.

"What did the woman look like?" asked Quinn.

"Well, she was tall…at least five feet nine inches, perhaps taller. Her head and neck were covered. She wore dark glasses," said Ms. Price. "But there was one thing…"

"What was that?" asked Quinn.

"She wore a grey and white checkered neck scarf. Looked like wool or cashmere. She caught the scarf on part of the car as she pulled the man out from the backseat. A small piece of her scarf tore off. I saw it after they left and picked it up off the ground. When they left, they took off so quickly. I've kept it just in case…let me get it for you Sergeant," said Ms. Price.

She opened up a small drawer on the top of her large desk, and she took out a small cloth bag. She handed the bag to Quinn. Inside was a soiled, torn piece of cloth 3 x 2 inches with some knitted wool strands on one side. It obviously came from a larger garment. And it looked to be the end of a scarf.

"Thanks so much," stated Quinn. "I'll take this for investigation. I may be back at a later time to ask some additional questions," he said.

"That's fine, Sergeant," she said. "I think I've told you everything…but if I remember something else, I'll make sure to write it down for you."

All in all…not a bad day at the Grand Marquee , Quinn thought to himself. *Hell, it's a start. I'll find the truth eventually.*

He made two more trips over to the hotel after that day to canvass the residents and staff, but didn't learn much new information. Everyone's story was about the same. Nobody spoke to or recognized the two strangers that had removed Eisenbach from the back of the car. Had Eisenbach been alive or dead at that point? Did the two strangers who showed up help keep Eisenbach alive, or did they finish the job and kill him? With the sketchy information Quinn had, it was impossible to tell. He had to fully find out what had happened, before he could ever begin to answer the real question…why?

But now, Quinn had to take care of himself. After more rest, therapy and exercises eventually he was allowed back at the PD on limited duty.

He returned to the police department in an administrative capacity in mid-September, and to his job at the citizen complaint desk. But that's not what Quinn wanted. Quinn wanted desperately to regain his status as detective. He thought about everything he and Ethan Clark had been through. In Quinn's mind, not only had they earned their spots on the force, but commendations for their sacrifice and an appropriate reward.

We should be treated like the celebrities of this department!

CHAPTER XI

Quinn had gone through rehab at the hospital and had returned to work and limited duty when during the first week of October he received word Captain Garrett wanted to see him again. He hadn't been up to the captain's office since his last briefing. This meeting would take place in a large conference room on the first floor due to Quinn's injuries.

"Well I'll be!…There's Quinn Chase!" said Garrett with his outstretched hand and a broad smile. "It's so damn good to see you!! Let me start by saying we're very proud of the sacrifice you and Ethan made on behalf of the department, and for our country, in safeguarding Professor Eisenbach. It's too bad it ended the way it did, Quinn…but from our internal investigation I'm overjoyed to report that no blame will ever be placed on you or Ethan. You performed just as you were trained and expected to. Everything you did was right. What happened was totally unexpected and a complete surprise. It was beyond your control."

"Who else knew we were there, Chief?" asked Quinn.

"What do you mean?" responded Garrett.

"Well, there had to be a leak somewhere for the other side to be waiting for us like that. They had inside information…I mean, we can't even trace the truck that hit us, right? It had to be the Germans," Quinn said.

"I know what you're saying," said Chief Garrett. "And while I promise you, Quinn, that we'll investigate this to the hilt, sometimes bad luck and ill fate plays a role in our lives. Bad things just happen sometimes despite our best efforts. What I'm trying to say, Quinn, is that I'm not sure this was anything other than a kid who by coincidence lost control while driving on Central Ave, and hit you with his truck. Then he panicked and ran away," said Garrett.

"Captain, you're not serious? You're joking right?" Quinn replied.

"I'm not kidding at all," said Garrett. "We may never know. But one thing's for certain—Eisenbach is gone and us wondering and talking about who drove the truck won't bring him back," Garrett said.

Quinn simply stared at the chief of police with disbelief. "Ethan Clark and I have just spent a significant time recovering from this accident…and I'll tell you, Captain, it has been a painful experience," said Quinn. "We both may need canes for the rest of our lives."

"Quinn, nobody appreciates you and your partner's efforts more than I do …on behalf of the entire department, we are grateful for your and Clark's sacrifice. You are two very brave and loyal men. You have served the department and your country in a selfless manner. But this brings us to another matter we must unfortunately discuss. That's the matter of your future and tenure here at the police department."

Quinn's brows furrowed and the muscles in his face tightened.

"You've been on medical leave and limited duty, Quinn, since you were released from the hospital," said Garrett. "Our regulations don't allow for any officer to perform limited duty for an indefinite period of time, even for injuries sustained for valorous and exemplary duty such as you performed. Ethan Clark is facing the same unfortunate circumstance," Garrett said.

Quinn continued to stare at the captain with a look of disbelief.

"Quinn, don't look at me that way…I want to put you back on the street as a detective, but even though you have the judgment and experience, you can't perform the physical requirements. It may be years before you'll be physically fit for duty" said the captain. "I'm afraid…despite everything you've done for us…you're going to have to appear before a review board and the end result might be that you're separated from the department on medical grounds. I am aware you're in a tough position too because you're not eligible for retirement yet," Garrett said.

Of course he was technically correct. Quinn had a little over 14 years with the Albuquerque Police Department to date and didn't meet the minimum time for retirement, which was 18 years. Could this really be happening…after everything he had done and sacrificed for the Albuquerque Police Department and his country? Yes, in fact, Quinn's future as a police detective was in jeopardy. It had been over four months since the accident, and Quinn was still hobbling around using a cane and occasionally crutches. He went to physical therapy twice a week, but it was conceivable that he would never walk without use of some kind of aid again.

During the third week of October, 1941, the medical review board met. Quinn sat by himself at a table facing the chief and five senior police officers. Garrett, as Police Chief sat in the middle. The police department's physician sat with the group as well. Despite a letter from his treating physician at Parkside Hospital and another from his physical therapist, which stated that Quinn was making excellent progress, no timeline or even an estimate for recovery was provided.

At the end of the hearing, Quinn sat looking at the group seated before him. He was told a decision as to his continued employment with the police department would be reached within one week. He was told that he would be notified by mail of the board's decision.

Quinn received his letter. The board concluded Quinn's "adequate recovery to resume full duties as an officer could not be predicted with any specificity." Although he was making progress with therapy and the statements from his doctor and therapist were encouraging, Quinn's physical injuries—specifically to his back, neck, and leg—"may be permanent injuries." The retention board therefore decided on a medical discharge from the police department. Quinn would receive hazardous duty compensation, some money for future medical needs, and severance pay, but he would not receive retirement pay or any other long-term benefit for his years of service.

CHAPTER XII

In the late fall of 1941, both Quinn and Ethan Clark faced the sad reality that their careers as police officers as part of the Albuquerque PD were over. They met up with one another on a Wednesday evening at The 9:15. It was a strange reunion. Both men had lost their livelihood and career after nearly 15 years on the force. They were the only ones who might empathize and relate to one another's plight after losing their badges. Maybe they had to meet to mark this moment in their lives.

Quinn was sitting at the bar in his usual chair, at the south end. The chair next to his was empty. The normal group of train travelers and a few soldiers had all the booths occupied. Ethan Clark hobbled in with his cane. "There you are, dammit! Good to see ya', buddy. What the hell you been doin' these days?" Clark asked as he extended his hand to Quinn and sat down.

"Same as you…tryin' to recover from the shock of all this. Tryin' to make some sense of it all," replied Quinn as they shook hands. "What'll ya' have, Ethan? I get credit for booze here, 'cause this is basically my second home these days," said Quinn.

"I like my vodka martinis," said Clark.

"Vodka martini, please!" Quinn said to the bartender.

"One minute I'm a valued detective on the force," Ethan said, shaking his head, "and the next thing I know my legs are strung up in a sling and I'm pissin' into a plastic bag in a hospital bed. Now I'm off the force and hobbling around with a cane!"

"I'm just like you, Ethan. I'll be usin' this cane for a while. I wonder constantly what the hell happened that day. Everything seemed to be going fine, and then out of the corner of my eye there's this huge thing comin' at us from the side," said Quinn.

"I don't know," replied Ethan. "Chief Garrett seems to think it was just a random accident, and the kid who was driving panicked and ran away."

Both Quinn and Ethan looked at one another and then laughed.

"Like hell it was just a random accident!" said Quinn. "You know I went back and spoke to a few of the residents in those apartments on the top two floors. Nobody I talked to actually saw the accident. And nobody seems to know exactly what happened, but all three people came down to the street afterwards. Apparently we were unconscious," said Quinn. "And it appears that Professor Eisenbach was still alive then when they came down to check on us. Apparently some man and woman showed up and moved him from my car to the sidewalk across the street! I need to follow up on that. Moving an injured man like that could have killed him right then and there," said Quinn.

"That's right," replied Ethan.

"I don't know about you, but I'm not gonna rest easy till I find out what happened that day," said Quinn.

"We put our lives on the line for the police department and the Army… and this is our reward?" asked Ethan with a sarcastic tone. "I had a lot of time in. Don't know what I'm gonna do next," Ethan said.

"I have no clue as to what I'll do," said Quinn.

"My cousin owns a garage in town. I used to repair cars in my early 20s before I became a cop," Ethan said.

"Yeah, there'll always be a need for mechanics. Hell, what need is there for two broken-down detectives who drink too much? I'm guessing not much need!" said Quinn.

With that pronouncement, both men took liberal drinks from their glasses and ordered two more. A Tommy Dorsey big band song played on the jukebox in the stark and simple bar of the early 1940s. The sound of clinking glass was heard as the bartender quickly cleaned up behind the bar.

"You ever thought about doing some investigative work, Quinn? Asked Ethan.

"Being a PI?" responded Quinn.

"We could partner up. Hell, we might do alright with our experience," said Ethan.

"No, I've never thought of becoming a PI," said Quinn. "To do any-thing like that, we'd need some serious cash. And that's one thing in my life that's in short supply at the moment."

"Well, I've been poor my whole life," said Ethan. "I've never been able to hold onto it even when I had it. Any money I ever made went to one of my family members sooner or later. Even when I ranked lieutenant on the force, most of the time I never had two nickels to rub together....It took me my whole life to save up a little money," he said.

The two men paused for a long drink.

Ethan started again. "Several years ago, I loaned my entire savings to my sister for her house. Her husband now owns a rubber factory that makes belts and tires for cars in town. He's starting to do well. In fact, he just got a contract with the Army. She owes me, and I can use the severance pay I received from the department," said Ethan. "I think I could put the money up," he said.

"So you're not just dreamin'? You're serious about this?" asked Quinn.

"When it comes to my money, Quinn, or what little I normally have, I'm always serious," Ethan said. "It would take us some time to get started and make a reputation for ourselves…but we've been doin' this now for over a decade or so. It's what we know and we're good at. Or at least we'll know in a short time whether we're any good at it. We'll be paid directly for our efforts," Ethan said. "I'm not sure I even want to be here in Albuquerque. We might do better in Santa Fe."

"What would we name the business?" asked Quinn.

We'll come up with something…maybe Clark and Chase Private Investigations," said Ethan. "I think my name should go first since I'll be puttin' up most of the cash…I hope that's not a big deal to you, Quinn. Well, how 'bout it?" Ethan said.

"It's a lot to think about, but I don't know what else I'm gonna do with myself. Maybe we can even help the police solve a few crimes up there," he said. "As PIs, what would we be investigating?" asked Quinn.

"We'd probably be running around snoopin' on cheating husbands or their wives most of the time. It might be dangerous, but it might also be fun and better yet, we can make some good money. And let's be honest here… that's something we both need. Right, buddy?"

CHAPTER XIII

The devastating attack on Pearl Harbor occurred on December 7, 1941. The United States declared war immediately and was now officially at war with both Japan and Germany. Things were changing quickly in America, and world events were transpiring to draw the United States fully into the Second World War at a sprinter's pace. But for Quinn and Ethan, despite the new national state of affairs, the winter of '41 and early '42 was when they were busy opening their office in a small adobe building on the outskirts of Santa Fe, New Mexico.

At one point in time the building had been a tortilla factory at the south end of town. There was a sizeable window in the front of the building, which was rare for the time, and it gave their office a look of importance. Other than that, it was a simple building on Cerillos Road.

In March of 1942, Clark and Chase Private Investigation Agency was born in Santa Fe, New Mexico. The name Cerillos was taken from an actual village located about 20 miles south of the Santa Fe Plaza, where in the late 1800s there were several gold and silver mines. Now Cerillos Road extended south from the Plaza, but after about one mile, it became a gravel and dirt road.

There were many dirt roads in the city and surrounding communities. The main mode of transportation in New Mexico at the time was by train, but the surrounding Sangre de Cristo mountains prevented a direct rail line into the city. The AT&SF line ran from Denver, Colorado, through Lamy (18 miles east of Santa Fe) to Albuquerque…and onto California. If one wanted to travel from Lamy into Santa Fe, as most train travelers did, it was necessary to hop aboard a short commuter train (called the "spur"), and enjoy a 40-minute ride over uneven ground, around many curves, and over arroyos before getting to the city itself.

In late March, one day Quinn decided to take a self-guided tour through his newly adopted town. He started walking north to explore. But soon he got tired and hailed a cab to continue his journey. He got a good view of the effects of the war on the people of New Mexico. Many family and small businesses were closed. The car lots (those few still in operation) had fewer cars displayed. Quinn noticed long lines extending out onto the street at the Goodwill and Salvation Army stores, both of which he passed as he rode in the cab. He also noticed more homeless people (commonly referred to as hobos at that time) scavenging through the junk yards on the south side of town. Many substances and food items were already being rationed, including steel and other metals, gasoline, butter, canned milk, and lard. Shortages and rationing of many necessities would be common-place among the population during the war years of the early 40s.

It took nearly 20 minutes from office on foot to reach the heart of the city. Quinn marveled at the adobe churches and structures mixed in the new Western-styled architecture aptly referred to as "territorial style architecture" of Santa Fe. The experience of walking through town was like taking a step back in time, but viewing through a decidedly modern lens. After all, there were automobiles on dirt and old cobblestone streets. There were hitching posts for horses outside of buildings—some still being used. The main Catholic Cathedral, the Cathedral of St. Francis of Assisi, was built and finished in 1885, and there was a statue of Santa Fe's first Archbishop originally from France—Jean Baptiste Lamy—in the front courtyard of the cathedral. Santa Fe had a completely different feel to it than Albuquerque…in Santa Fe, the generations of time intertwined and blended together. The past was given a space of reverence—a place at the head of the table. It could be seen in the architecture of the city's buildings and ancient roadways. That is why Santa Fe is where they decided to set up shop. They would soon find either success or failure here.

In 1942 Santa Fe still had a small-town atmosphere with many Hispanic families that had lived there for generations. Native American pueblos that had been there for hundreds of years surrounded Santa Fe and blended in as part of the culture. The city was developing its art society in the late 1930s and was becoming a destination for creatives due to its diverse population and the beauty of its mountains. Ever since the railroad came to town, Santa Fe had become a tourist destination, and a place of rehabilitation for tuberculosis patients. An influx of newcomers trickled into the old town and settled into its rhythms, or they moved on. Clark and Chase Private Investigations was one such newcomer, and they occupied the last building accessible by paved road on Cerillos. Traveling south from their building on Cerillos Road was all dirt, a path marked for centuries by locals coming into Santa Fe from the south with cart and oxen from the town of Cerillos and running parallel to the old Camino de Real Spanish highway. It was a start, and they had to start somewhere.

Ethan's brother-in-law bought them a metal sign to place above the entrance to the building. It all looked simple and plain…but it was a beginning, and it was their beginning. Would they be able to make a living here during wartime? Only time would tell.

The first few cases Quinn took on as a private detective were laughable. A local family who had chickens and sold eggs as a side business accused their neighbor of purposefully sending two dogs onto their land every night to attack and kill the chickens. The woman and owner of the henhouse had suffered the loss of eight chickens that had been killed over the last six weeks. Quinn ended up surveilling both homes over a two-week time period. He solved the mystery, but he had to spend the entire night one evening surveilling the henhouse. What he discovered was that it wasn't the neighbor's dogs, but a coyote that was sneaking onto the property through a break in the outer wire-mesh fence that gave access to the chickens. Quinn made hardly any money on that one, but was proud of himself that he had solved the case. He considered it a bonus that he was a factor in restoring neighborly relations.

The subject for Quinn's second case was the nearly ancient water distribution process of the Spanish canals in Santa Fe, known as acequias. These canals were built in the late 1700s or early 1800s and carried runoff snow water down to Santa Fe from the surrounding hills and mountains, but were in use all year long. There were four actively used acequias in 1942; and these canals serviced the water needs of many local farmers in the community and out into the adjacent towns for up to 20 miles.

There was a public water board and a Mayordomo that regulated the water flow and usage by farmers from the canals. Farmers could only draw from the water canals at set times, and they were limited in the amount of water they could use. The nickname given to the Mayordomo in Santa Fe was "Ditch Rider," but that didn't mean he wasn't a very powerful man.

One farmer in town accused his neighbor of diverting water away from his land and siphoning it off. So Quinn had to first inspect the canal to see if the acequia had been tampered with in some manner, and then find a vantage point where he could watch and see if any mischief took place with the water distribution and flow of water from the canal. What he discovered was that the offending farmer rigged his own sort of dam in the canal that would block water on occasion when it was his neighbor's time to irrigate with water from the acequia. The offending neighbor then pumped the water from the canal with a motorized siphon and hose he had built. It was a lot of work for a little water, but then again water was the lifeblood of the farming community. The farmer who was being shortchanged was losing produce and money, and his land was being harmed by the lack of water. Quinn was paid well for his work on this case, and the offending farmer was turned in and received a hefty fine for his malfeasance.

Quinn and Ethan worked on an insurance fraud case where two old warehouses had caught fire and burned to the ground. There was suspicion that they were intentionally set ablaze for the insurance money. Ethan discovered evidence where the fuse of a junction box had seemingly been tampered with to make it look like an electrical fire had taken place...but then discovered evidence of gasoline-soaked towels spread throughout both buildings. Ethan was also able to establish that the owners of both large buildings were related to one another, being distant cousins, and one of them had applied to the zoning commission to redesignate the property for commercial purposes in the hopes of building a large hotel there.

So Quinn and Ethan discovered there was work to be had in Santa Fe for two old former police detectives. Even though the pay wasn't great and the work wasn't exactly the kind the two had desired or had planned on, it seemed like Santa Fe and Clark and Chase Private Investigations fit together well enough. It was a beginning.

CHAPTER XIV

J. Robert Oppenheimer had just finished writing his last theorem of the day on the large blackboard for his Theoretical Physics class at the University of California, at Berkeley, in mid-January 1942 when he noticed two men wearing overcoats and Fedoras, reminiscent of the G-Men of the 1920s. The two strangers walked into his classroom and took up positions on each side of the door. In the 1920s and 30s, America's research into theoretical physics, including nuclear physics, was conducted at major universities. J. Robert Oppenheimer, a fairly young man at the time, was the head professor of theoretical physics at UC Berkeley.

Disregarding his outstanding academic achievements, Oppenheimer was an interesting man in other ways. He was very liberal with his political views and had many acquaintances and friends who were considered radical at that time. He had friends who were members of the Communist Party of America. Oppenheimer himself had attended meetings and had donated money to the Communist Party and what were considered other controversial causes. He was under investigation by the FBI and several other national security agencies several times in his life for his political associations. Despite his political leanings, Oppenheimer would be chosen to lead America's research into atomic energy in the early 1940's. He would be the chief research scientist of The Manhattan Project. While there were several more facilities in other parts of the country (Tennessee and Washington State), the main location for research and development of America's nuclear program was at Los Alamos, New Mexico.

In early 1941, months prior to the US entry into World War II, President Roosevelt signed an Executive Order establishing a national nuclear development program, and placing an Army officer, General Leslie Groves, in charge of the program. General Groves, in the Army Corps of Engineers, was not a physicist or scientist. Groves was the director for the Manhattan Project, and he needed a lead scientist he could coordinate with, a scientist he could work with to manage the effort at Los Alamos and get the job done. "The job," in this instance, was researching and creating the world's first atomic bomb. It was Groves in the end who chose J. Robert Oppenheimer to head up the research in New Mexico. And just by coincidence, Oppenheimer was Jewish.

"Professor, do you have the vision and drive I need to complete this job not only for America's war effort but for the sake of humanity?" asked Groves.

"I'm not completely sure exactly what the job is, General," said Oppenheimer. "I know the effort will be to create atomic energy for the war effort…but I'm not exactly sure what it will entail."

"Professor, we must have a way to end this war with finality. We cannot allow the Axis Powers to continue their war effort and capabilities in any form. Post wartime Japan and Germany cannot have the means to wage war. One problem we will face is if either Japan or Germany refuse to surrender. If we have a super-weapon such as an atomic bomb and are forced to use it to end the war, there may be many military and civilian casualties.

But it also may save millions of lives that would otherwise be lost as we attempt to conquer our fanatical enemies city by city," Groves continued.

"I need a leader who can manage the scientists, who will work on the project, keep them focused and moving forward towards solutions and the end result. So, here's what I expect you to do, pure and simple. Create a bomb for us," said Groves.

"But we don't even have a reactor where we can simulate an atomic reaction. We are literally starting from scratch, General. Most of this research is still theory, and I would have to be in charge of scientists far more accomplished academically and brilliant than myself," said Oppenheimer.

"I know you're the right man for the job," said Groves. "You've just gotta convince yourself of that, Professor. Our nation is counting on you!"

"We don't even know how a weapon as powerful as this would work in real time, General. First, it may be beyond our capability to ever construct such a bomb. Second, if we did, and it actually worked, we may not be able to control it. Such an uncontrolled reaction could literally destroy the world!" said Oppenheimer.

"Listen," said Groves, "if the Nazis discover how to harness and use this energy inside a normal-sized bomb, they won't hesitate to use it to achieve their aims…guaranteed! They won't discriminate when and how they use it."

Groves stared at Oppenheimer. "Can you appreciate and imagine what a weapon like this would do in the wrong hands? We have to be the first to develop this weapon and technology!"

Oppenheimer paused as he reflected upon that scenario.

"Professor, I have been authorized to issue US Army officer commissions to all scientists you recruit for this project. They will either be captains, majors, or lieutenant colonels during the course of this project. You, as their commander, will receive the commission of lieutenant colonel. You may start to order your uniforms. Obviously, I will be your military superior and be in overall command of this research project, but since you are a scientist—"

"Wait one minute, General," replied Oppenheimer. "Let's consider who these scientists are and where they come from. First of all, most of them teach at our nation's universities and conduct research there. We will be removing them and bringing them here to New Mexico...almost by force. Throwing a uniform on them and giving them a rank won't inspire them or get this project completed any faster. These men and women are professors and scientists, not soldiers. In my opinion, to get the most out of these scientific minds, and achieve your goals in the fastest manner possible—maintain an academic atmosphere here. Few, if any of these men and women have any desire to be in any military. It will be my chore to convince many of them to work on a project for the purpose of building a weapon. Some of them will refuse to do so on moral grounds. On the other hand, some of them know firsthand the brutality of the Nazis as their families have been harassed or sent to concentration camps, set upon and torn apart by men wearing the Nazi uniform. They want more than anything to end the reign of Nazi terror."

So in February 1942, Leslie Groves and J. Robert Oppenheimer together scouted out potential sites for Project Y of the new Manhattan Project. Oppenheimer liked New Mexico, and actually owned property northeast of Santa Fe in the nearby mountains. They looked at sites close to Oppenheimer's ranch, about 40 miles northwest of Santa Fe in the Jemez Mountains. Eventually, they settled on a location in the mountain pines that was for the most part a mesa divided up by some fairly steep canyons. This mesa would in time become the site of the Los Alamos National Laboratories. There were already buildings on the 125-acre site. The area was a "Boys' Ranch" for youth, originally built in 1913, but had been abandoned and left in disrepair. The Army could use the buildings already there and quickly construct other buildings to make the area functional. The site would be private, as it was miles away from the closest city (Santa Fe), and secure. Work began to make Los Alamos into America's wartime atomic research center in October 1942. In reality, the community that served as the scientists' home on the mesa resembled a hastily put together enclave resembling an old Western boomtown like those that sprung up during the gold rush or cattle drive years, with mostly dirt roads, dirt sidewalks, flimsy wooden buildings, and chain-link fences that seemed to have permanent gaps and holes.

CHAPTER XV

Quinn was still exploring Santa Fe. The city was a strange combination of different cultures, architecture, art, and religion. It was a city with old traditions and architecture being propelled by necessity into the modern 20th century by World War II. Life in Santa Fe in early 1942, as in most other traditional Hispanic cities or towns, revolved around the downtown plaza. The Santa Fe Plaza was a large square in the middle of the city with a government building on the north side; a gazebo and monument to the Army in the center; and a variety of art galleries and other shops surrounding its sides. Just off the plaza at the southeast corner was the large Catholic Cathedral of St. Francis of Assisi. Along the east side of the square was The Palace of the Governors. This was the building raised in the 1600s by the Spanish when they marched into Santa Fe. Governor Pedro de Peralta was the territorial ruler for New Mexico, most of the American Southwest, and part of Mexico at the time. Now the building housed a museum and some sort of office at 109 E. Palace Ave. Joel Finebaum's art gallery stood at the far north end of Palace Avenue at 104 ½ E. Palace Ave. It had a wooden sign above the doorway that read "Art Gallery, Joel Finebaum, Proprietor."

Mr. Finebaum was there that day as Quinn walked by. Finebaum had on display mostly nature scenes with an Impressionist bent, but he loved the territorial-style architecture of Santa Fe, which also often appeared in one form or another in his paintings. Also, Finebaum loved to paint women. In the corner of the front window was a painting on an easel that stopped Quinn cold in his tracks. He stared through the gallery window at the portrait and face that had haunted him for the last eighteen months. It was Katrina, the blonde girl with the incredible pale blue eyes, from Albuquerque. It was unmistakenly her. Quinn just stared, his feet seemingly implanted in the sidewalk cement before he broke out of his trance and entered the gallery. As he entered, he saw scenes of Santa Fe and nature painted in a style he had never before experienced. The mix of colors—light yellows and earthtones—were amazing. Finebaum's paintings and scenes at 104 1/2 E. Palace Ave. were mostly of the surrounding mountains and woods, yet they were unique, unlike other similar scenes in color, shape, and form. Some were hazy in appearance with the main subject hidden within the haze. Others were a collage of colors; like that of the painting of the field filled with natural flowers in springtime. Every painting on display was worthy of attention, but to Quinn the most stunning of all was Katrina's portrait. Finebaum had created an Impressionist-type background to the portrait of his niece. With her blond silky hair and blue eyes peering through the haze, she resembled an angel emerging from the clouds.

"Can I help you?" said the man's voice from behind Quinn. Quinn was startled and nearly jumped as he was transfixed on the girl's portrait. He quickly turned around and saw Joel Finebaum, a slightly built man of about 5'8" with grey hair and a noticeable grey and black goatee.

"Hello, I was just admiring the work and the young lady's portrait in the corner. My compliments to the artist," replied Quinn.

"Thank you. That would be me," said the man. "She's beautiful, isn't she?" said the artist, pointing at the young woman's picture.

"Yes, beautiful on her own in real life, but the artist brings it out more!" said Quinn.

"She's my niece," said the man. "My name is Joel Finebaum and I own this gallery."

Quinn's jaw nearly dropped when the man said this. "I know her," said Quinn. "Well, what I mean is, I've met her before."

"Really, where did you meet her?" asked Joel.

"Oh it was in Albuquerque some time ago. I talked with her a little… but I've never forgotten how pretty she is…her pretty eyes," said Quinn.

"Well, she's still pretty. You should come back then, Mr.….eeh…," said the bearded man.

"Chase," said Quinn. "My name is Quinn Chase. How do you do?" Quinn outstretched his hand. The two men shook hands.

"My niece Katrina works here on Sunday and Monday afternoons," said the artist. "You'll have to stop by sometime and renew acquaintances," he said.

"Well, I'll do that," said Quinn. "You have some other stunning paintings," said Quinn.

"Thank you," said the man. "I can't take credit for all of them. Some of these are European artists."

Quinn took his time gazing at the pieces nearby.

"What brings you to Santa Fe, Mr. Chase? What is it that you do?" asked the man.

"I'm a private detective now," replied Quinn. "I used to work for the Albuquerque Police Department." Finebaum's facial expression changed almost instantaneously.

"Really, and what do you investigate now?" he asked.

"Oh, I've just started here in Santa Fe. So far my partner and I have been hired on small cases…mostly disputes between neighbors, lost pets, or an occasional domestic dispute or insurance investigation."

Right then some people walked into the gallery and diverted Joel's attention. But before walking away from Quinn, he said, "Well, I hope you find success and enjoy your time here in Santa Fe. If you are at all interested in art, you're in the right place. Take a walk up Canyon Street and you'll see all sorts of art. I hope you come back and see my niece Katrina," he said.

"I will," said Quinn.

"Excuse me now while I tend to my other guests," said Finebaum.

"Thank you again," replied Quinn.

CHAPTER XVI

Quinn was slowly getting used to his new city. Now it was time he felt to familiarize himself with the recreational opportunities of Santa Fe. What he most wanted to do was find a good bar in town and indulge himself in his favorite pastime…drinking. Deep inside he knew he could never stay away from the libations for very long. From experience, Quinn knew the best way to discover the best bars in any new place was to ask a cabby. It has been accepted as fact the world over that cabdrivers generally know the best points of interest, locations and adventures any city has to offer. He just had to find the right cabby with whom he could bond a little. He checked the phone book out and saw a listing for "Manny's Taxi Service."

This has a nice ring to it. Let's give this one a try, Quinn thought to himself. About one hour later, a Hispanic man in his 50s picked Quinn up in front of his hotel.

"How are you today, sir? I'm Manny, and where can I take you?"

"So you're the infamous Manny," Quinn said. "Where can I go to get a good drink around here?"

"Well, sir, there are several places I would recommend," Manny said. "The La Fonda is very popular on the weekends…and then there's Okies, and there are a few others, but my favorite is Alex's."

"Oh," said Quinn. "What is Alex's like?"

"Well, sir, I don't think you've been to a bar like Alex's before. It's a fixture in Santa Fe, but it is different. There's all sorts of different people there. Alex's is never dull. Artists, the local crowd, the music…keep it lively, sir. Alex the owner is normally there. There's a piano that anybody can play. Normally an old guy named Clyde is there playing. And sometimes there is entertainment like Flamenco dancing or a combo playing. It's…how do you say…avant-garde," said Manny.

"Let's go check Alex's out," said Quinn.

"Yes, sir, it'll take about ten minutes. It's on the street with all the artists, Canyon Street. There's just one thing you should know ahead of time. Alex is a woman."

"A woman?" said Quinn in a startled manner. "And she's the owner?"

"Yes, I can take you somewhere else?" said Manny.

"No-no," replied Quinn. "I haven't had any real fun for a while. Let's go there…this sounds like something different and interesting," replied Quinn.

Alexandra Farmendale, or Alex as she was known, had bought a large old adobe home at the top of Canyon Street in Santa Fe and converted the entire building into her bar. The bar attracted a mixture of eclectic people, including many of the artists living on Canyon Street, people of various ethnic backgrounds, and visitors to Santa Fe as well. While Alex's wasn't a gay bar, per se (and the term wasn't widely used at that time), gay people frequented Alex's bar. It was a place where social stigmas, norms, and conventions did not apply. You could be yourself at Alex's no matter who you were. If fights broke out or if other disruptive behavior was exhibited from anyone there, one of the bouncers or Alex herself would handle the situation. She stood 5'10" and was imposing in appearance—a tall woman for the 1940s.

Several local artists had donated their time and skill and painted murals of patrons on the inside adobe walls there, of typical scenes and of the clientele of Alex's. The bar itself was a work of art.

The large four-door Buick Manny used for his cab stopped in front of an old adobe building along the heavily sloped Canyon Street, in Santa Fe. It's a good thing Quinn took a cab because walking up the steep hill to Alex's would have been exhausting.

Manny dropped him off, and Quinn asked him to come back in 2 ½ hours. "I normally don't stay anywhere longer than a couple hours if I'm not familiar with the place," said Quinn.

Manny indicated he would return as requested. Quinn went inside.

Quinn immediately began to feel the strangeness of the place and of the environment he'd never experienced before. Compared to The 9:15 in Albuquerque, this bar was very different. The 9:15 was a drab place with a long bar, many booths, and a jukebox in the corner. Alex's was more colorful and upscale from the start. This place was larger with a long bar on one end, high barchairs with many tables spread out around the large room. One waiter who Quinn noted walked a little odd for a man, and three waitresses quickly moved throughout the main room delivering drinks to the throng of patrons there. Quinn gazed at the colorful murals that took up several walls. There was another backroom, which had fancy couches, large tables, another bar and a small stage. Instead of the blue-collar atmosphere of The 9:15, Alex's had nicely dressed people; even men and women in suits. Some of the women had short, cropped hair. There were Hispanic patrons in the bar as well. This was something that wasn't seen at The 9:15 in Albuqerque. There was a baby grand piano in the main room, and a woman wearing a pinstripe suit playing it. Quinn sat down in a free chair at the bar.

"How can I help you, amigo?" said the bartender. "What are you drinking tonight?"

"Bourbon and soda," replied Quinn. "Nice place you have here…seems a little different from what I'm used to," said Quinn.

"You should go and thank Alex for that," replied the Hispanic bartender. "It's her place. First time here?" said the bartender.

"I'm new to Santa Fe," said Quinn.

The bartender set Quinn's drink in front of him. "Here, try this," he said. "Bourbon, soda, and a hit of my secret liquor, Curacoa. Tell me what you think."

Quinn took a sip, and then replied, "Not bad…not too bad at all. Who painted the murals on the walls?" asked Quinn.

"Several local artists have contributed, but the main painter is Alfred Mahone. He's an odd guy who likes this bar. He's here a lot," said the bartender. "He's a strange guy. He walks up here from his studio and house, just down the street. Always smoking a cigarette and always wearing his sunglasses in here, even at night. He did a real good job on the wall murals though," said the bartender.

"Yes, he sure did," said Quinn. "I'll have another of your concoctions," Quinn said to the bartender as he pulled a cigarette out and lit it.

A lady with short, cropped blonde hair came and sat in the chair next to Quinn. " Fidel, I'll have my usual Manhattan with a twist," she said to the bartender in a low-pitched voice. The lady appeared to be around 30 years old. "Do you have a light?" she asked as she opened up a cigarette case and pulled one out.

"Here, allow me," said Quinn as he pulled his lighter out of his pocket.

Quinn lit her cigarette and she began smoking. "Thank you," the young blonde said as she pulled the lit cigarette out of her red colored lips with her right hand. The smoke from the lit cigarette filtered up to the ceiling. She wore a fairly tight-fitting dress. Once again, not the norm for ladies' fashion of the 1940s. She had an attractive face with high pronounced cheeks. She had light blue eyes and seemed to be either English or German. "What brings you to Alex's tonight?" she asked.

"Oh, I heard this was an interesting place, and different, and I felt like something different tonight," he said.

"Are you new to Santa Fe?" she asked.

"Yes…I've only been in town a short while. My name is Quinn Chase. What's yours?"

"Marika Kraus," she said as she stuck her hand out, palm down. "Happy to meet you. What do you do, Mr. Chase?"

"I'm a private investigator," replied Quinn.

"How exciting!" she replied.

"I was a police detective," Quinn stated. "As small as Santa Fe is I'm surprised there is work up here. But so far I've been busy," he said.

"Where do you come from?" she asked.

"I've lived my whole life in Albuquerque, but my partner and I decided to come up here to Santa Fe."

"Well, welcome to you again!"

"And what brings you here?" Quinn asked.

"I'm in the art business," she said. "My father owned an art gallery in Chicago, and I inherited it. So my work involves a lot of travel, buying and selling…and please, call me Marika," she said. "Recently some works by well-known European artists have found their way to Santa Fe, and I'm here to check them out. Art is a fickle business," she said.

"So is the average woman," said Quinn.

"Yes, I suppose that's true as well," she replied.

Quinn then said, "I was just in a gallery on the Plaza, 104 ½ East Palace Avenue…and I met the owner who said he had some paintings by Europeans."

"Yes, that's what I've heard, and I have to go look at his display. Do you know his name by chance?" she asked.

"Joel Finebaum," Quinn said.

"Is he Jewish?" she asked.

"I don't know…I really don't," said Quinn. "He's one hell of an artist, though, I do know that."

"It truly is a shame," Marika said, "but many European works of art… sculptures and paintings are being smuggled out of Europe on the black market by the Nazis. Priceless original works of art by Monet, Renoir, Matisse, and other masters," she said. "The Nazis have basically rejected and condemned any modern art made after 1910. Or at least that's what their public stance is," she said. "They've publicly burned some of the art they classify as degenerate. Someone has to locate and protect these masterpieces, or they'll be lost forever."

"So you travel around looking for art?" Quinn asked.

"Among other things," she said. Another woman then approached and sat on the other side of Marika. She was a younger woman with long auburn hair. "Hi, baby," Marika said as she kissed the younger, more fragile appearing woman on the lips for a considerable length of time.

Quinn's eyes widened, and he nearly dropped his drink...and just stared in shocked silence.

The two women giggled about something, and Marika Kraus then briefly turned back to Quinn. "It was nice meeting you, Mr. Chase. Maybe I'll see you again sometime?" she said as she winked at Quinn.

He was speechless as the attractive blonde and her apparent lover stepped off their chairs and retreated into the hoard of patrons at Alex's that evening, most likely to some other area of the bar. The bartender walked over to Quinn again.

"Can I get you another one of those?" he asked. Quinn had a look of disbelief on his face. "Didn't anyone tell you, this is not your typical bar...it's really an open lounge...there's all sorts of people here on any given night. Stick around...you'll see things you won't believe." Quinn's expression never changed as he took the glass from the bartender and sat on the barstool continuing to drink.

About 90 minutes later, as Quinn was on his sixth drink that night and feeling the effects, he felt a tap on his right shoulder. He turned and the blonde woman with the short hair—Marika—was back with a smile on her face.

"Mind if I join you again?" she said. "I thought you might buy me a drink." She pulled another cigarette out of her case and sat down next to him at the bar. It was the 1940s, but she wore a tight blouse with the top two buttons undone, showing ample cleavage, along with the rest of her beige dress that seemed to hug her body. She held Quinn's attention. At near midnight and with a buzz, she looked extremely sexual and alluring.

Quinn wanted to comment on the sexy dress she wore, but then wondered, *Why is she interested in me?* But then he thought about it again...and really all that mattered to Quinn was that she was interested in him. They sat and talked for a while about nothing in particular. When Manny's cab came back to pick him up, two fares got in. A-40 year old man wearing his Fedora and London Fog overcoat, and a very attractive, tall, blonde with an athletic body and cropped haircut.

"Let's go back to your place and have a nightcap," she said. The two disappeared into Quinn's hotel at 1:20 a.m., and remained there till the sun shined brightly the next morning when she reemerged, and quietly left the premises.

CHAPTER XVII

It was about noon the following day when Quinn awoke. He made inaudible grumbling sounds as he opened his eyes and looked upon his disheveled hotel room that appeared slightly blurry. He accidentally swung his arm and knocked a pitcher of water on the adjoining nightstand down to the floor. The pewter pitcher crashed on the hardwood floor, and water spilled everywhere. He was by himself in bed now…with a pronounced hangover. He slowly got out of bed, stood up, and made his way carefully to the shower. He took a cold shower to wake up. Then he filled up half a shot glass from the bottle of Bourbon left over from the previous night and instead of chugging it, he sipped it. Marika Kraus had supplied the bourbon…and as he drank he asked himself, *What the hell was last night all about? Why did she come back? Who is this woman? I've gotta' find out.*

Marika Kraus was also thinking of her night with Quinn. In fact, she was contemplating how Quinn could serve as a helpful connection to her. Perhaps she might acquire from him information down the road that could be useful in dealing with the police, the identity of a mysterious figure known as The Merchant, or the alleged research and development center near Santa Fe. Marika Kraus was an alluring and sexy lady. She did deal in art. But Marika Kraus' main occupation at this time was as a Nazi spy.

While Quinn was taking his cold shower and thinking about his latest love conquest , Marika wrote a letter in coded message to her main contact and superior officer in New York. She then dropped it in the mailbox. The letter was short and read as follows:

Greetings Henry,

All is well here. Met many fine artists and possible buyers. Hope to contact our main prospect soon. May need additional funds…I'll let you know.

Yours truly,

"M"

She wasn't sure who "Henry" was because her superior contacts in New York were anonymous to her, but she had various names and addresses to send updates and correspondence to New York. She knew all messages and names were coded, but she followed her orders to the letter as best she could. She had her own P.O. Box and would receive similar letters back and occasional cashier's checks from "Armbridge Mortgage Company," which she promptly cashed at a local bank. Every letter she received also included additional instructions in code.

Marika had been recruited by the Abwher at the beginning of the war before Germany invaded Poland in 1939. She had personally met and been briefed by Admiral Wilhelm Franz Canaris, the head of the German Army Intelligence Agency, before traveling to America with a false passport and other supporting documents. Although Admiral Canaris had such an important position, he was not a member of the Nazi Party and at times openly voiced his opposition to Hitler and the Nazi Party. Marika's father formally held the title of Graf before the start of the war and was offered a high position in the Nazi government, but he declined to serve. Marika had been previously educated in Switzerland and didn't have Nazi political sympathies or leanings. She was well aware, however, of how powerful and insidious the Nazi officials were, and how vulnerable her position was. She knew she was the linchpin spy in this area, chosen to ensure the black-market trade of Nazi art went smoothly, and that the art was moved through Santa Fe to the west coast in California. Her father was Heinz von Lohseman, a respected aristocrat and landowner in Eastern Germany before the war. She knew as long as she made a reasonable attempt to fulfill her mission and kept in good contact with her superiors in New York, her mother and father would be safe. And Marika would go to any length to ensure her family's safety.

CHAPTER XVIII

It was two weeks later, and Quinn was meandering around Santa Fe on a Sunday afternoon. The bars in town didn't open until 4:00 p.m. on Sundays, so he had to occupy himself for a few hours. He meandered on foot over to 104 ½ E. Palace Ave, the Finebaum Gallery on the Santa Fe Plaza. He looked through the divided window and saw her sitting at the desk in the front of the gallery. She was speaking with an elderly man who was holding a watercolor up to the light. Her blonde hair reflected the light beaming from the gallery's spotlights above. She looked just like she did eighteen months ago when he drove her home that cold wintry night from The 9:15. But would Katrina remember him?

Quinn walked in and removed his hat. At first she didn't notice him, but when she finally turned her head and saw him, her eyes lit up and she flashed a broad, beautiful smile. "Oh, my lord," she said. "My uncle said a man stopped in who recognized my portrait, but I didn't make the connection that it was you! What are you doing in Santa Fe?"

"I live and work here now," said Quinn.

"Are you a policeman here?" she asked.

"No, I'm not on the force anymore. I'm a private investigator…a detective," said Quinn.

She smiled, and the two just enjoyed the moment of meeting again after so much time and in another place.

"So you painted all of these?" Quinn asked, sarcastically.

"No…no," she answered. "But my uncle Joel painted many of them. They're beautiful, aren't they?" she said.

"Yes, especially the portrait of the lady in the corner. I wonder who she is?" Quinn asked, feeling emboldened.

Katrina blushed.

Quinn said, "I think I'll take a self-guided tour around your gallery if that's okay? I'll be back, and maybe we can talk some more."

"Okay, and if you have any questions about any of the paintings, just ask. This is modern art you won't see everywhere," she said.

"Hey…what's that noise coming from the ceiling?" Quinn asked.

"What noise?" Katrina said, listening intently. "Oh…I know what you're talking about," she said. "It's my uncle's pigeon coop from up on the roof. He raises pigeons. It's his hobby, besides painting. He had one in New York when we lived there."

Quinn embarked on a self-guided tour of the art gallery, which had several rooms with about 50 paintings and 10 sculptures placed on small tables. The paintings were nicely framed and were a mixture of oils, water-colors, and pastel sketches. Joel Finebaum painted many of them, but there were other artists represented too. Quinn, being a novice to the world of art, didn't know what he was looking at except that he had to spend consid-erable time with the images before he could figure them out. Most of them didn't have a clearly defined subject. The Impressionists painted natural scenes, but not in the classical sense. What made it to the canvas was what the artist saw and interpreted the very instant a scene hit their eyes. This could be different from what others saw while looking at the same scene. The Expressionists took it one step further into the realm of imagination. Artists like Matisse painted forms and subtle shapes on canvas, which were sometimes vague and ill defined—wanting to express a scene, but a mood or feeling as well. Quinn was fascinated by what he saw in the gallery, but he really didn't come there to look at art. His attention was drawn back to Katrina. To Quinn, Katrina's natural beauty was prettier than any painted or sculpted work of art.

"I never really got a chance to speak with you when I drove you home that night. You ran off so quickly. Maybe we could have dinner and catch up on our lives since then?"

"Yes, I'd like that, Mr.—"

"My name's Chase…Quinn Chase."

"I'd really like that, Mr. Chase."

"Everyone calls me Quinn. Please call me Quinn."

"In fact, why don't we set a date?" she said.

"Wonderful…how about next Wednesday night, say around 7:00?" Quinn asked.

"Sounds great, I look forward to it. And why don't you pick me up here at the art gallery, Quinn?" Katrina said.

On the prescribed date and time, Quinn came as a passenger in Manny's cab up to 104 ½ E. Palace Avenue. The gallery was the last store-front on the east side of the plaza, closest to the Palace of the Governors off to its left, as one faced the gallery. Quinn could see a pretty blonde staring out of the main window as he got closer. Katrina was nicely dressed, and Quinn was dressed in a suit and tie for the occasion too. He presented her with a bouquet of flowers. He had made reservations at one of the nicer restaurants in town, about a six-minute drive from the Plaza; *Le Meilleur Boeuf* was upscale for Santa Fe at that time and required coat and tie for men and dresses for women. It was known for its French cooking, so that night Quinn and Katrina would be treated to some of the best French cooking in Santa Fe. Quinn ordered a Beef Burgundy meal, and Katrina ordered *Lapin a la Cocotte,* a fancy name for "rabbit stew."

Once the wine was poured, Quinn raised his glass for a toast. "Katrina, may you find happiness here in Santa Fe, and hopefully two years won't pass by before we see each other again," Quinn said as he touched his glass to hers.

"And may you find the same here as well," she replied.

They ate their dinner while a pianist played background music. "I am curious," he said. "When did your uncle come to New Mexico?"

"He came to New Mexico three years ago. He was an art dealer in New York before coming here."

"Oh," replied Quinn, "it must be a big climate change from New York to here?"

"Yes, well that's one reason my uncle came here, because of the climate. Tuberculosis has been a problem for him for many years. He needed a drier, less humid climate for his health," she said. "Since being here, he's felt much better."

They talked on and on that night. He learned some about her and her family, and she learned about his history and his time in the Albuquerque Police Department. Once they finished dinner, they decided to take a walk. "Let's walk back to the gallery. We could both use the fresh air," said Quinn.

"Okay," she said, "there are several things I want to show you along the way. "

They got back to the gallery after dinner that night around 10:00pm. If he was going to show her he was romantically interested, Quinn figured that the appropriate time was now. He had the urge to kiss her, and she wanted the same. They were outside the gallery front, and before either could say a word, he took her in his arms. He knew once started he couldn't hesitate. Their lips touched for the first time. To Quinn, Katrina's kiss felt like the sweetest fruit he'd ever tasted. It was a moment of bliss for him. He drew her body close and held her.

"I imagined what this might feel like as I drove you home that evening," he said as he kissed her again.

"How does the reality match up with your expectations? I hope you're not disappointed," she said.

"No, not in the least," Quinn said as he smiled. "It was definitely worth the wait," he said. "You know now I'm gonna be hanging around the gallery...or at least when I know you're there," he said.

"You're always welcome here, you know that. And I hope to see much more of you," she said.

CHAPTER XIX

Vitali Chetkin took a sip from his teacup while sitting in the ornate restaurant at the La Fonda Hotel, Santa Fe, New Mexico, in early March 1942. He had heard how backwards and unsophisticated Americans were, especially in the Western United States, but he was discovering just the opposite. Chetkin was impressed by the décor of brightly colored hand-painted clay tiles and the wood carvings of the La Fonda Hotel. The food and alcohol was good too, which made it all the more desirable. He was a Russian agent posing as a Hungarian art dealer in Santa Fe. For this mission, he had chosen the name Laszlo Tibor. Vitali also knew there was at least one Nazi agent in Santa Fe at that time, and he knew this agent's identity—Marika Kraus.

He was an odd-looking man, which made him an unlikely spy from any country. But that's what made him so effective. He appeared absolutely harmless. As a short man, significantly overweight and mild in appearance who wore bifocals—a criminal of espionage was the last thing Vitali looked like. The different personas Vitali assumed were purposefully odd. Some were generally comical. But this was intentional and part of his act. Short, heavyset, and in his late 50s with a round face, Vitali played the role of a wealthy, well-traveled but naive, European aristocrat very well. The Russians were well aware that degenerate art, and stolen European Jewish art, was somehow making its way into New Mexico and Santa Fe. Vitali's main assignment was to discover how the art was being smuggled into the United States; which pieces were in Santa Fe; where they were being stored; and for what purpose.

But he had a secondary mission in Santa Fe. Chetkin was aware there was secret research being conducted by the military somewhere around Santa Fe. Unbeknownst to most American intelligence officers, Santa Fe had been used by Russian agents as a location to hide out and base their operations from for some time. Stalin's agents had planned and launched the first assassination attempt on ex-Soviet dissident Leon Trotsky right from Santa Fe. The lead spy, Josef Grigelevich, was stationed here and with his team of agents, they traveled to Mexico to kill Trotsky in early 1940.

Vitali Chetkin, alias Laszlo Tibor, was given a sizable budget for his role—to determine if the degenerate art was being funneled by the Germans through Santa Fe, and in what numbers. He was then to acquire the specific paintings and get them back through his contacts in New York to the U.S.S.R. What better way to start his mission than to engage the services of two American private detectives while using his cover... they, in turn, would help him locate the art. That's what Laszlo Tibor was thinking the afternoon he walked into the office of Clark and Chase Private Investigatons for the first time.

Ethan Clark was there when he came in. "Can I help you?" asked Clark.

"Yes, I would like to talk to you and possibly engage your services to assist me in recovering some stolen art. My clients believe it has been brought here to Santa Fe," stated Tibor.

"Sit down, Mr.—"

"My surname is Tibor."

"Is that a Russian name?" asked Ethan.

"No, no, I am Hungarian. From Budapest, Hungary, sir," replied Tibor.

"May I offer you some coffee, tea, or a brandy?" asked Ethan.

"No, thank you, sir, but do you mind if I smoke?" replied Tibor.

"By all means….My name is Clark, Ethan Clark. So you are Hungarian… long way from home, out here in the American West Mr. Tibor," said Ethan.

"Well, yes, I suppose so…but I've been sent here for a specific purpose, sir. My clients, some of whom are from the wealthiest families in Hungary, are seeking to recover stolen oil paintings that are rightfully theirs. I have spent the last year tracing these paintings, and to my astonishment, the trail leads me here. Since I am a foreigner…I realize that enlisting the assistance of some local investigators might help my efforts immensely. I want to avoid involving the local police and…how you say it…stepping on toes here if I can help it," said Tibor.

"Interesting. I have a partner who is not here at the moment," stated Ethan.

"I wish to employ your entire firm to assist me," said Tibor. "And I believe I can afford your retainer and whatever your rates are," he said. "I've brought $300 with me today," he said.

"Well, our rates are $20 per day that we actually work on your case, plus expenses. We require an initial deposit of $100," said Ethan.

"Here, sir, take the entire $300. Work off that amount, and I'll pay more when it is used up," said Tibor.

"Well, we may be able to help you, Mr. Tibor, but I'd like my partner, Mr. Chase, to meet you, and the three of us can discuss exactly what you want and any leads or clues you may already have," replied Ethan. "I'm staying at the La Fonda Hotel, and I eat breakfast at 9:00 every morning in the hotel restaurant. Please, why don't you both join me there for breakfast tomorrow morning in the restaurant," said Tibor, as he moved towards the door to leave.

"That sounds wonderful, Mr. Tibor. Expect myself and Mr. Chase tomorrow morning at the La Fonda at 9:00. I'm sure we'll be able to help you in some manner," said Ethan Clark as Tibor walked out the front door.

When Quinn returned, he and Ethan spoke. "I'm not sure what to make of our new client, Laszlo Tibor. I don't think I completely believe his story, but if he's only tryin' to locate some missing artwork, what's the difference?" Ethan asked. "We're in this to make a name for ourselves, help people out, but also to make money doing what we like, right?"

"Something doesn't sound right about this," said Quinn, "but if he's got the money...? Let's meet with him at 9:00 tomorrow morning."

The following morning, Ethan and Quinn showed up at La Fonda on the Santa Fe Plaza. "Good to see you, gentlemen. Please have a seat. The view from this spot across the plaza is nice in the morning. The way the sun shines...I get the same table every day," said Tibor.

"Mr. Tibor, this is my partner, Quinn Chase," said Clark as Quinn shook hands with Laszlo Tibor.

"It's nice to meet you, sir," stated Quinn.

"Call me Laszlo, please. My first name is Laszlo."

"Okay, fine Laszlo. While your project sounds very intriguing, I do have a few questions," said Quinn.

"By all means," replied Laszlo.

"To begin with, and I apologize for mentioning this, we need some verification of your identity. May we see your passport or visa authorization, please?" asked Quinn.

"Of course, sir…actually I was expecting this," replied Laszlo as he handed his fake passport to Quinn. "What I seek is the return of my client's artwork, Mr. Chase. After all, that is what I have been hired for," he said.

"What specifically is missing, and why do you think it's here in Santa Fe?" asked Quinn.

"I was sent here to find several specific paintings. All were previously taken by the Nazis," said Laszlo. "They are masterpieces and, by our standards, are beyond valuable. The Nazis took control of them and have funneled them for sale through the black market. The first one is by the French artist Degas, Edgar Degas. It is a pastel and beautiful example of 19th century Impressionism. Degas named the painting - *Five Dancing Women*. The next two are more recent, and the Nazis labeled them Degenerate Art. *En Canot* and *Man with a Pipe*. These two are by the Modernist French painter Jean Metzinger." With that Laszlo pulled out photos of all three paintings.

"My clients believe other paintings, and possibly sculptures, from museums in Germany and other countries have made their way to Santa Fe. In the scheme of things, Mr. Chase, Santa Fe may appear to be a sleepy small Catholic town, but there are many illicit activities taking place here. You may be wondering, Mr. Chase, why I would come all this way for three paintings. You should know, since I'm hiring you and Mr. Clark, that the paintings are considered priceless in the art world. I would think this would be important to you and the local police. And as I told your partner yesterday, I will pay you liberally for your services," said Laszlo. "By cooperating together, we can do the right thing, save some of the world's great art treasures, and…how you say…make a few nickels in the process." Laszlo displayed a slight grin.

"Where do you think the art is stored here?" asked Ethan.

"I have no idea at this time, Mr. Clark. I do believe, however that a man by the name of Mr. Berndt Kruger, a wealthy German art dealer from New York, will be in Santa Fe within the next few weeks to pick up some of these paintings and move them to Los Angeles and then probably to South America. Kruger will be meeting with someone and collecting several paintings while here. My understanding is that there is great demand for these paintings in South America—Argentina, Paraguay, Bolivia, Brazil," said Tibor.

"How did you come about this information? Are you sure about his name, and how did you learn about him?" asked Quinn.

"Mr. Chase, you are a man who asks many questions. Please bear in mind while I am hiring both you and Mr. Clark to work with me to locate these paintings, a certain amount of discretion must be shown by all parties. And while I will share much information with my 'team,' Mr. Chase, I also have my own methods of investigation that must remain private."

Quinn and Ethan looked at one another. Laszlo Tibor had proper identification, or at least what appeared to be proper identification, and seemed very sure of himself. He talked a good game. He was well informed and had done his homework. They finished eating and said their goodbyes. They felt good now because they appeared to be in the employ of a well off and generous client, and they were convinced Tibor's story was real. In small part, it was real.

CHAPTER XX

The Santa Fe Police Department was located in the same building as City Hall. The police department was small compared to their larger neighbor, Albuquerque. "We're running background checks on both you and your partner, so we'll start with fingerprints and registering your firearms," said Detective Frank Huff in the presence of several other detectives of the Santa Fe Police, in May 1942. "We should have had this discussion long before now, but better late than never," said Huff.

"We know about your backgrounds with the Albuquerque PD," said the Santa Fe detective, as both Quinn Chase and Ethan Clark presented their handguns to him. Huff began to record the serial numbers from each handgun. "Well, listen up, men, and listen good," Huff said. "I'm not a fan of PI's in general. Investigations are what the police are for. I don't even think you should be allowed to carry guns," Huff continued.

"We've got a quiet, safe town here, boys. And it's gonna stay that way as long as I'm here, understand? We know about your little botched babysitting job for the Army down in Albuquerque," Huff said. "I don't even think two old retread detectives should be allowed to stick their noses in our business up here, but it's a free country, and as long as you don't interfere with our work on the force, I guess you can stay. But if I start getting reports of either of you stepping over the line…I'll personally run both of you out of town and do my best to put you in jail."

"You don't have to worry about a thing, detective," Ethan replied. "We were cops once. We're just here to help people out and try and make a living."

"Well, here's the deal…the three of us will have a little monthly meeting here at the police department," Huff replied. "I have to know what you're working on, so like I said, you're not getting too involved in police matters. So you will share with me your cases and the extent of your involvement," he said.

"We may not be able to reveal our clients," said Quinn. "Most of our clients will not want us to reveal any personal information, and as you know, detective, certain things are confidential."

"Well, I want to know what you're up to at any given time," replied Huff. "And remember, gentlemen, I can shut you down in a minute—just remember that!"

Huff took his time returning the men's guns, making a show of signing the paperwork.

"Do you have any information for me now?" Huff asked as he handed both Quinn and Ethan their revolvers back.

"You ever heard of the term Degenerate Art, detective?" said Quinn.

"No, can't say that I have," replied Huff.

"Well, you might want to become acquainted with that term," advised Quinn.

"I'll do that," said Huff. "In the meantime, you two Dick Tracys stay out of my way, and be back in here next month on the 15th at noontime for our meeting," Huff concluded.

"Thanks, detective. We can't wait," replied Ethan, as he and Quinn got up to leave.

"Remember, we've got eyes on you!" Huff said as Ethan and Quinn walked out of the police meeting room that spring day.

"Boy, don't you just love the warm welcome we're receiving from the locals here, Ethan?" asked Quinn.

"I expected that from the police. They are going to try and monitor what we do to some extent," Ethan said. "Our investigation on various cases could easily overlap theirs. Remember, the PI's in Albuquerque were always walking around the department, trying to get information from Lt. Smith. And Smith got tips from them as well. One hand washed the other Quinn. It's a new game up here. There is no choice but to play by their rules and adjust," he said.

CHAPTER XXI

Quinn returned to the hotel room he had been renting at the Santa Fe Inn that night around 8 p.m. Since he had only been in Santa Fe a short time, renting a room at the Inn seemed to be the best solution for lodging. He opened the door and walked in, and the room was entirely black with the drapes shut. That wasn't the way he remembered leaving it.

"Come in, Mr. Chase," said the voice from the back of the room. He had heard this voice before. "Have a seat…I took the liberty of letting myself in," came the alluring voice as the small table lamp was turned on.

Marika Kraus was sitting on the small chair adjoining the round table with her legs crossed looking very alluring. On the table was a bottle of Old Forester Kentucky Bourbon, a container of ice, and two glasses. "Let's have a drink or two for old time's sake…what do you say?" she asked.

"I didn't realize the lock on the door was so easy to pick," said Quinn. "I'll have to talk to the front desk about that," he said.

"Who said it was easy?" Marika replied with a devilish smile as she poured the bourbon over ice and handed the glass to Quinn.

"You know, you could have left a note under the door if you wanted to see me," said Quinn.

"I prefer the more direct approach, Mr. Chase," she replied as she raised her glass and clicked it against his. "To your prosperity and health," she toasted.

"Great to see you. We really didn't say goodbye properly before," said Quinn. "What do I owe the honor to this time?" he asked.

"Oh, I just wanted to meet with you and have a little talk about love, art, and your well-being," she said. "It's amazing how the three topics all intersect with one another."

Quinn downed his bourbon and soda in one gulp and took off his jacket.

"You may not believe me, Mr. Chase, but among other things I can be a good friend to you," Marika said. "And you may need a good friend in the near future. It has come to my attention that recently you've been in contact with a Mr. Laszlo Tibor," she said.

"So you've been following me?" Quinn asked as he poured himself another drink.

"No, I'd never do that, but I have my little birdy friends here and there that chirp to me about various things they notice," she said.

"Okay, so sharing a meal with someone is worth notice?" Quinn asked.

"To be forewarned is to be forearmed. I don't know what he represents himself as…or why he's in Santa Fe, but be very careful with that man. I'm here to give you that warning," she said. "Remember, dear, I am here as your friend."

"And what is your basis for stating this warning about Tibor? How do you know him?" Quinn replied.

"I can't really go into it here. Let's just say I've had business dealings with him before, and my experience brings me to this conclusion," she said as she sipped her liquor. "He's absolutely ruthless when he wants something," she said. "If he's asking you to help him look for various paintings, I'd turn the job down and go back to investigating cheating wives. He's a dangerous man who should not be underestimated or trusted," Marika said.

Quinn was listening to her speak, but felt his eyelids getting heavy and his eyesight a little blurry. He became aware that he was falling asleep. Quinn said in a semi-groggy voice, "You've drugged me. Why?"

"Listen to me."

He heard her voice as it started to fade and saw her devilish smile right before he blacked out.

"I'm telling you this as a friend. I wouldn't want you to involve yourself in something that could get you hurt," she said. "Leave the art investigation alone and forget about crazy code names like The Merchant. Go back to resolving water rights and spying on cheating spouses, Mr. Chase. It'll be better for your health in the long run."

And that's all Quinn remembered when he woke up five and a half hours later. When he woke up, his head was pounding and the clock read 1:15 a.m. *That's impossible,* he thought to himself. *I've been out for nearly six hours? How did I fall asleep?* Then he saw the bottle and glasses on the table, and a few small granules of white powder in a paper pouch, and it came back to him.

She's good, he said to himself. *She's damn good at what she does, but what the hell's goin on?*

Quinn, without even thinking grabbed the bottle and chugged some bourbon, straight. After he finished guzzling the alcohol, he laid down again, sprawled across the bed, and fell asleep within three minutes.

CHAPTER XXII

"Katrina, we've got to talk," said Quinn after stopping by the Finebaum gallery. "Let's have dinner tonight. There are some things I need to discuss with you," Quinn said.

"I can't tonight, but tomorrow night I'm free," she said.

At 7:00 the next evening he picked Katrina up, and the two went to *Le Meillier Beouf* again for dinner. "I have some questions for you and your uncle, but I don't want to upset him. Have you ever heard the term Degenerate Art?" Quinn asked. "This is art that the Nazis don't like; mostly Modern or Expressionist-type art that's beyond their scope of understanding and toleration," he said.

"No, I've never heard of the term before," with a quizzical look she said. "Why do you ask?"

"Well, I wonder whether your uncle has heard of the term before and knows anything about this type of art in Santa Fe," he said.

"Well, I'm sure he'll be honest with you if he knows anything. You should ask him. I've never heard of this before," Katrina stated. "I know my uncle was not allowed in one of the Modern painting groups…because his paintings were not abstract enough," she said. "Maybe you should talk with them," she said as she laughed and tousled her blonde locks to the side of her forehead. Katrina had a vulnerable beauty about her that was undeniable; she looked so easily breakable and precious.

"He'll be at the gallery working tonight," she said. "My uncle always paints on Wednesday nights. It's when he thinks he's most creative," she said. They finished their dinner, a simple yet delicious French dish accompanied with blush wine. Then they returned to the Finebaum Gallery. It was dark when they arrived, but just as she told him, Joel Finebaum was found with a brush in his hand painting. He was in the back storeroom with the light on. His current project was on an easel and appeared to be an oil painting, but there were dozens of paintings lying around in the large room. It seemed as if each one was a work in progress.

"Sorry to bother you, sir, I know it's late, but I was wondering if I could speak with you for a moment," Quinn asked.

"I normally don't like to be interrupted while I'm working, Mr. Chase. It stops my concentration. Can you come tomorrow, say around three o'clock? It would be better for me," Joel said.

"Of course," Quinn said, and made to leave with respect.

"But what is it you want to talk about?" Finebaum said, before Quinn took more than five steps.

"Sir, have you ever heard the term Degenerate Art?" asked Quinn.

"Oh, yes," replied Finebaum. "It's the name given to abstract Modern art, or really anything not Realist or Classical, but I do not refer to this art as Degenerate. Some of the world's great artists paint as Impressionist or in the Expressionist genre. I would hardly refer to artists like Monet, Renoir, Cezanne, or Van Gogh as Degenerate, but the Nazis do. They've been confiscating this art as they occupy various countries in Europe, Mr. Chase. Or, at least that's what the papers say. I've heard they even burned many pieces in a public rally last year. Apparently this art is a threat to their ideology and their belief system."

A cloud passed through Finebaum's expression, and he abruptly turned back to his work. "Let's talk more about it tomorrow, Mr. Chase."

"Fine then, I'll see you at three in the afternoon tomorrow," said Quinn.

"If you'll excuse me, I must return to my work now. Goodnight, Mr. Chase."

"Goodnight, sir," said Quinn.

Well, if Finebaum's involved in this he's not acting like he's concealing anything, Quinn said to himself as he rode in the backseat of the cab that night. *It's only natural that he would not approve of the Nazis' contempt for Modern art, and I could see no sign that he was hiding insider knowledge of a black market. I'll find out for sure tomorrow.* The rest of the night passed without incident, and Quinn got a decent night's sleep, after many restless and chaotic nights. The next day at 3:00 p.m., Quinn came back to the gallery and met with Finebaum again.

"Hello, Mr. Chase, come in please," said Finebaum. "Now what else can I help you with?" he asked.

"Mr. Finebaum, I've heard reports that this Degenerate Art from Europe is making its way out to Santa Fe and is in this city in large quantity. I have no proof of any kind other than rumor to back that up. If it is being brought here at all, it is a matter for the police and the FBI. I'm sure they would be very interested in locating this art, as it is most likely stolen from its rightful owners in Europe. Do you know, or have you heard, anything about this?" asked Quinn.

"No, I haven't. No, not at all, Mr. Chase. Renoir and Chagall originals and other works from the great Modern artists in Santa Fe? I surely wish that were true, but I haven't heard a word and I am friendly with most of the artists in town. As you know Mr. Chase I have some European Art, but it isn't Degenerate Art from the great artists. My paintings are from lesser known artists and are my personal collection I brought with me when I came to America. It would be an honor just to study and examine the works of the great painters. But unfortunately the pleasure would be bitter sweet, as the paintings would be stolen from their rightful owners in Europe. At any rate, I haven't seen or heard anything. If I do, I'll surely alert you immediately!"

"One more question. Does the name Berndt Kruger mean anything to you?"

At this question, Finebaum paused and his look noticeably changed. *This artist is no actor,* Quinn said to himself. "Yes, I've heard the name before. He was an art dealer I knew back in New York several years ago, Mr. Chase. Why do you ask?"

"Well, his name has been brought up as being involved somehow with this Degenerate Art," said Quinn.

"I highly doubt he's involved, Mr. Chase," said Finebaum.

"Why would that be?" asked Quinn.

"Because the Berndt Kruger, the former art dealer I knew in New York, died in an apartment fire 10 years ago in Brooklyn," said Finebaum.

CHAPTER XXIII

"Katrina, we must talk," Joel said to his niece. "What have you told this man, Mr. Chase?"

"Nothing, uncle…really," she said. "We've gone out to eat twice and talked about Santa Fe a little and the art gallery. Nothing much. He's a nice man," she said.

"What has he asked you about the gallery? About our family?"

"He hasn't asked much of anything, uncle," Katrina replied. "He asked where we came from back East in New York, and how long we've been here in Santa Fe."

"And what have you told him?"

"That you bought and sold art in Manhattan and traveled outside New York every now and then for your business."

"Katrina, you know what it is we have to do…and you know how many people's lives depend on us completing our mission here," Joel said. "We can't fail, Katrina. We must succeed for their safety and well-being. I think it was a mistake that I encouraged this man to renew his friendship with you. Maybe you shouldn't spend so much time with him right now."

"Whatever you think is best, uncle. He has been a friend to me, and I don't think he means us any harm," she said.

"I'm sure he is well-intentioned," said Joel, "but he's a former police officer and now a private detective. His instincts are to prod for answers, search and expose whatever is being concealed. We don't have a choice with regards to our behavior, Katrina. And you are aware we are committing a crime by assisting the German government. But our families' lives back there are being held as ransom. Over 50 of our immediate family could face terrible consequences, Katrina, if we don't do as we're told here. Do you understand?"

Katrina looked at her hands as a blush crept across her pale face.

"You cannot talk about any matters involving our family with him. Our background, relatives, or anything about the gallery, Katrina. The next few months will be important. Berndt Kruger will be here at the gallery and at the warehouse. You cannot mention his name or our association with anyone arriving from Europe. Once we get the inventory cleared from the warehouse, we can concentrate on our next mission. I will explain that to you at the proper time, Katrina. Be very careful what you say to anyone about the gallery—and especially to Mr. Quinn Chase. I know he's your friend, but without even intending to, he can cause us great harm!" said Joel.

"Then I won't see him at all, uncle. I'll make up an excuse or something," she said.

"No, no, don't do that," replied Finebaum. "We can't withdraw completely from public life. Now more than ever we must try to go about our daily lives and be normal in our behavior. Just be careful of what you say to this man or anyone else about our family and about the gallery. We won't act differently right now. It could create too much suspicion about us, and we don't want that. After all, we're not from Santa Fe or New Mexico, and we are Jewish. You must let me know if he keeps questioning you about our family, the gallery and particularly about me."

CHAPTER XXIV

Marika Kraus went to the bar at the La Fonda Hotel on Sunday afternoons because she knew FBI agents would be there. If she became romantically involved with the right one, much information could be gained. But she underestimated the loyalty and professionalism of the FBI. She was aware the United States government was starting some scientific project near Santa Fe, but that's all she knew. Her mission was to find out as much as possible by any means. Marika knew what that meant. This was a first step in making a contact. Marika had all the necessary tools. She was alluring, and cunning. She had used her sexuality in many ways with both men and women to get what she wanted. And now she was perfectly positioned to act as a spy for Germany. She showed up at the La Fonda around 3:00 p.m. that Sunday wearing a bright red dress. She sat by herself in a small corner table in the dimly lit, ornate bar decorated with a carved wood ceiling and colorful hand painted wall tiles. A lone guitarist was strumming and singing a slow Spanish ballad. The mood was easygoing and melancholy compared to the hustle of tourists and people outside in the plaza that day. The Hispanic bartender was measuring and organizing the bottles of wine and other liquor on the counter and on the shelves behind the bar. This was an upscale Spanish bar. Several different brands of tequila made up the most popular liquor in this establishment. Here, women generally preferred wine or mixed tequila drinks, like the margarita. Men normally drank their tequila, whiskey, or brandy straight on the rocks. Sometimes even with the worm from the bottle in their shot glasses. This was a familiar environment for Marika where she thought she would do well.

She didn't have to wait long. About 20 minutes after her arrival, a group of 10 walked in and sat around two tables in the middle of the bar area. These did not look like normal citizenry. With them came three tall men wearing dark suits and fedoras. The men sat at another table just off to the side of the large group in the middle. Two other men similarly dressed entered and sat at the bar. All of the men sat positioning themselves where they could keep watch on the large group at the table. Marika could only guess this group had something to do with the government project. She would do what she could to find out. She moved up to the bar counter and took a seat on a stool. The bar counter was made of heavy wood with colored tiles on top.

She sat next to one of the men there. Then she took out her silver monogrammed cigarette case and pulled out a cigarette. "Do you have a light?" she asked the man with the crew cut.

"Yes, of course," said the man as he pulled out his lighter and flipped the top, thus igniting the wick. He lit Marika's cigarette.

"Thank you," she said. She looked at him. "I'm Marika," and she stuck out her right hand, palm down. The man did not kiss her hand, but reluctantly shook hands and mumbled his name.

"What brings you here on a Sunday afternoon?" she asked the man as she stared at him and took a drag on her cigarette.

"I should be asking you that question," he said.

"Oh, I want to drink a little, and meet a nice man," she smiled and said matter-of-factly.

The man's facial expression changed. "Excuse me," he said as he got up and relocated to the other side of the bar away from Marika.

What did I do wrong? This is obviously the wrong tactic, she said to herself. *Something's very strange here.*

The table of 10 burst out laughing. "George, you always come up with the corniest stories," said one of the women to the tall man sitting at the table. What seemed strange to Marika was that everyone at the table appeared to be young. Under the age of 40, for sure. And it was a mixed group. The women sat together, and the men all sat together around the large table. Some of the men appeared to be Spanish, Italian, or Eastern European. Marika couldn't tell whether or not the women and men were together as couples or not.

"Brigid…you know we have to be back by seven tonight," said one of the young women. One of the other women raised her index finger to her lips as a sign for the first girl to "shut up."

"Oh, what's the big deal?" the first girl asked as she looked up at Marika who sat on the barstool. "This is still the USA. It's not like Nazi spies are hanging around listening to us," she said while laughing.

"Jeanny, shut up now," the older woman said.

The younger woman stared at Marika and asked, "Why don't you sit down and join us?"

Marika smiled her semi-mischievous grin and said, "Thanks so much, but I really must be going soon. It's very kind of you, though. Perhaps some other time," as she smiled at the younger woman. The slightly intoxicated miss looked back at Marika and said, "Where are you from?"

Marika answered, "I'm Dutch…I'm from Amsterdam, Holland."

"Oh," said the girl, her mouth setting into a pretty pout.

Marika could sense the girl was interested in her. "Excuse me, please, I'll be right back," said Marika as she got up, leaving her cigarette case on the bartop. She headed for the ladies' restroom. It didn't take long before the young woman with auburn hair stood up and said she'd be back soon as well…and headed for the restroom.

When the younger woman entered, Marika was staring into the mirror, applying red lipstick while combing her short blond hair. Marika was tall for a woman at that time, about five feet ten inches, and she had a well defined hourglass figure.

"I hope I didn't put you on the spot back there," the younger woman said.

"Oh, no, it was a very kind gesture," said Marika smiling. The girl stood next to her and stared into the mirror as well, checking her lipstick, and Marika's.

"My name's Jeanny," said the younger woman as she extended her hand.

"I'm Marika," said the blonde as she shook hands in a gentle fashion. Marika's light blue eyes sparkled in the light. When the two women touched hands, a mild shock of excitement was felt by both. "Where are you from?" asked Marika.

"Oh…up on the hill. That's what we call it," said the younger woman. "I'm not supposed to talk about it," she whispered.

"How often do you come here?" asked Marika.

"Well, we're allowed to come every Sunday afternoon for a little while," said Jeanny. "I look forward to the break every week."

"Oh, you must work hard up there…on the hill," said Marika.

"We're really not supposed to talk about that, either," said the young woman.

"I see," said Marika. "Why did you ask me to join your group?"

"Well, you look interesting and I thought I might want to get to know you," said Jeanny.

"That was very nice of you...I would like to get to know you too," said Marika.

"Well, I'll be back next Sunday," said Jeanny.

"You have such pretty hair," said Marika with her melodic, deep voice of seduction. She then took her right hand and fluffed up the younger woman's hair on her right side and gently caressed Jeanny's ear. The younger woman nearly melted into Marika's arms.

"I hope to see you again, Jeanny," Marika then said as she made an impromptu about-face showing her tight dress and body. When Marika turned, her well-defined buttocks' cheeks protruded seductively in outline form. Jeanny watched in mesmerized fashion as Marika walked out the door.

CHAPTER XXV

The next Sunday afternoon, the group was back at the La Fonda. The accompanying FBI agents were there, too, and Marika Kraus was there. Jeanny sat with her chatty group of Los Alamos scientists but couldn't help looking up at Marika and at her blonde hair nearly every 20 seconds or so. Marika, for her part, was wearing an attractive green dress. Marika flirted and laughed with the bartender, but every now and then she would sneak a look over at Jeanny. Finally, after a few minutes passed, their eyes met and locked for about 10 seconds. And Jeanny couldn't stand it any longer…she excused herself from the group and headed towards the restroom. About a minute later, Marika got up from her barstool, leaving her silver cigarette case and drink at the bar.

When Marika opened the door, Jeanny was alone and waiting for her. "Hi, again," Jeanny said. This time there was no hesitation on Marika's part. She walked up, grabbed Jeanny behind her head, and gently kissed her on the mouth. To Jeanny, this was a surprise that approached ecstasy. Jeanny couldn't resist the alluring older woman. The two held this kiss for the next 45 seconds as Marika roamed over Jeanny's body with her free hand. "We don't have enough time or privacy now," said Marika. "We have to find a way to meet…where we can be alone." Marika stated.

Jeanny groaned and pressed closer against Marika as she broke the kiss.

"Can you leave from up there ever?" Marika asked.

"No, not right now…they watch us too closely. I can only leave from up there with the group. But some of the more senior people have their own cars and can come and go. Maybe I can ask for a ride or stow away to sneak out sometime," Jeanny answered.

"Here is my home address and P.O. Box in Santa Fe…I wrote it down for you. Write to me or come by if you can get away. We can write to each other and maybe plan something," Marika said as she slipped a piece of paper with her name and address down Jeanny's blouse.

"I think we should go now," Jeanny said, "they'll be expecting me soon and they'll send someone in here to check on me."

"Okay…write to me," Marika said as she kissed Jeanny on her lips again and gently ran her hands down Jeanny's side and over her hips. "Clean yourself up before you go back. You've got my lipstick all over," Marika said.

And with that, Marika was gone. Jeanny stepped back while holding onto the sink, took a deep breath and then exhaled. Jeanny then quickly looked in the mirror and tried to clean the red lipstick from her mouth, while straightening her hair.

CHAPTER XXVI

It was fall of 1942. The leaves were falling off the large trees in Santa Fe and seemed to be everywhere, but especially on the sidewalks and in the parks. They covered the park benches and had to be routinely cleaned off so visitors could sit down. Clifton Park in Santa Fe was named after Colonel Sylvester Clifton who fought in the Mexican-American War of 1843. Quinn went there to meet with an old friend of his. Eddie "Skitts" Jones was a Fence Quinn knew from his detective days in Albuquerque. Quinn had busted Skitts many times for possession of stolen property. During the Depression it happened so much with Skitts that Quinn began looking the other way. Skitts was a petty criminal who, aside from trying to hock cheap watches and other small items, was essentially harmless. Skitts didn't steal the items himself, so he wasn't on Quinn's radar as a serious criminal. And Skitts knew the city and the game. He always seemed to have information on the more serious criminals in Albuquerque at any given time. Quinn wanted information on these more dangerous criminals, and Skitts always seemed to have dirt on somebody. They became a team of sorts. It was part of the game of cops and robbers.

Quinn had heard Skitts was in Santa Fe and arranged through a mutual friend to meet him at Clifton Park. Skitts generally made sure Quinn always had a new lead during his detective years on the police force. Sometimes the small criminals narked on the big criminals in the city; at their own risk, of course, but this never seemed to bother Skitts. The cops had to have some way of gaining information. And there always seemed to be a few hoodlums that had to be taken down.

"This town's different from Albuquerque, isn't it, Skitts?" asked Quinn as he cleared the leaves off one of the park benches and handed Skitts a Philadelphia "Perfecto" cigar. In the past this had been Skitts' favorite.

"Yeah, it's different all right," replied Skitts as he took the cigar and cut off one of the ends with his pocket knife. "But you know what," Skitts said as he struck a match and lit the stogie… "I like it like this…nice and quiet. And up here it's nice and quiet. I'm getting old, detective," Skitts said as he puffed on his newly acquired cigar.

"I'm not sure how quiet it is up here," said Quinn. "And quit calling me detective. I'm not on the force anymore. My name's Quinn," he said.

"To me you'll always be Detective Chase," replied Skitts. "Now what do I owe the honor of this meeting to, detective?"

"There's some stuff goin' down up here, Skitts… stolen paintings from Europe coming in to Santa Fe. You hear anything about it?" asked Quinn.

Skitts pressed his hands together and looked deep in thought, but didn't reply right away.

"Actually, it's three paintings specifically I'm trying to find."

"You talkin' about the stolen Jewish paintings being' smuggled in?" said Skitts finally.

"So you know what I'm talking' about?" said Quinn.

"Yeah…I might have heard something' about it," replied Skitts.

"Well, I want to find these paintings. The problem is I've got competition. There's others in town trying to find this stuff too," Quinn said. "You know Skitts I'd be very appreciative of anything you can help me with."

"Skitts is always happy to help the detective out! And any return assistance from the detective is always much appreciated!" Skitts stated while displaying a broad grin.

Quinn reached into his coat and pulled out a $20 bill. Quinn put it in Skitts' shirt pocket. "I've always believed in one friend helpin' another out," said Quinn. "I do remember a little bird telling me, Detective, that there's supposed to be a new shipment of some stolen art coming into Santa Fe within the next two weeks," Skitts said. "Comin' in by train on the AT&SF on a Saturday…that's what I've heard."

Quinn took out another $20 bill. "Daytime or night?" Quinn asked.

"Don't know at the moment," Skitts stated. "But I'll see what I can do about findin' out."

"Have you ever heard of the painting, *Five Dancing Women* by the painter Degas?" asked Quinn.

"I've heard of it…I recently heard it mentioned, which makes me think it could be here," Skitts said. "Is that what you're lookin' for?" he asked.

"Yeah, that and two other paintings by the Modern French artist Jean Metzinger," said Quinn.

"Metzinger…never heard of him, but I'll keep my eyes and ears open," said Skitts.

"I would very much appreciate it if you did," said Quinn as he took another $20 bill, folded it in half, and stuck it in his informant's shirt pocket.

"Where can I find you normally?" asked Quinn.

"Oh, during the week I'm generally at the community center on St. Francis, with all the other old folks playin' cards and pool," said Skitts.

"Now you wouldn't be hangin' out at the community center and hustling those unsuspecting nice folks there, would you, Skitts?"

"Who…me, detective? Damn, I thought you knew me better than that!" said Skitts smiling.

"I know you, oh so well—why do you think I'm asking?"

Both men laughed out loud.

"Well, I'll look for you there," said Quinn. "And keep your eyes and ears open…I need to find these paintings."

"It's been good talking with you, Skitts," said Quinn as he stood up and handed him another cigar. "You take care now!" Quinn said as he turned and began to walk away.

"Thanks, and good seein' you detective," said Skitts. Skitts smiled as he leaned back on the park bench and gave a two finger salute from the brim of his fedora as Quinn walked away.

CHAPTER XXVII

The Atchison, Topeka & Santa Fe commuter train came to a slow stop on a Saturday afternoon at the train station in Lamy, New Mexico, on November 19, 1942. A tall man with a thin face and dark hair and a finely trimmed mustache walked off the train carrying his briefcase. He wore a long wool overcoat and a fedora. Berndt Kruger, a top Nazi spy in New York and the man Marika Kraus communicated with had been on the train from New York for the last six days. The train stopped in several major US cities before continuing to Denver, and then, from Denver, on to Lamy, New Mexico, outside of Santa Fe.

Lamy was a small town of several hundred people, several miles outside of Santa Fe. The small town was specifically built as a train stop in 1881. Any visitor or vendor coming to Santa Fe by train had to stop first at the Lamy, New Mexico, station. Then, a 50-minute spur connecting train chugged from Lamy around the many curves and over arroyos to the main Santa Fe Station. Thousands traveled to Santa Fe in this manner at that time.

After arriving at Lamy, Berndt was tired from the long train trip and wanted to wait an hour or two before getting onto another train. There was a bar across the street called the Velvet Garter, and he headed there. About two hours later, Kruger saw that his luggage being loaded onto the spur connecting train from Lamy into Santa Fe, so he jumped onto that train. He brought with him eight oil paintings and 10 watercolors by various artists unframed and concealed in a special cylindrical tube. As a Nazi spy and double agent also working for the British, Berndt was in the profiteering business. He was loyal to the Third Reich and had given false information to his British contacts before, but money was Kruger's real boss. The opportunity for cash while finding and then selling the stolen Degenerate Art was too much to pass up. This meant that Berndt Kruger had no qualms about committing a host of crimes if necessary, to preserve his own self-interest. He also knew the painting *Five Dancing Women,* by the French artist Edgar Degas was in Santa Fe. His personal mission was to find it. He had potential buyers in South America who would pay a fortune for this and other Impressionist paintings by the masters. He had to acquire the artwork. And while Kruger knew he would have to part with considerable sums of the Reich's money, one way or another he would acquire these paintings. This was an opportunity that wouldn't present itself again.

Kruger walked into the Finebaum art gallery the next morning, and Katrina was there. He was elegantly dressed. He wore a dark blue coat with tie, and highly polished black shoes. He also used a fancy engraved cane with a silver top molded into the shape of a boar's head. The cane made a sharp sound as it tapped on the cobblestone walkway leading up to the gallery door. "Good morning, Frauline, my name is Kruger. Berndt Kruger, and I'm here to see Joel Finebaum," he said. "I'm an old friend."

"He is not here. He had to go out of town briefly and won't be back for two days," Katrina said.

"When you see him, please tell him that his old friend Berndt is in town and would like to meet with him if he has a chance. I'll be here for a full week, Frauline," said Kruger. "I would very much like to see him."

"How may he contact you, sir?"

"I'm staying at the DeVargas Hotel. Tell him to give the desk clerk my name. That's all he needs to do, and they'll direct him to my room," Kruger said as he bowed, turned, and proceeded out of the gallery.

Katrina was speechless as the tall, polite and impeccably dressed German man with the goatee left the gallery. She could hear the metal tip of his cane tapping against the cobblestone sidewalk outside as he walked away. Katrina couldn't help but say to herself, *Impressive…so well mannered and elegant!*

The DeVargas Hotel was not located on the Santa Fe Plaza but on the nearby Don Gaspar Street. It was an elegant hotel; more traditionally European in design than the La Fonda and known for its bar, which was a traditional Santa Fe meeting spot. Berndt Kruger was in Room 310 two nights later, when there was a knock on his door. Kruger quickly turned the lights off except for a small spotlight he carried with him and he shined it on the chair at the room's entrance.

"Come in," Kruger said.

Joel Finebaum walked into the room with the curtains drawn and because of the spotlight, he couldn't see to his front. Joel could just make out the silhouette of a man on the other side of the room about 12 feet away.

"Sit down, Mr. Finebaum," said Kruger. Joel complied with that instruction.

"I'm here to—" Finebaum started to speak the words, but before he could finish, Kruger stated, "I know why you're here, Mr. Finebaum. We don't have much time. First of all, did you come alone and does anyone else know you came here tonight?"

"I am here alone, and no one else knows," replied Joel.

"Good, when can I pick up the paintings?" Kruger asked.

"Come to the gallery on Sunday night at midnight. Come to the back entrance in the alleyway," said Finebaum. "I will meet you and transfer the paintings. Now, Herr Kruger, I need something from you. What assurances do I have that my family is alive and in good health?" asked Joel.

"Here." With that, Kruger tossed Joel an envelope-sized package with photographs inside. "The dates of the photos are stamped on the back of each one. These were taken just two weeks ago. As you can see, the members of your family are in good health and appear to be happy. They are in a special camp, and receive special privileges at Theresienstadt, near Terezin in the province of Bohemia. Your family will be protected as long as you fulfill your obligation to the Fatherland!" said Kruger.

Joel audibly sighed in the darkness.

"You know your mission changes soon, and will be even more dangerous!" said Kruger.

"Yes, I know. I am very conflicted about completing this second part for your heinous regime," said Joel.

"Careful with your tongue and choice of words, Herr Finebaum. I want you to know that I am not anti-Semetic personally. Many of my good friends prior to this war were Jewish. But I am a loyal German and would do anything for the Fatherland, although I don't agree with all its policies and tactics. And while I do have some sympathy for your family's plight, Finebaum, you will comply if you ever want to see your family members at Theresienstadt alive again!"

"I understand," said Joel.

"I will be at the back entrance of the gallery on Sunday night at the appropriate time. I expect you to be there and to be prepared. We will have to work quickly. Do you have any questions for me, Herr Finebaum?"

"No, I understand and will be waiting for you Sunday night, " replied Joel.

"Till then," Kruger said as he flicked the lights completely off in the room. Seeing that the meeting was over and there was nothing more to say, Joel departed quickly with the package of photographs of his family tightly clutched in his hand.

CHAPTER XXVIII

At midnight on Sunday night, Joel turned the light on in the small room filled with paintings at his gallery. It was a foggy night and the alleyway behind the gallery was unlit and misty. He peered out into the alley and saw something move a few yards away. Then he saw two flashes of light from a flashlight and more movement. The man approached. It was Kruger.

Finebaum opened the back door and let him in.

"Are you ready? Where are they?" Kruger asked.

"On the table," Joel replied.

Kruger walked over to the table. His eyes widened with near amazement as he carefully examined the oil paintings layered within protective parchment paper. "My god, most of these are masterpieces. They should fetch a million marks each for the Reich," Kruger stated. "Roll them up and place them carefully in the tube," Kruger ordered as he gave Joel the round canister.

The entire transaction was completed within a few minutes, and Kruger then vanished into the dark alleyway almost as quickly as he had appeared. Kruger disappeared out into the foggy night, but before leaving he gave Joel Finebaum a final message. "Finebaum, you may be receiving additional paintings from one of our couriers in the future. Safeguard them in the same manner. Your service to Germany is appreciated and your name will be known in the highest ranks of the Reich. You have my word your family will be kept safe during this time." With that, Kruger quickly left the art gallery and began walking down the alleyway through the fog.

Joel exhaled heavily, breathing a sigh of relief, and turned his light off. He locked the back door. *My god, I could have just been killed...*Joel thought to himself.

It took sometime before Joel learned exactly what happened to Berndt Kruger after he left the gallery that night, and who fired the fatal shots that took Kruger's life. Kruger's body jerked back from the impact of the round fired into his chest by the assassin that night. The killer used a handgun and a silencer. Kruger was still on his feet and tried to run in the opposite direction to find cover. He did make it to the opposite end of the alleyway before collapsing against a wall to hold himself up. The second shot fired pierced through his right arm and into his side. He could feel the blood oozing out of his body. It had punctured and tore apart his ribcage, eventually settling into his right lung. Kruger tried to move forward, but it was too painful to move. He was extremely weary, and had already lost considerable blood. He quickly collapsed to the ground.

The assailant appeared from the fog behind him and, walking fast, grabbed the canister out of the hands of Berndt Kruger's weakened grip just before Kruger blacked out. Kruger groaned loudly and the killer seeing that Kruger was still alive, fired one final shot into Kruger's chest immediately killing him. The assailant then disappeared into the dense fog that night with the cylinder-shaped container of priceless paintings.

It wasn't until the night's fog lifted that Kruger's body was found at the end of the alley behind Finebaum's art gallery. Someone walking his dog in the early morning hours found the body. The police then conducted their own investigation. Even the police didn't realize someone else had been to the scene, searched the body and removed evidence before they arrived.

The police found in the dead man's possession, a current Dutch passport with a photo matching the dead man, and belonging to a Mr. Gustaf Vondolen. They also found $400 in cash, US currency. What they did not find, was a hotel key to the DeVargas Hotel, Room 310. The key had already been located and removed from the body long before the police had been alerted to the man's untimely demise.

CHAPTER XXIX

I'll have to work fast and not be seen, Quinn said to himself as he milled his way through the streets towards the DeVargas Hotel on Don Gaspar Avenue. The DeVargas Hotel had been built in the early 1900s at another location in Santa Fe, but had burned down in 1922 in the largest fire Santa Fe had experienced in 300 years. The hotel then moved locations and was rebuilt on Don Gaspar Avenue in early 1924. In the 20s and 30s the DeVargas hotel had been the place where state and local politicians hung out, drank, and solved their unofficial and sometimes official business. It was a landmark in Santa Fe.

Quinn didn't normally enjoy the surveillance part and duty of being a detective. But now Quinn knew the room key he had would open up more than a door to a hotel room. Hopefully, a treasure-trove of evidence and clues to this art mystery awaited Quinn. It was a cold day, and he wore his overcoat with a scarf and fedora. He would cover up as much of himself as he could to get in and make it up to the room...and at that time Quinn didn't know the true identity of the dead man. He was hoping to find out. He passed a few people on the way, but Quinn was so innocuous by the manner in which he moved that no one really noticed him. He caught a break as he approached the entrance to the hotel. A large group of people, possibly tourists, were entering, and he quickly got in the middle of the group as they entered. The concierge was standing not far from the entranceway ready to say something to the group of 30. Quinn mulled momentarily with the group as they entered and listened to the concierge direct them, then he slipped behind the concierge and started up the staircase of the De Vargas to the third floor while lowering his head as he ascended. He needed to go up two more flights of stairs to get to the third floor, and Room 310.

He passed some people coming down the staircase who were loudly engaged in conversation. He ducked his head again and faked a cough to appear to be a man with a cold who didn't want to speak to anyone, and then Quinn proceeded on. The third floor of the DeVargas Hotel was a long, plain-looking corridor. The hotel had a very simple charm, but could not be called a luxury hotel.

He reached Room 310, looked to his right and left but saw no one in the hallway. He quickly tried the key. It opened the door, and Quinn entered. He didn't see much in the room. Quinn experienced the chills as he would be literally rummaging through the personal effects of a dead man. What was he hoping to find? Anything that could shed light on what the hell was really happening in Santa Fe, and could explain the murder of the man. He knew he didn't have much time. The police were inefficient here, but they would soon start checking area hotel lists for a visitor from Holland named Gustaf Vondolen.

Vondolen (Berndt Kruger) had an open suitcase on top of his bed. Quinn chose that place to start looking. He took out all the neatly folded clothes and laid them on the edge of the bed. All the clothes would need to be searched as well. Vondolen, or whatever his name really was, was a traveler as he had many maps and travel guides from various cities in the

US and Europe; including New York, Chicago, Berlin, Copenhagen, and Zurich, Switzerland. He had nothing from Holland.

Quinn next checked the three jackets hanging neatly in the coat rack. Just as he was ready to abandon further search of the suitcase, something caught his eye. A small slit at the bottom of the suitcase concealed something underneath. The suitcase on one side had a false bottom. He tried to stick his hand through the opening to lift the false cover up. It was zippered shut with a small zipper. He located it and opened the cover. He found what he was looking for. Inside were what appeared to be several small notebooks, a key with no markings of any kind, and cash. About $100 in US currency, some English pound notes, and German Reichmarks. One of the notebooks was actually another passport; this one from the German Reich, the official name of Nazi Germany

Bingo! Quinn thought. The picture was definitely that of the man in the alley who had been murdered, only with a different name. This passport showed the name, Berndt Kruger.

Quinn heard a noise outside the room. Someone was trying to open the door, and Quinn heard muffled voices from the hallway outside. The room was small, and if he had to hide quickly, the only possible place was under the bed. The doorknob to the room was turned again, but the door was locked. Whoever it was mumbled something and began to walk away. Quinn could hear the footsteps walking on the carpet of the old hardwood corridor floor.

Time to get outta here, he thought. *If that was the police, they'll be back soon.* He went through the pockets of the jackets hanging up. Nothing. Before leaving, Quinn quickly opened the chest of drawers in the clothes cabinet. Nothing. Having located the most valuable piece of evidence and information he could—the dead man's actual passport—Quinn placed the clothes back in the suitcase and slipped out of Room 310.

There was an exit; another staircase at the far end of the corridor. Quinn quickly headed for it. The staircase went all the way down to a cellar where the boiler room for the hotel was located. Another small staircase led back up to the first floor and to an exit to the rear parking lot. Quinn exited the hotel and quickly left the premises, walking at a fast pace. As far as he could tell, no one knew he had been there. Now he knew instinctively, that he was involved in something big…a murder investigation now gave new meaning and made this larger than searching for some paintings.

CHAPTER XXX

They met at Laszlo Tibor's suite at La Fonda on San Francisco Street on Wednesday of the next week. "Gentlemen, it's good to see you. I'm sure there is much to discuss about our case," said Tibor. "I am anxious to learn what information you've uncovered so far, but first please join me in a glass of a native Hungarian drink, Pilanka. It's very much like Brandy only with a fruity taste." He filled three shot glasses and handed one each to the two men.

"Laszlo, I brought my partner Ethan with me today because this may not be a completely pleasant conversation, and I want a witness."

"A witness…to what, Mr. Chase? I have no quarrel with either of you," replied Tibor. "We are supposed to be working on this case together…or so that was my belief. What have you found so far, and what is happening now?"

"I think you know what we've found, Laszlo. Berndt Kruger came to Santa Fe as you predicted, and within a short time of his arrival he was found dead in the alleyway behind the Finebaum art gallery, shot three times. The murderer used a silencer on his handgun. That tells me this was a planned hit by a professional…not a random robbery or argument that resulted in violence. Also, I think the murder weapon was a foreign-made handgun. I believe it was a German Luger."

Laszlo took a seat.

"You knew Kruger would be here. I need some questions answered to decide whether or not I share your name and information with the police," said Quinn.

"Gentlemen, just because I knew of the man and what he did gives you no basis to suspect me of wrongdoing or to conclude that I had anything to do with the murder of this man. For god's sake, get a grip!" said Laszlo.

"Yes, that's true, but it's one hell of a coincidence," said Quinn.

"So, are you going to tell me more about what happened?" Tibor asked.

Quinn and Ethan looked at one another.

Tibor continued, "Oh, I see. Since I am the killer, I must know all the pertinent details…right?"

"Who is this man again, and how is it you knew about him?" asked Quinn.

Berndt Kruger was a German art dealer who for years specialized in the very art the Nazis hate so much; such as Impressionist, Expressionist, and Abstract works, like Picasso, Cezanne, Monet, and Kandinsky," said Tibor.

"But that makes no sense. Why was he permitted to come here to conduct business as a German citizen if the Nazis hate what he was doing and what it stands for? He should have been in jail in Germany. They're not shy about locking people up," said Quinn.

"You're not acknowledging the evidence in front of you, Mr. Chase," said Tibor. "The Nazi's are using their own art professionals and any other contacts who will work with them to smuggle this art out of Germany and anywhere else they occupy and sell it on the black-market. Kruger was probably here to do just that."

"So you didn't know he was actually here in Santa Fe now? Is that what you're saying?"

"On my life, gentlemen, I had no idea he was here!" said Tibor. "Again, gentlemen, my only concern is finding specific paintings for my clients. I am somewhat offended by your questions and tone, Mr. Chase, and I am beginning to wonder if this partnership is the right thing for us or not."

"Listen, Tibor, this case is beginning to cut across many lines. There is a war on that my country is involved in as you are aware. There is now a homicide involving an art dealer. Gustaf Vondolen…or whoever the hell he really is. There seem to be valuable stolen paintings from Europe that might be hidden somewhere in Santa Fe."

Tibor stroked his beard, thinking through the recent events.

"He was only here a short time before being knocked off," Quinn continued. "It would make sense that anyone associated with this man at all… even remotely…should be concerned for their own safety too. We're meeting with Detective Huff from the Santa Fe Police in a few days. He'll press us for information about the murder and who we're representing. We have to decide what to tell him."

"I ask, gentlemen, that you not mention me…or any knowledge you may have about Kruger's death at all. Whoever did this and for whatever motive, they probably won't stop there. As your client, I am asking you not to reveal my name to the police. I was not involved in Kruger's killing in any way, so please don't reveal your client's identity or any predetermined conclusions based on pure speculation. I have enough trouble in other areas of my life to have the police snooping around. But, I still need assistance tracking down this art I am looking for. So I need to know, do we still have a business relationship, gentlemen? And am I still your client?"

"Of course you are, Mr. Tibor. We're in this investigation together!" replied Ethan, and he continued. "Please understand, my partner and I were police detectives ourselves not too long ago. My partner gets a little too serious and overzealous at times… no offense intended. I completely agree with you and we will maintain your confidentiality when we meet with the police later in the week. There are some additional leads we want to pursue and maybe more information about your paintings will develop there, but right now we have very few answers," said Ethan.

Tibor smoothed a wrinkle in his sleeve.

Ethan continued. "Now, I do hate to bring up formalities, but I was checking over our employment agreement, and looking at our ledger of time spent on this demanding case, we must ask now for an additional $230 to continue working on your behalf," he said as he handed Tibor the ledger.

"Gentlemen, money was never an issue between us. Please give me a moment, and I will pay you your requested amount," said Tibor.

"Mr. Tibor, and also if it's not too much trouble…I'll have that fruit Brandy now," said Quinn.

CHAPTER XXXI

"Okay, dammit, enough double talk! What the hell's going on here?" Quinn's voice rose as he stood in the front of the art gallery staring at Joel Finebaum and Katrina. "A man is dead with a suspicious Dutch passport. He was shot two or three times in the alley behind your gallery. What the hell happened, Finebaum? Don't tell me you don't know this man. I want the truth or from here on out you won't have a minute's peace. Oh, and by the way, the victim wasn't Dutch." Quinn continued, "Here's a clipping of a German newspaper *Das Reich,* dated August 20, 1936. It shows the picture of a man holding up a painting he had just purchased. The caption under the photo in German reads, *Berndt Kruger is smiling after buying a new portrait by Ludwig Dettmann…one of Germany's top artists, at a recent auction in Munich.* Does the man in the photo look familiar? Berndt Kruger looks very much alive in this photo to me!"

"No more double talk and no more lies, Finebaum, if that's even your real name. What was your connection to Berndt Kruger? Tell me now, or I will go right to the police."

"No, no, they don't need to be involved in this," said Finebaum. "Alright, alright…I think I can tell you what you have to know," he said. "Life at times can be complicated and unforgiving, Mr. Chase," said Finebaum.

"We all have a past…sometimes things we're not proud of. And such is my story," Joel said.

"You see, Mr. Chase, I'm a German-Jewish immigrant who didn't grow up in the US. My family, including Katrina, has been here less than 10 years," Finebaum said.

"So, Mr. Chase, are you aware of what is happening to Jewish people in Germany and the rest of occupied Europe? Well, tragedy sometimes makes for strange bedfellows. To get out and get my family out of Germany nearly seven years ago, I did things I never want to discuss, but I had to do these things, Mr. Chase. For no sane reason…no sane reason other than ideological hatred and greed, the Nazis are systematically murdering hundreds of thousands of innocent people. They've refined their murder to an industrial scale. I couldn't let this happen to my family, and Katrina. Berndt Kruger was my underground contact, and I paid him a lot of money to get us out. There were others too. But he paid off various officials to get us out of Europe. In the process, someone else tried to blackmail us for money… and then double-crossed us and nearly turned us in. I killed the man to save my family. I have never thought of myself as a murderer, but in this instance it was for self-preservation and preservation of my family. I deeply regret it just the same."

"Kruger disposed of the body and covered for me while we escaped with false identities and passports and came through Lisbon, to America. We have since cleared customs and are in the process of gaining citizenship, but Kruger located us and began harassing us with letters, trying to blackmail us for more money. He's threatened to turn us into the authorities here. We've been through so much and are so grateful to be here that we submitted to his demands. Last night he came by and I gave him more money. He left through the back door to the alleyway, but I didn't shoot him. I swear I didn't! I don't know what happened when he left, but he had cash on him," said Finebaum.

"Interesting story. Does anyone know this besides me?" asked Quinn.

"No, and I want to keep it that way, Mr. Chase. I have money, and we can work out a deal. Katrina deserves a chance at a free and decent life here in America, and a chance to put an ugly past she didn't cause, behind her," he said.

"Don't worry, Finebaum," Quinn said. "I believe even though you lied to me earlier about Berndt Kruger...basically you're an honest man. If you're telling the truth now about this and you haven't committed a crime here, you should be able to live in peace. The police will be here soon to talk to you...but I don't want your money and I won't say a word unless I have reason to think you've committed crimes here," Quinn said.

"So, Finebaum, this murder had nothing to do with paintings...this Degenerate Art?" Quinn asked.

"As I told you before, Mr. Chase, I know what the term refers to, but that's all. I haven't heard anything, seen or come in contact with it in Santa Fe. As to Kruger's murder...I have no idea what happened. Maybe someone saw him leave through the back door and was lying in wait and robbed him?"

"You understand that you had a very strong motive to kill him, Finebaum. He was extorting money from you with the threat of turning you into the authorities," said Quinn.

"Yes, that's true, but there's another fact you're not aware of, Mr. Chase. I have relatives in Germany and I was ensuring their security and safety through Kruger and the money I paid him. Because of his unexplained death, now they are all at much greater risk. I will have to make other arrangements somehow to ensure my family overseas remains safe. Mr. Chase, I am never surprised when I'm visited by adversity and misfortune…these two evils always seem to locate me and harass me in life."

CHAPTER XXXII

Quinn had always followed his instincts as a detective. Now his instincts led him to the two suspicious art dealers he knew. Laszlo Tibor's story about Kruger made sense, but so did Joel Finebaum's. It was possible that they could both be telling the truth. But why would two foreign art dealers be spending their time in Santa Fe, if there wasn't some prize to make their efforts here worthwhile? And then it occurred to Quinn that Marika Kraus and Laszlo Tibor may not be the art dealers they claimed to be. Quinn knew it wouldn't be long before Detective Huff would put two and two together and begin looking at both of them.

Quinn called a meeting with both of them at Tibor's hotel suite. "Alright, I asked both of you to meet me here for one reason," Quinn said to Marika and Laszlo Tibor. "What the hell is going on in this town?" he asked. "The man who was supposedly from Holland wasn't Dutch and is found dead shot to death in the alleyway behind an art gallery. You two are supposedly art dealers, but is that who you really are? We haven't seen violence and a murder up here like this in many years. It's too much of a coincidence. You know more than you've told me. Tell me what's going on and maybe I can keep the police and FBI away," he demanded. "Otherwise, I'm afraid either the FBI or Detective Frank Huff will be breathing down your necks in a week or so," Quinn said.

Laszlo seemed as if he might say something to Quinn, but then he turned and looked at Marika…"You harlot!" yelled Laszlo. She answered right back, "Old swine!" Quinn wasn't sure whether or not to intervene at this particular moment.

"You're the perfect spy," said Laszlo. "Underhanded and slippery as an eel! Have you ever told the truth in your entire life?" he asked.

"Your people will be under our domination very soon! Then we'll crush you like the cockroaches you are!" she replied.

Quinn thought he should say something as this argument was getting nastier by the second. "You two…screaming at each other isn't gonna solve your problem," as he pointed at Laszlo, "or your problem," as he pointed at Marika.

"You've done this to me before…I know you're hiding my paintings!" yelled Laszlo, pointing at her.

"I don't have your stupid paintings, you old fool!" retorted Marika. "Someone's playing both of us…can't you see that?" she said.

Laszlo drew a pistol and pointed it at her. "Tell me where the paintings are, you Nazi!" he yelled.

"I don't know anything about them, but even if I did, I wouldn't tell you…just to see you squirm, old man!" she yelled.

"Are you trying to get us all thrown in jail…?" yelled Quinn. "Put that away, Tibor…" he yelled as he went to grab the gun from Laszlo, pushing the older man's arm downward, then taking the gun away from him.

"Berndt Kruger was your contact. He brought those paintings in for you!" Tibor yelled. "And then you took the paintings and killed him!"

"Crazy old man!" she answered. "I don't know who killed him, but it wasn't me. And I told you I don't have your damned paintings!" yelled

Marika again. "Next time you point a gun at me you better aim well and it better work! It will be the last time you ever get the chance!" she said as she turned and slammed the door to Tibor's suite as she left.

"What the hell were you doing? What was that all about?" demanded Quinn.

"I told you that woman is evil through and through!" said Laszlo.

"Tibor, if that gun had actually fired you'd be on your way to jail right now, probably charged with murder. I don't know where you got this pistol from, but I'm gonna keep this for a while," said Quinn. "It'll be locked in the safe at our office. You can retrieve it when you leave Santa Fe."

"I need that gun for my protection.!" Laszlo replied.

"Listen, dammit! You leave her alone!" Quinn retorted. "You're either gonna shoot yourself or someone else by accident. You're much safer without it, and that's the way it's gonna be!"

"Okay, Mr. Chase, okay...you keep it," said Laszlo. The two exhausted men paused for about forty seconds before Tibor muttered, "You know Mr. Chase as much as I hate to say it, I don't think she killed Berndt Kruger. And she could be right about something else," Laszlo said. "Somebody else in Santa Fe is involved searching for this Nazi stolen art, and maybe manipulating all of us. Manipulating all of us like puppets attached to strings. We have to find out who it is!"

CHAPTER XXXIII

Springtime in Santa Fe was exceptionally beautiful in 1943. The foliage was green, and there were colorful roses, lilacs, and wildflowers blooming all over the small city. The temperatures warmed up in the daytime, but cooled down to a comfortable point by late afternoon and remained all evening long. A fair amount of snow had fallen in the Jemez and Sangre de Cristo Mountains in the wintertime several months earlier, so the rivers and streams seemed alive with runoff water jumping over the various rocks in their way. About the only drawback to spring in Santa Fe was the pollen in the air, which made some eyes water and other people sneeze constantly. Baseball was the national pastime and popular game at the time. Due to the war, major league baseball had shut down so there were no professional games to listen to on the radio or follow in the newspapers. There were many informal games, however played around town on any given day... and it seemed like every church and organization in town had a team.

Springtime was also the time for romance. Those staying back home still lead their lives; and fell in love. In one way or another, however, every physically and mentally able adult contributed to the war effort whether they knew it or not. Even if it was through the purchase of US Savings Bonds. Rubber and gasoline were just two of the staples of life that were rationed during the war years. People had ration coupon books and points for their coupons, allowing them to purchase varying amounts of gasoline if they owned a vehicle. Also, gasoline was dispensed on an as-needed basis, depending on where one lived and where they had to travel for work. Anyone needing an automobile for transport to and from Los Alamos New Mexico during this time had no problem acquiring coupons and fuel whenever they needed it.

Jeanny, the young woman from The Hill wrote a letter to Marika Kraus. Jeanny was eager to continue their dalliance and desperately wanted to see her again. Marika, for her part, never expected to hear from Jeanny again, and was surprised to receive her letter.

"My dearest Marika," Jeanny began. "Even though we only spent a little time together, you have had a profound influence on me. Being away from you makes me feel empty inside. It is a feeling I hope can be overcome shortly. I am planning a trip to Santa Fe on Saturday, the 18th of May. Although we only spent, a short time together…I ache for more. You have provided your address to me…I will stop by at your home at three in the afternoon on Saturday, May 18th. I hope with all my heart to see you then."

In Jeanny's letter, she also stated that she could only be gone that afternoon. Eventually they would notice her absence, and she would be in great trouble as they tried to find her. And Jeanny noted that the consequences would be severe if her superiors discovered what had happened. But, where romance is involved, obstacles are overcome and things have a way of working out.

On Saturday May 18, 1943, Jeanny Conway jumped into the backseat of an administrator's sedan who was leaving the compound, pulled a blanket over her body as she hid under the blanket in the backseat of a 1939 Buick Century Coupe as it rolled out the Los Alamos front gate. She rode in that backseat, concealed under the blanket on roads that were unfinished for an hour and 20 minutes, until she reached Santa Fe. Her chauffer and friend had offered to wait till dusk before driving back to The Hill, about 40 miles away.

Jeanny hadn't said a word to anyone about her previous meetings with Marika at the La Fonda bar. Jeanny had never experienced a romantic, let alone sexual, encounter with a woman before, but at times found various women attractive. Back home in New Jersey she always had a boyfriend and was raised in a traditional Methodist family. But she couldn't deny her curiosity or feelings. These feelings confused her as she never thought of herself as gay. She would just admire the personalities and sheer beauty of various women she had seen or encountered randomly. This was a first time for her. She was a little reckless in this new and strange environment. She had to satisfy this curiosity.

On the afternoon of May 18th she searched and found Marika's place. It was a small casita in a row of small houses on the northwest side about a mile from the plaza. Marika's casita was quaint but with a fairly large front window. There was a chimney, so there was a fireplace that most likely saw much use during the year, especially during winter. It appeared cozy.

Jeanny walked up to the front door and took the door knocker in hand. She hit it against the large wooden door distinctively two times. At first she didn't hear a thing, but then she heard a noise on the other side of the door. The doorknob turned slightly, and then the door began to creak open. Standing before her was a blond tall woman, about 5 feet 10 inches, with a slender, athletic body, wearing a beige top and black tights like that of a dancer. Marika displayed a wry, mischievous smile as she stood aside and motioned for Jeanny to enter. As Jeanny walked through the door into the small home, Marika pulled her beige top completely off and threw it on the floor.

The thing that made Marika Kraus so sexy to both mean and women was difficult to define. Her mysterious and alluring charm? Her shapely figure? It was a combination of all things most likely. But there was no question that Marika exuded sexuality and appeal.

Two and a half hours later, Jeanny left Marika's little home. She exited through the back door. Her hair was disheveled, and her face was flushed. She had a half bewildered look about her. If she wasn't confused about her emotional and sexual identity before, there was no doubt she was now. But she didn't have time to contemplate much at that moment. She had to find her ride back to The Hill. She only guessed at the trouble she'd be in if it was discovered she had snuck out and stowed away on a ride to Santa Fe.

As for Marika…she smiled as Jeanny walked away. She was now privy to a limited, but still top-secret information about America's efforts to design and construct an atomic bomb at the Los Alamos National Laboratory. Marika showered and then slipped into her outfit for the evening. She actually had developed real feelings for Jeanny that she could not deny, which was the exception from most of her other sexual conquests and relationships. Foremost, Marika was a German spy, and everything she did had to support and benefit her mission in some way. This was her reality. For Marika, relationships and sex had more to do with her mission in America than with her own personal enjoyment. It was the way things had to be, and she knew it.

CHAPTER XXXIV

"You've had quite a few tonight. You sure you want another one, buddy?" Mario, the bartender at Lorenzo's on the plaza, said to Quinn on an abnormally cold night in late May 1943.

"Another shot, bartender! You got nothin' to worry about. It's not your health we're talkin' about…it's mine!"

Based on that command, the bartender poured another shot of bourbon into Quinn's glass.

"Wonderful! Someone who listens!" said Quinn, noticeably slurring his words.

"Anyway, how you getting home tonight, buddy?" said the bartender.

"I use Manny's Cabs," said Quinn. "Well, we close in 45 minutes, and it's pretty cold out there tonight. Maybe we should call Manny now?" he said.

Quinn then felt a tap again on his right shoulder. "A thirsty girl needs a drink. How about buying me one?" The sexy deep voice that came from behind him was unmistakable. Marika took the chair next to his. She pulled her cigarette case out, pulled out a cigarette, and turned towards the bartender. Mario struck a match, and the scent of tobacco from a newly lit cigarette filled the air.

"What are you doing here?" Quinn asked. "This isn't Alex's."

"Oh, I just happened to be walking by when I noticed someone wearing his G-man hat at the bar. That could only be one person I know in this town," she said.

"What would you like, Marika?" the bartender asked.

"I'll have my usual champagne," she replied. When the bartender was out of hearing range, Marika said, "The better question, Mr. Chase, is what information may I provide you with?"

Quinn, noticeably drunk, turned in his chair, displaying a silly grin. "What did you just say?"

The bartender came back. "Marika do you know this...this gentleman?"

"Oh, yes," she said, "you might say we're old friends."

"Well, he's had a few too many as you can see," said Mario.

"How dare you question my sobriety, sir!" Quinn said with a sarcastic look on his face while slurring his words.

"Believe me, mister, nothing personal, but tonight it's not hard to do! I've called him a cab. He's probably gonna' need some help getting to it when it arrives," the bartender said to Marika.

"It's okay, Mario," she said. "I'll make sure he gets home."

She looked at Quinn with her sharp, well-defined looks and sparkling blue eyes and took a drag on her cigarette. "I may have some important information for you regarding the Degenerate Art," she said.

"Oh, yeah?" said Quinn. "You're not gonna tell me Lazslo Tibor is smuggling art here, are you?"

"Please, Mr. Chase, don't insult my intelligence...that's no way to treat a lady," she replied. "Listen to this, ten Impressionist original paintings were seized by authorities last week in Los Angeles as they were being loaded into an unmarked crate for transport on a ship bound for Buenos Aires.

These are the types of paintings I want to buy for my gallery, Mr. Chase. Rumor also has it they originated from here. If true, what an interesting and strange little coincidence!" she said.

She had caught Quinn's attention, even in his drunken state. "Well, that's very interesting, lady!" he stated. "But I have it on very good authority that there is no connection between the Finebaum Gallery and this so-called Degenerate Art that everyone's after," Quinn stated.

"Mr. Chase, the paintings I mentioned were confiscated on the docks in California. Guess whose initials were written as "Sender" on the Bill of Lading? JF. And from of all places…Santa Fe, New Mexico! As I said… what a curious little coincidence."

Quinn just stared at his drink.

"Why are you telling me this?" he asked.

"Because you need to know that the very people you think are your friends, may be involved in this. You're looking into something so dangerous that it can get you hurt or even killed.…I told you this before. Remember Berndt Kruger," she said.

"So then you're obviously involved," Quinn said.

"No, but I have my suspicions of those who are," she said. "And they're not nice people …starting with the most obvious, Laszlo Tibor. And yes, I believe Joel Finebaum is involved as well," she said.

"Okay, folks, the bar closes in five minutes!" yelled Mario from the other end of the room, interrupting their tense conversation. "Buddy, your cab just pulled up in front. Here's your tab for the night," Mario said as he slid a small piece of paper under Quinn's glass.

Quinn took his wallet out and pulled out a $20 and then a $10 bill. Then, enunciating his words clearly, as if he was sober and with no slur at all, Quinn replied to the bartender, "I'll take care of the lady's drink…and by the way Mario, my name's not Buddy…it's Quinn," he said as he stuck his hand out and shook the bartender's hand.

He then turned to Marika and asked with slurred speech again, "Can I give you a ride somewhere?"

"That would be very nice," Marika replied as she allowed Quinn to help her with her coat before they both walked to the door. "Have a good evening, Mario!" she yelled from the door as she grabbed Quinn's arm to help escort him out. They both stumbled out of the bar and to the waiting yellow cab that was idling outside, spewing exhaust into the cold night air of Santa Fe. Their eventual destination would be Marika's small home on Guadalupe Street, about two miles away. Quinn attempted unsuccessfully to kiss her on the neck as they drove to her flat. He was so drunk that all Marika could do was help get him inside to her couch and then watch as he quickly passed out and began to snore loudly.

CHAPTER XXXV

A few days later both Quinn and Ethan Clark were at Lieutenant Huff's office at the police station. "What do ya' have for me?" said Detective Huff. "Some strange shit's goin' on around here. If you know something, you're duty bound to tell me," Huff said.

Quinn and Ethan just stared at the obese and homely-looking police detective, whose hair was noticeably disheveled and whose clothes struggled to fit properly.

"Detective, why don't you tell us what's happening around here?" Ethan retorted. "A man with a Dutch passport who is basically a stranger to Santa Fe is killed in an alleyway several months ago. The shell casings found at the scene were from a German Luger. How many murders does that make in the last three years?" Ethan asked.

"That fact, Mr. Clark, is irrelevant unless you're suggesting some type of a connection or trend. Actually, we've only had two other incidents we've investigated for murder in the last three years. But those cases eventually were ruled as accidents. I'm gonna ask again, what information do you have for me concerning this murder?"

"The gallery owner Joel Finebaum didn't do it," said Quinn.

"And how can you be sure of that, Chase?" spat back Huff as he looked at Quinn with indignation.

"I know it," answered Quinn. "I can't reveal my source, but you're lookin' down the wrong alleyway, pardon the pun, detective, if you suspect Joel Finebaum."

"We plan to interview him, and his niece too," said Huff, "when we gather some more details to check on their stories."

"Last time we were here, Lieutenant, I asked if you had ever heard the term Degenerate Art. Did you check up on that term?" asked Quinn.

"Once again, boys," said Huff as he pointed at Quinn, "I'll be the one asking the questions here."

"Just so you know," said Quinn, "it's Modern and Abstract art from Europe that the Nazis have targeted as being anti-fascist. The art is a threat to their regime. Hitler himself and a few of his henchmen, including his Minister of Propaganda Joseph Goebbels, have identified works of art they call Degenerate. They're trying to either hide them away, auction them off, or burn them. Many paintings they want to get rid of are works from the great painters of the world. Well, the rumor is that some of these great works are in Santa Fe right now, Huff," said Quinn.

"That's 'Detective Huff' or 'Lieutenant Huff' to you, Chase!" replied the police detective. "I wouldn't advise irritating me. My job is hard enough!"

"It very well could have had something to do with the Dutchman's murder several months ago," Quinn said.

"Perhaps your friend Finebaum and his pretty niece are hiding some of this art? They'd make the perfect front. They're outsiders nobody really knows much about. Maybe it's time for a good old-fashioned police search, with a warrant," said Huff.

"As you see fit, but I think that would be a total waste of your time," said Quinn.

"We'll see," said the police detective. "We'll see if they willingly cooperate or not."

Quinn could have easily turned Joel and Katrina in to Detective Huff based on what he had learned from Marika Kraus – but something prevented him from doing so. The two PI's had much more criminal investigation experience than the small, awkward, and sloppy-looking police detective, but they had no other choice than to indulge this man and make him think they took him seriously. But Lieutenant Frank Huff was right about one thing. He could make their lives absolutely miserable if he wanted to.

So right in the middle of Lt. Huff's speech, a well-dressed older man opened the door and walked into the meeting room. He appeared to be in his 50s.

"Mayor Harper, it's good to see you," said Huff. "Can I help you?"

"No, thank you, Lieutenant," said the man. "I'm looking for the police chief. I need to speak with Chief Sutherland," the mayor said. With that, the man walked over to Ethan and Quinn and extended his hand.

"Hi, I don't know you...I'm Dan Harper, Mayor of Santa Fe," he said as he shook both Ethan and Quinn's hands while they stood with surprised looks on their faces.

"Hello, Mayor," said Ethan. "It's our honor to meet you. My name is Ethan Clark, and this is my partner, Quinn Chase. We're former police officers from Albuquerque, and we've opened up our own office here offering private investigations," Ethan said.

"Oh, my god!" said the mayor. "More detectives in town, that's all we need now!" he said sarcastically while giving a hearty and good-natured laugh. "Well, welcome to the City Different, gentlemen...as we call it. I hope you have a wonderful experience in our little city," the mayor said. "I'm sure Lt. Huff will fill you in on all the attractions of Santa Fe and the surrounding area."

Lt. Huff's face broke out in a red flush.

"Make sure you get around town when you get the chance and check out our fine art galleries. Some of the most beautiful art in the world is created and sold right here in Santa Fe."

"Yes, your Honor, I've heard," said Quinn.

"In fact just walk through our City Hall and you'll see some great examples of Southwestern and Modern art...or check out my personal collection in my office," said Harper.

"I'd enjoy that very much," Quinn said.

"If I can ever do anything for you, don't hesitate to let me know. My office is in City Hall... the door is always open. Great to meet both of you!" the Mayor said, waving as he walked out of the same door he entered.

"That was nice of him," said Ethan after the mayor had left.

"Yeah...Mayor Harper is a great guy," said Huff. "But don't take his easygoing nature for granted. Just like me, he's a serious and cunning man when he needs to be...I'm cunning and I can be a real son-of-a-bitch when I want to be!" Huff said. "So, back to my little speech, boys....Things will be much better for both of us if you can provide me with some information I can use every month," Huff said.

"We fully intend to provide you with information as we can, Lieutenant. After all, it is for the common good," said Quinn.

"How are you two paying your bills these days?" Huff asked. "What I mean is, what cases are you working on and who's hired you? The police department has an interest in knowing."

"Oh, just your standard husband-wife cheating, and an occasional farmer complaint because someone else's cows were grazing on his land. Every now and then employee theft from a department store or a bar that's losing money and the owners want their bartenders checked out," said Quinn.

"Enough to pay rent, but nothin' really exciting," said Ethan.

"Well, boys, that sounds nice…a lot of simple cases. I don't believe it, but I haven't heard any complaints about you either. Cooperation, boys, is the way to keep me off your backs. If you hear anything or get any leads at all – especially anything about Gustaf Vondolen, the Dutchman – I need to know. Okay, that's all for now. Let's see if we can cooperate with one another. I got nothing' personally against you. I did some askin' around, and there are strong opinions in the Albuquerque PD that you both got a raw deal. But that doesn't change anything between us. Get me some real information next time!"

"That guy's so damn charming!" Quinn mumbled as the two men walked out of the police station after the meeting that day.

CHAPTER XXXVI

The community center or "rec center" in Santa Fe was a gathering place for many people in Santa Fe over 50. It was basically just a plain building with two large rooms. The front room was a lounge area with simple chairs and a few sofas. A large radio and phonograph was set up in the front room to play big band and ballad music of the day. Posters adorned the bulletin board in the front room with news clippings of various battles taking place around the world, and news of any local men or women in the armed forces. An American Flag hung noticeably in the foyer as guests walked into the center. Various posters, including "Uncle Sam Wants You," "Support the USO," "Rosie the Riveter," and a Navy recruiting poster, were displayed as well.

The back part of the community center was a larger room with no decorations but with ten card tables and four pool tables set up. This wasn't a place where the wealthy and artistic crowd of Santa Fe went to socialize. That crowd, the eccentric crowd, would be found at places like Alex's or at one of Santa Fe's fine restaurants or museums. But at around 2:00 in the afternoon, the center was generally packed with 40 or so card players who bet on card games like Gin Rummy, Bridge, and Five Card Stud, even though the rules forbid gambling.

Tommy Dorsey records were played, often with the enticing voice of their new young singer, Frank Sinatra, echoing throughout the center. So when Quinn walked into the rec center that Wednesday afternoon, everyone appeared to be listening to the music, playing cards, or talking with their friends.

Skitts Jones was there too that day when Quinn walked in. Skitts was playing cards in the back section of the card room. These were the tables where the big money was bet. It wasn't unusual for $100 to change hands on any given day at these tables.

Quinn noticed Skitts almost immediately by his fedora, which Skitts wore all the time—even indoors. Skitts also gave his location away by raising and slamming his hand of cards down on the poker table when he won. And Skitts had just raised the current hand of his table ten bucks with the straight he was holding. Two of the four players at the table quickly folded, with one calling the bet. A pair of 10's did not beat Skitts' straight. Skitts raised his five cards up in the air with his right hand before slamming the cards on the table and laughing with his familiar cackle as he did so.

"Gentlemen, Skitts Jones is so happy for your donations to his for-profit foundation this afternoon! Your generosity is so much appreciated! Now, shall we play some more?"

Quinn flashed a quick smile. Quinn knew Skitts was the best card shark in town. If you played against him, sooner or later you'd be broke. *Hell,* thought Quinn, *I've got to hand it to him. He's found a place where he can make a livin' playing cards.*

Quinn started to walk over to the table, when Skitts turned and saw him. "Gents, before the next hand is dealt…I gotta' take a break. I'm gonna be out for about 20 minutes, so if I lose my seat, I understand. I'll be back tomorrow. You can try to beat me then, but you better be wearing your lucky shirt!" He laughed while collecting his chips.

"Detective Chase, what's been goin' on with you since our last meeting?" said Skitts.

"If you got the time, let's walk over to the park and talk about that stuff, Skitts," said Quinn.

"I got the time for you, detective!" replied Skitts, as he got up and the two walked out.

"Some strange shit's going on around here," Quinn said.

"You know, I sure could use a cold one, detective! It would help me think and remember so much better," Skitts said with a sly smile.

"Skitts, you old hustler…for a damned beer?" Quinn asked sarcastically.

"A man's got to stay hydrated, Detective!" Skitts said.

"Okay, we'll stop at the corner grocery store and get a couple of beers," said Quinn.

"Much obliged, detective…much obliged," replied Skitts.

They ended up with two cigars and two beers. They walked over to Clifton Park, which was the only park in Santa Fe that permitted public consumption of alcohol. "So…what's on your mind, detective? What can old Skitts do for his friend today?"

"I've got to find these three paintings, Skitts. Did you hear anything more about the stolen artwork in town?" asked Quinn.

"Oh, a little bit here…a little bit there," answered Skitts as he tilted his Coors bottle upwards, taking a liberal gulp. Quinn had played this game so many times before he was better at it than playing cards. "Got a light?" Skitts asked Quinn with a smirk on his face. He simultaneously cut off the end of his cigar.

Quinn quickly pulled a match out of his box of matches, struck it, then lit Skitts' cigar. He then pulled out a $20 bill and stuffed it in Skitts' shirt pocket.

"Well, I believe you were askin' about three paintings in particular, right, Detective?" Quinn nodded. "Well, I got mixed news for you," said Skitts. "The paintings you're looking for…all three of them are here in Santa Fe. I'm sure of that. But I don't know where. And that's unusual for me, detective. But give me some time," Skitts said with a smile. "Rumor around town is that there's some new cat known as The Merchant —the big kingpin in charge of all the paintings coming in and out of town," said Skitts. "Rumor also has it that there's more comin' in and goin' out in the next few weeks," Skitts said.

"Well, I'll be damned!" said Quinn.

"Well, that's the interesting part," said Skitts. "There's supposed to be a show from Paris comin' into town booked at the Lensic in the next few weeks. The rumor is they'll be doin' more than their vaudeville act…they're part of the smugglin' ring," said Skitts.

"Where are you getting your information from?" asked Quinn.

"A little birdie told me, detective, but this little birdie sings true songs. You know I can't give away everything," replied Skitts.

"My friend, I hope you're not bein'fed bad information!" Quinn stated as he stuffed another $20 bill down Skitts' shirt pocket.

"That's not likely, detective…not likely," said Skitts brandishing a smile.

CHAPTER XXXVII

Quinn had Manny drive him up to Alex's around 10:00 that night. Immediately he noticed things had been rearranged inside the large bar. The tables, chairs, and almost everything else was moved around the small stage set up in the rear of the building. The front bar with the high barstools was still open with a few people sitting there, but just about everyone else that night gravitated toward the back stage. Several portable spotlights had been set up above and to the side of the stage.

"What's going on tonight?" asked Quinn as he motioned for a drink.

"It's Cabaret night," said the bartender. "Every so often Alex brings in entertainment. Last month we had a ventriloquist from back East. Tonight it's a Cabaret-style burlesque show. Supposedly a touring show from Paris."

"What?" replied Quinn. Just then he felt a tap on his shoulder and heard a familiar voice in his ear.

"So you are a man of culture after all," the voice whispered. He turned to his right and came face to face with Marika Kraus. "I have a table close to the stage. Come sit with us up front," she said. With that she grabbed his hand and essentially pulled him off of the barstool. "Leave your drink here. We've got champagne at the table. Hurry, I want to get there before the show starts!" she said. Quinn followed as she pulled him towards the stage.

Marika led him to a round table about five feet from the front of the small stage. The tables and chairs were jammed fairly close together as the patrons were settling in to watch the show. Quinn and Marika got there as the lights were dimming. Soon the lights were so low that it was nearly pitch-black inside. The next sound Quinn heard was a drumroll, and then the spotlight shined on the stage. A thin man of medium height with slicked back hair, wearing a black tuxedo with a slight layer of white paste on his face, dark makeup around his eyes and colored lips like a harlequin, walked onto the stage. Only this was no harlequin. He talked loudly.

He spoke with a high-pitched voice that otherwise might have been annoying, but was strangely perfect for this occasion. His raspy voice pierced the air in the room.

"Madames and Messieurs, Ladies and Gentlemen, Fine peoples of good character, and ahh maybe not so good character…Good Evening! Welcome to Cabaret Le Paradis from Paris! Ha! Ha!" he yelled out. "Here, you can drink a little, relax a little, and dream a lot about our beautiful ladies from Europe for you tonight! Here you can let your inhibitions down, your imaginations run free. There is no need to worry. If your husband, wife, or girlfriend thinks you're having too much fun! They let you know with a pain to your side with their elbow! Ha…! Tonight, we give you a sample of our show. Our complete show will play at the Lensic Theater starting next Wednesday and then every night for two weeks. Therefore, enjoy a taste of our program tonight. "We hope you enjoy and we see you at the Lensic Theatre during the next two weeks."

"Now I present to you a woman of the Romani Gypsys of Eastern Europe. A beauty of risqué pleasures and mystery…Lady Lavinia!" And with that the small combo played a short introduction. The lights went out on the stage, and when they came back on, a dark-complexioned lady wearing a colorful free-flowing dress of orange, yellow, and purple that showed her midriff danced out. She wore a necklace of ivory trinkets and wore a red bandana. She also wore many rings on both hands. She danced out and sat at a small table with what appeared to be a crystal ball. The piano, accordion, and clarinet played some background music.

"Welcome, my friends, to Lady Lavinia's parlor!" the woman said. "Here, for a small fee, I will look at your palms, stare into my sphere, and stare into your hearts and minds, and tell you what your future is." The music became slightly louder, and a rhythmical accordion and drumbeat ensued. The woman got out of her chair, spun around, and began to sing. She sang and danced to the pulsating drumbeat with two other similarly dressed ladies who came to join her. The clarinetist and other musicians played a melody that was repetitive and pulsated, sounding like a Bohemian or Jewish Horah wedding dance.

The three women moved in unison swinging their hips and gyrating their midsections. They locked their hands and arms behind each other's backs, and sang about the men that came to watch them. In unison they shed parts of their dresses, and their outfits became skimpier. At the end, all three well-endowed women were scantily dressed compared to when they started. They sang of traveling to other villages to perform for other people. One by one they danced off the stage with Lady Lavinia bowing to the audience. Then she untied a cloth bag affixed to her waist, opened it and ran along the edge of the stage inviting the audience to deposit money. The band played on. Most people sitting in the front dropped coins into the bag. She circled the stage, spun in a complete revolution, and then was gone.

The combo band began to play again. The Master of Ceremonies in his tuxedo walked back out on stage. "Ha! Ha!" he said, pointing at the crowd with raised eyebrows and a sly smile. "You like?" he asked. "You like Lady Lavinia and her friends? Come to the Lensic next week to see them again!"

Quinn and the people of the audience clapped. Marika and Quinn were hypnotized by the gypsies, caught up in their intoxicating perfumes, and their rhythmic dance. "My fine Ladies and Gentlemen," the Master of Ceremonies then said. "That was only the beginning, Ha! Now we bring to you an act of death-defying bravery of human being against the dangerous vicious snarling beasts of the world!

"Madames and Messieurs, please welcome Giselle and Simon and their trained poodles!" The lights went out briefly, and when they came on again, six small poodles ran out onstage with their handlers, performing various stunts and tricks. The poodles were decorated with sparkling sequins. They ran around the stage as the band played. They ran under and jumped over chairs, through hoops, and down a miniature slide with stairs. There was a bell at the top of the slide with a string hanging down, and the dogs rang the bell by yanking down on the string before they slid down the slide.

A fat man in costume with an oversized mustache and necktie, wearing suspenders, baggy pants with two flaps extending about six inches out from his waist rearwards, and a beautiful woman scantily clad wearing a garter belt and high heels, were the dog handlers. The woman directed the dogs by blowing a whistle and pointing a riding crop as the poodles performed various stunts. The fat man stumbled around the stage mumbling at the dogs and trying to chase them as they ran from obstacle to obstacle. But he could never catch them. At the end of the show, and in total sync with the band...two of the poodles came from behind the man as he wiped his forehead following his arduous chase, jumped up, grabbed onto the two flaps, and refused to let go. The weight of the two poodles brought their handler's pants down to his ankles, thus exposing his polka-dotted shorts beneath. The crowd gasped, and laughed loudly. The large handler, obviously embarrassed, even though this was a planned stunt, displayed a look of surprise and tried to cover up. The crowd continued laughing. The man then chased the poodles from the stage floor, pumping his fists at the dogs as they all ran off the stage.

The Master of Ceremonies came back out onstage gesturing to the couple and their poodles by raising his arm and pointing. "Giselle, Simon, and their killer poodles, Ladies and Gentlemen!" the MC yelled. The crowd responded with clapping and whistles of approval.

"I introduce to you now, straight from Paris, a lady whose beauty has been compared to the Goddess Venus!" The drummer started a low-pitched drumroll. "This is a lady who captivates with sight, sound, her incomparable charm and grace....Please welcome Mademoiselle Sadira and friends!"

The crowd clapped enthusiastically. The piano began a very light entr'acte again, and the lights went out. When they came back on, five scantily clad women were onstage straddling and leaning over the tops of their chairs. All had short black or blond hair, and wore tight nylon blouses with garter straps and belts. All wore tight-fitting hose with high-heeled black shoes. The spotlights focused on the one in the middle, as she was extremely well-endowed with unnaturally large bosoms.

She looked up and got up from her chair. Her well-toned body was accentuated by the spotlight. She leaned back and stuck out one of her long legs. Then she began...more speaking than singing. "A woman is like a flower in the springtime, Monsieur…With care and love she blooms before your eyes, Monsieur! She only asks a little of your time, Monsieur…"

Then the orchestra started their tune, and she slowly transitioned into song. "A little bit of your time and attention, Monsieur! Will you come talk to me? Will you come walk with me? Will you come sing with me into the night, Monsieur? I only seek your time, let's have a glass of wine, and get to know each other through the night, Monsieur. I don't want opulence, I seek your confidence…let's watch the moon glow in the starry sky, Monsieur."

The tune accelerated in tempo as it went on, with all the instruments— drums, clarinet, accordion, and violin—joining in to keep the rhythmic, pulsating beat lively. It was a group dance scene with the other female dancers moving in unison, snapping their fingers, and repeating Mademoiselle Sadira's phrases and movements at times. Sometimes dancing with her, and other times dancing behind her as she sang.

As for Quinn and Marika, they were captivated by the mysterious and alluring Sadira until the very end. The song was meant to be an invitation by Sadira for her lover to shower her with attention, money, and time. This, of course, with risqué and sexual innuendos and dancing mixed throughout. In the end, Mademoiselle Sadira and her group sat back down straddling their chairs, backrests facing the audience—all signaling for their lovers to join them in unison, curling their index fingers and beckoning their lovers forward. The lights dimmed to black, and the crowd—obviously pleased—again whistled loudly and cheered with approval.

The Master of Ceremonies was back onstage, and the band started to play an Umpa-Umpa two-beat tempo tune, where two different notes are repeated over and over again. He performed his own soft-shoe routine to the beat, singing and talking about a young woman as he danced. He danced for a few minutes, and then ended his dance routine as the performers that evening reappeared onstage behind him.

"Ladies and Gentlemens, I hope you have enjoyed our performance as we have tonight!" he yelled. "Lady Lavinia and her exotic women!"

Lady Lavinia and her group stepped forward, and brandishing mischevious smiles, bowed . "Ha!" he yelled again. The women rejoined the performers in line in the back. The crowd clapped, whistled and shouted with approval.

"Ha! Ha!...Giselle and Simon." Both Giselle and Simon walked forward, each with one of the small poodles in their arms. They bowed to the crowd. Again the crowd applauded enthusiastically. They rejoined the line of performers behind the MC.

"And finally, Ladies and Gentlemen, Mademoiselle Sadira and her group of lovely ladies!" Mademoiselle and her fellow dancers stepped forward and bowed to the audience, acknowledging their loud applause and approval.

The lights began to brighten in the large room, but the MC was still speaking as the lights were raised. "Come please friends and attend our entire show at the Lensic Theatre next Wednesday and for two straight weeks. We hope you enjoyed our short presentation. Ha! Ha! We have much, much more for you!"

Quinn cheered and applauded with approval like the rest. Then he looked over briefly to his right, and saw him there. Quinn later couldn't recall the final words of the eccentric Master of Ceremonies. He was too transfixed and staring at the familiar face off to his right with keen interest. Ethan Clark was about four tables over watching the burlesque show, and sitting at a table with some people Quinn didn't recognize. The lights were fully on now, and the show was over. The band was still playing as the performers exited the stage as a group.

It was Ethan…he was sure of it. Marika drew his attention away briefly by grabbing his arm and exclaiming, "Fantastic! We must go see the whole show…what do you say?"

Quinn didn't say a thing, but when he looked back to the right, Ethan was gone. In only a few seconds' time, he had blended into the large crowd and soon afterwards disappeared from the bar as well. Did he see Quinn? Did he panic and leave? Quinn looked all over Alex's as the crowd thinned, but Ethan, or someone Quinn had mistaken for Ethan, had vanished.

CHAPTER XXXVIII

On June 5, 1943, they met with Lt. Huff at the police station again. "Well, what's happening this week in the lives of our town Dicks?" Huff mused. "Someday, I hope you have some useful information for me," he said. "I would love to go back to my superiors and be able to justify your existence in Santa Fe," Huff said sarcastically.

Quinn spoke out. "Well, Huff—"

"That's Detective Huff to you, Chase," Huff quipped. "When will you gain some respect for your superiors?"

"It just so happens we do have a lead we think you're gonna find very interesting," stated Quinn.

"It would have to result in an arrest for it to be interesting to me, Chase! Then again, as desperate as I am to find out what the hell's going on in this town,…Well, what is it?" Huff arrogantly asked. "Unlike you two, I have a busy schedule and taxpayers to satisfy."

"A large quantity of Degenerate Art was recently brought into Santa Fe, detective…if that is of interest to you!" Quinn retorted.

"Okay, I'm interested…tell me more!" responded Huff.

Quinn divulged what he had learned from Skitts Jones several days before. That the burlesque show was also a cover for smuggled Degenerate

Art and a large amount had been brought into the city. And the troupe might be leaving with some when their show was finished at the Lensic Theater.

When Huff received this news, he made Quinn and Ethan stand by while he informed the Chief of Police. The Chief, Captain Sutherland then wanted to speak with Quinn and Ethan. "Thank you, boys, for this information," the captain said. "May I ask where you got this information from?"

"It's a very reliable source, sir, but I can't be more specific at this time," answered Quinn.

"You better start singing, detective, if you wanna' keep the doors to your business open!" said Huff.

"Lieutenant," said Captain Sutherland, "one thing you've never learned is the art of diplomacy...at any level. Please excuse Lt. Huff's rudeness," said the captain.

"What do you think we should do, boys?" asked Captain Sutherland.

"These most likely are paintings the Nazis have scarfed up from the countries they've invaded and the churches, museums, and civilian populations there. Much of it has come from the Jews the Nazis are rounding up and persecuting. These unfortunate people have lost everything. Also, this is art from the world's great painters...Picasso, Van Gogh, Renoir, Matisse, just to name some of them. The stuff is very valuable, sir," stated Quinn.

The captain looked at Detective Huff and said, "Despite my hesitation, this is your investigation, Lieutenant. Take whatever resources you need. We'll get a search warrant signed. See if you can make a bust and recover the art. And, although I hate to bring them in on this, we probably should inform the FBI since this artwork was stolen and brought here and smuggled in from overseas," said the captain.

CHAPTER XXXIX

For the small city of Santa Fe, it was the "bust of all busts." It was the most significant recovery of stolen property based on pure value in Santa Fe ever, and quickly became the talk of the town. Twelve of the world's most sought after and expensive Modern works of art…stolen from their helpless Jewish owners in Europe and smuggled across the Atlantic Ocean all the way to this point.

Based on Skitts Jones' tip to Quinn; and Quinn's subsequent tip; Lt. Frank Huff had obtained a search warrant and planned a major raid on the burlesque troupe.

The police raided the burlesque troupe in their hotel rooms down the street from the Lensic Theatre, in the afternoon before their first performance. Lt. Frank Huff, "The Bumbler," as he was called behind his back by other police officers, recovered 12 paintings and three small sculptures, all identified as Degenerate Art. The artwork included two sketches by Emil Nolde, Elfreide Lohse-Wachtler, and Paul Klee, and pastels by Gustav Klimt, Otto Dix, and Oskar Kokoschka. The artwork was found concealed inside the troupe's equipment wagon. The Master of Ceremonies, Mr. Goran Sebo, was immediately arrested and charged by Lt. Huff and his team.

Lt. Huff was so sure he would make a bust that day and recover significant amounts of stolen artwork, that he didn't inform the FBI ahead of time as he was ordered to do, but he did notify two local newspapers. Many staged photos taken were poses of Huff holding up the paintings with his men. The headline of the *New Mexican* read, "Local Detective Uncovers Nazi Stolen Art!"

Lieutenant Frank Huff was now a celebrity of sorts, even though his detective skills had little to do with the discovery of this large quantity of stolen artwork. Huff publicly announced that the mystery of the Degenerate Art had been solved, and he and his men could now focus on more "important local" crimes and cases. As far as Huff was concerned, all Degenerate Art had been discovered in Santa Fe and all criminals who were responsible had been arrested and were soon to be brought to justice. The paintings and other works eventually would be turned over to the FBI who would do the best they could to find the rightful owners. In Huff's mind, the case was solved and closed.

CHAPTER XL

"But Goran is completely innocent. He had nothing to do with this! My show can't go on without our main performer, Lieutenant…He is our Master of Ceremonies," said the owner of the Cabaret Company to Lt. Huff. "He is essential for us."

"Well, that's too damn bad. He was the one who held the keys to the equipment wagon where the paintings were discovered, Sir!" said Huff. "How could he not know those paintings were there? Nobody could get access, load or unload that wagon without going through him first," Huff said. "He stays in jail. Go hire yourself a good lawyer." Huff laughed. "Maybe if you go plead with the Judge, he'll let him out of jail for your show!"

The Cabaret Le Paradis was cancelled, or at least indefinitely postponed, one day before it was scheduled to open. The negative publicity of the police raid didn't help ticket sales either. The owner was close to hysterics as Goran Sebo was arraigned in court. "I am going to lose thousands of dollars, Your Honor!" he said to the judge.

"Bail is set at $ 3,000!" the judge said as he pounded his gavel down.

"Your Honor, it will take me a week to get that kind of money," the owner exclaimed.

"I'm sorry, sir," said the judge. "But because you all travel around so much, I have to ensure Mr. Sebo remains here for his trial date. I really shouldn't offer bail at all!"

So Goran Sebo remained in the Santa Fe City jail unable to post bond for his charges; *Possession and Trafficking of Illegal Contraband, and Grand Larceny (Stolen Artwork)*. There weren't many in the jail at that time. A few local drunks were brought in each night to sober up, and then they were released the following day. That was about it. Goran sat on the bench in his cell, counting the hours till dinnertime, and pondering his future as a performer with the show. Tomorrow night was opening night. Over 500 tickets had been sold. He was the Master of Ceremonies and the main performer, but Goran was aware of the saying, "The Show Must Go On!" The question in his mind was, *will this show go on without me?*

That night about 10:00 p.m. was when it happened. One of the two night jail guards briefly left to go home to care for his sick daughter. The other guard remained at the jail. The front bell rang, signaling someone outside was there wanting to speak to the guard. When the guard went to check the front entrance, he didn't see a thing but the lit walkway outside. He turned to walk back to his desk when the bell rang again. This time the guard, unable to see anyone again, unlocked the door to look quickly outside. He briefly stepped through the door of the jailhouse entrance to see if anyone was there, when he felt a hard blow to the top of his skull. Everything was blurry as he was struck a second violent blow. Then all was black.

Goran Sebo, back in his locked cell, heard the bell ring twice and the commotion at the front of the jailhouse. He instinctively had an uneasy feeling. He was the sole prisoner in the jail. And he was powerless to do anything, locked in his cell. There was an access door the guards had to unlock and pass through to the prison cells in the back of the jailhouse, but Goran was still anxious. He then heard the access door unlock and squeak open. From where he was, he couldn't view the access door, but he heard footsteps approaching on the tile floor. The next thing he saw was a man wearing a dark coat with a scarf tied around his mouth and nose, similar to depictions of old train robbers, step in front of the cell. Only the man's eyes were visible. They stared at each other briefly.

Goran barely got the words out, "No! I won't say anything," But the figure raised his right hand, pointing a gun with a silencer directly at him. He simultaneously pulled the trigger. A red spot immediately appeared on Goran's forehead and the pupils of Goran's eyes dilated. The impact from the bullet knocked Goran back to the bench, extending out from the back wall held up by chains. Goran collapsed onto the bench.

The killer successfully completing his hit, calmly slipped the gun into the wide pocket of his coat, turned and calmly walked back to the front of the jailhouse to the front door. Goran's body twitched and jerked for the next 40 seconds until it finally stopped. The guard on duty remained unconscious and sprawled out on the ground outside. The entire execution took only several moments to complete. The assassin appeared briefly at the front entrance, still wearing his facial cover, and remained unseen by anyone who could possibly give a description. He then slipped quietly away into the night.

CHAPTER XLI

"Why was he killed, Marika?" Quinn asked two days later. "I'll tell you why…it was me. I'm responsible for that man…Goran Sebo's death! I had a tip that I passed on to that idiot Huff at the police department. Huff and his boys went after him. I started the process that got this man killed!" said Quinn.

"You cannot blame yourself for this," Marika said. "I've warned you several times that this art investigation is dangerous. I'm scared as well. He was killed because he knew too much and to keep him from talking…but about what?" she asked.

"Maybe he had some connection to The Merchant. This figure nobody knows anything about who's supposedly controlling the illegal art that comes here," Quinn said.

"Where are the paintings Huff recovered in his raid?" she asked.

"I have no idea," replied Quinn. "My guess is the FBI has them."

"These were also world-famous artists like Gustav Klimt, Picasso, and Monet. You know it's possible that the police are in on this too," she said.

"Not Huff," said Quinn. "He's not smart enough to figure any of this out. Maybe now that he made a bust he'll go back and turn his attention to the local drunks and petty crooks stealing from the drugstores," Quinn retorted.

Later that same day Quinn was back at the office talking with Ethan Clark. "What's going on in this town, Ethan? Two killings now tied to these smuggled paintings."

"I wish I had the answer to that question as well," replied Ethan.

"Have you heard any scuttlebutt around town about this figure called The Merchant ?" asked Quinn.

"No. I've just been trying to solve Laszlo's case and find that picture he wants so bad...*Five Dancing Women*. I've come up with a big zero on that so far," Ethan said. "He just paid us another $300 dollars by the way, so I think I'll be spending some more time on his case now."

Ethan took a sip of his coffee. "You know it's quite a coincidence that this Master of Ceremonies for the Cabaret is killed while in Huff's custody at the jail," Ethan said.

"Yeah, but Huff didn't have anything to do with it," Quinn said.

"You believe what you want to believe, buddy, but if Huff is part of this, then he certainly had a motive to keep this Goran Sebo quiet. And as we both know, there's a failsafe way to make sure someone never sings again. I think Huff deserves a closer look," said Ethan.

"Interesting hypothesis, Ethan," said Quinn, "but my gut doesn't tell me so."

Ethan shrugged and returned to his paperwork.

"Speaking of singing, Ethan. How'd you enjoy the festivities at the Cabaret show up at Alex's last Friday night?" asked Quinn.

"Alex's...what are you talking about?" replied Ethan.

"You know, the Cabaret show up at the bar last week...I saw you sitting at a table with some people up there," Quinn said again.

"I don't know what you're talking about. I've never been up to that place before, and I have no plans to ever go there, alone anyway . I'm a married man, Quinn. I don't go out without my wife—you know that," Ethan said.

"Oh, come on, I was sitting just off to your side about three tables over. It was you Ethan, and you were sitting with four other people I didn't recognize."

Ethan's laugh sounded strained, and the grin was a weak attempt to hide either fear or concern. "I'm telling you, I don't know what you're talking about. And be careful what you say to Beth next time you see her. If she thinks I'm going out on her, that'll be the end of my marriage. In fact, it would be the end of me!" Ethan said.

"Well, you must have a twin brother around you don't know a thing about, that's all I gotta' say!" said Quinn.

"Maybe it's the booze you're drinking buddy," replied Ethan. "I often wonder, my friend, how you can be as lucid as you are with as much as you drink. Down a few shots of the hard stuff and you start seein' the darndest things!"

CHAPTER XLII

Amidst the craziness of events in Santa Fe, and to maintain his sense of emotional stability, Quinn gravitated towards Katrina. She was the one who he felt the most comfortable with and who could make sense of things in times of chaos. As the summer of 1943 moved into fall, they saw one another nearly every night. Quinn would show up around 7:00 each night, and he and Katrina would go walking around Santa Fe. Sometimes they would walk up Canyon Road, stopping to look at the artwork various artists would place on the edge of the street for the public to inspect. Sometimes they would walk to the north to Fort Marcy Park, formerly home to the US Army's Fort Marcy. Even as the weather was getting cooler, there was a mysterious and odd beauty about the park. The change of seasons caused the trees to turn colors, showing beautiful shades of orange and yellow that couldn't be found anywhere else in New Mexico. The two of them melded into this scene as they walked and talked late into the day.

Quinn could see that there was something bothering Katrina that day. "My uncle Joel doesn't want me to spend time with you," she said.

"I can sense that," said Quinn. "He's hardly ever there anymore when I come over."

"It's not that he doesn't like you," she said. "It takes him a long time to open up to strangers," she said.

"Let me ask something, Katrina. Are you able to correspond with your family in Germany at all?" asked Quinn.

"No, I don't think so…I don't know the last time we heard anything from them. I don't know how they're getting along. Things were getting bad when we left several years ago," she said.

"There are stories coming out of Germany and the other occupied countries, and they don't sound good, "Quinn said. "Many people have been displaced from their homes, and Jews in particular have had all their possessions, money, and property taken from them."

"I try not to think about it too much, but my family back in Germany really has suffered," Katrina said. Her shoulder-length blonde hair fluttered in the air as a breeze picked up.

They walked through Fort Marcy Park that evening. The moon was about three-quarters full. The unique sounds and noises of the animals of the night began to come alive. Several sparrows tweeted in the background, and the crickets started making their unique chirping sounds. There were other romantics in the park that night, all attempting to be as discreet as possible. Quinn pulled out a cigarette and lit it as they walked. You could tell where lovers in the park were that night by the lit cigarettes exposed like fireflies in the darkness.

"Why do you come by the gallery so often?" Katrina asked.

"I like the art, but that's not the real reason. It's because of you," he finally said. "I come by to see you," Quinn said again.

"I'm so happy it's because of me," she said. "That's very nice of you." The two stopped. They were standing less than one foot from one another. Quinn pulled her to him in a close embrace, and they kissed for a significant amount of time. "Ever since I met you on that cold night in Albuquerque you've been on my mind," Quinn said.

"You've been on my mind too," she said.

"Once this war is over, maybe we can make some real plans," he said.

"I don't think the war's ever gonna end," she said. "I pray every day for my family overseas. I told you that my uncle and I haven't heard anything from my family in Germany, but my other Uncle Ariel sometimes gets information about them," she said.

"Your other uncle?" said Quinn. "I thought your Uncle Joel was your only relative in the US?"

"Oh I never told you…I have another uncle here too," said Katrina.

"Where is he at?" asked Quinn.

"Well, I'm not really sure right now," she said. "He travels around a lot. Sometimes we don't hear from him for a while and then…"

"What does he do?" asked Quinn.

"Oh, I really don't know…He works for the government, I think," she said.

"Well, maybe I'll get to meet him someday?" said Quinn.

"He only contacts us by letter every now and then. But you never know," she said.

They were in a section of the park where there were other lovers hiding in the small forested area. Quinn placed his hand on her waist and brought her to him. "Katrina, no matter what happens with this crazy war, and this crazy town…I want you to know I'll be here for you as long as you want," he said.

Their lips met again. For that brief period of time that night in early October 1943, all that mattered was that they were in each other's arms. All that mattered was that they had each other.

CHAPTER XLIII

As 1943 turned into 1944, there was good news for the Allies on the war front, but things didn't appear to change much in Santa Fe. In fact, the weather was unusually warm and there was little to no snow. The roads were dry. Quinn worked his day job, staking out the only real department store in town, F. W. Woolworth Co., located on the southwest corner of the Santa Fe Plaza. It wasn't a bad gig, and the pay was good. His job was to watch employees suspected of stealing; and then mingle around in the store to see if he could catch any shoplifters. He had been doing this for about three weeks now, and had actually caught three shoplifters. He even was able to buy another car. He bought a used shiny 1942 Buick Coupe with a detachable roof with whitewalls.

Quinn left the store about 4:00 in the afternoon that Thursday. The sun was still shining. Surprisingly, it was a perfect day to take a little drive along the newly constructed and paved State Highway 20, built through the foothills surrounding Santa Fe. Quinn got behind the wheel of his new Buick and started to drive. This was a two-lane road that wound its way up into the foothills for about five miles and then twisted back down out of the hills to the east side of the main plaza.

Part of the drive was totally obscured from the general public as the road had been cut into and through the foothills. The road was designed to be a shortcut into Santa Fe from the main highway. Quinn drove at a leisurely 35 mph. On his right side was the side of the mountain; on his left was a steep, rocky embankment descending hundreds of feet to the canyon below. Quinn had the entire road to himself, climbing into the foothills for about three miles before he looked in his rearview mirror and saw the black car behind him. The sedan either had a tinted windshield or some sort of a screen in the glass as Quinn couldn't get a glimpse of the driver at all.

The car approached quickly from behind. Smash!... the large black sedan crashed into the rear of Quinn's smaller Buick as Quinn jammed on the brakes, causing him to lose traction and nearly spin out of control on the narrow road. The big black car rushed in again and crashed into Quinn's Buick again, obviously no accident.

Quinn's Buick swerved back and forth and nearly careened off the road and over the edge of the steep hill and into the canyon below. The black sedan sped by as Quinn's car teetered, balancing on the edge of the cliff. Quinn had a bloody gash across his forehead and felt acute pain above his left knee. He was badly injured, and he knew it. He sensed the momentum of his vehicle and its weight going over the cliff. With a herculean push he was able to jump out of the driver's side door just as his car went over the cliff's edge. Quinn now lay face up on the shoulder of the road as his Buick rolled down the steep and rocky slope. The vehicle hit a large rock and somersaulted backwards vertically in the air, landing upside down. The buick continued to slide down the hill before stopping and coming to rest against a large tree stump. Quinn could smell the gasoline leaking from the vehicle nearly 400 feet away and permeating the air. Quinn had suffered a bad wound to his head and a broken left leg. About 30 seconds later, the Buick exploded and erupted into flames. Had he not jumped from the vehicle when he did…Quinn would have either been crushed by the weight of his own car as it tumbled down the rocky slope or simply blown to bits.

The pain to his head was excruciating, but luck was on Quinn's side that day. His Buick had broken through the guardrail adjacent to the roadway and his left rear tire and left rear quarter panel had been ripped from the car on the roadway's edge prior to the Buick coupe descending the hillside. The evidence was plain for any passerby to see that an accident had just happened there. A city utility vehicle passed by 15 minutes later, and the driver noticed the debris. Quinn ended up being rescued before he bled to death on the side of that obscure road.

CHAPTER XLIV

Quinn was transported and treated at Bruns Army Hospital in Santa Fe. The hospital was built as a military hospital but handled civilian injuries in the community as well. It didn't look like your typical hospital. It was a plain, long, thin building constructed in the shape of a bland military barracks. The accident had severed two arteries in Quinn's left leg. Quinn had also suffered severe head trauma. He was treated and admitted for recovery.

Three days after his accident, he had some visitors. The first was Katrina. "I heard you were here," she started out. "What happened?" she asked.

"While I was driving, I think another car hit me from behind and ran me off the road, Katrina."

"You could have been killed!" she exclaimed.

"You're right," Quinn retorted.

"I brought some flowers for you," she said as she held up a brightly colored bouquet.

"Thanks, you can put them in the empty vase on the window sill," Quinn said.

"I've missed you," she said. "When I heard you were here, I had to come and see you right away," Katrina exclaimed. "Is there anything I can do?" Quinn struggled for a moment with his thoughts before remembering.

"Actually, yes, there is…and I would be grateful, " Quinn stated. "My weekly rent is due at my motel. My wallet is in the first drawer of the armoire. Take $23 out of my wallet and pay my rent for me, please," Quinn requested. "Tell the guy at the front desk I'll be back in a few days. And remember to get a receipt. Thank you so much, Katrina. I'll be by the gallery, and we can go out as soon as I'm released," Quinn said as his eyelids started getting heavy and he began to nod off.

Katrina came to the side of his bed. "I'm going now Quinn, but I'll be back. I'll take care of your rent at the motel, don't worry. If you need help with anything else I'm here for you. I've missed you terribly!" she said as several tears rolled down her face. They kissed goodbye before Katrina left that day.

Later that afternoon Quinn had another visitor. It was Marika. Quinn was asleep when she entered. She gasped as she entered his hospital room and saw his head nearly fully bandaged. As she entered his room she woke Quinn up. "I heard about the accident from your partner when I came to your office. I hadn't seen you anywhere for a while and thought maybe you had left town. It looks like you took quite a spill, " she said.

"Oh, just another day in the life of a private detective," Quinn said.

"I told you to back off the art thing," she said as she looked out of the hospital window room. "I warned you…you're messing with some very dangerous people," she said.

"Who did this to me?" asked Quinn.

"I don't know," she answered, "but if I had to guess, Laszlo Tibor had something to do with it. You went too far, and you got closer than they wanted you to be. Look, I came here to see you," she stated, "but I may be in some trouble myself, and I may need your help. I can't talk about it now though. When are you being released?"

"I guess I'll be here for a few more days. They're worried about a hematoma or something like that," Quinn said.

"When you get out, come up to Alex's. I'm there just about every night. We can talk there or make plans," Marika said. Just then one of the nurses came in and announced visitation time would be over soon.

"Okay, I've got to leave now…but don't forget Alex's."

"I'll be up there when I'm released and I'll look for you," Quinn said.

"Wonderful," she said as she gave Quinn a liberal kiss on his right cheek.

"If I knew I'd be kissed like that, maybe I'd be here more often!" he said.

One week later, Quinn was released. His left leg was in a cast where it would remain for another month. He still had bandages wrapped around his head, and he used crutches to walk.

As soon as the bandages were removed, and despite his other injuries, he took Manny's Cab up to Alex's with the hope of seeing Marika there. A swing band was playing that night. The all-male band was comprised of several men on trumpets, trombones, one clarinet, two saxophones, and one set of drums. They all wore the same style jacket. A young woman in a nice dress provided the vocals. They played swing and slow ballads; Glen Miller, Artie Shaw and Benny Goodman type stuff.

Marika was sitting at a table with her lady paramour and several other people laughing and drinking when Quinn came in. Quinn went up to the bar, crutches and all, and took a seat. The place was packed that night, but he had to speak with Marika. He had a couple of his usual libations—bourbon, soda with a shot of Curacoa. The drinks brought his inhibitions down some.

During one of the band's breaks, he decided to approach Marika. As he approached the circular table, he noticed everyone was laughing profusely with one another. "Well, I see there's a festive crowd here tonight!" Quinn said with a smirk on his face as everyone turned their heads and stared at him.

Everyone was formally dressed that evening and Marika looked very sexy with one of her slinky dresses. "Darling!" she said. Just then the leader of the band announced a break. "Grab a chair and join us..."

"Well, thank you, and I don't mean to interrupt, but I'd like to talk with you for a minute if possible," Quinn said.

"Well, of course," Marika said. Several of the guests at the table indicated they had to leave, and three seats quickly opened up.

"Baby," Marika said to her paramour, "be so kind as to give us a few minutes, please," as she kissed her girlfriend on the side of the cheek. Her lady friend got up with her cigarette case and purse. She smiled and walked off.

"Well, I see you survived," Marika stated.

"I've got to find out who did this to me Marika," Quinn half asked and half stated. "Do you know anything? If you do, you've got to tell me!"

"Is it really worth knowing? After all, you survived," she said.

"Yes, I need to know! I could easily have been killed that day."

"As I've told you before, my little birdy friends clue me in on things every now and then," she said. "I've inquired, but I haven't heard anything yet about your accident," she said. "I would tell you if I knew.... But I've also told you before to walk away from the Degenerate Art investigation. There are people involved who will go to great lengths to avoid being identified or having their smuggling ring disrupted. You're a threat to expose these people if you keep looking. Somebody tried to kill you and failed this time. They may not fail next time!"

Just then the band at Alex's returned to the stage to start up again. "Listen," Marika said, "I need to talk with you about something else. I need your help. But not here, not now. We need to meet in private away from everyone and everything before I can talk about this."

"Anything for you Marika," Quinn said with a hint of tenderness.

"We'll meet on the north end of the Guadalupe Street bridge Thursday afternoon at four o'clock, if you're up to it. I can talk freely there," she said.

"Maybe you'll hear some chirps from one of your little birds that will be useful for me in the meantime," Quinn said.

CHAPTER XLV

The problem was he had now lost his vehicle, and his current living space was two miles from his work. New Mexico did not require motor vehicle operators to carry automobile insurance during the war years, and Quinn did not have insurance. He also did not have the available cash to replace his car at that time. He was now at the mercy of local cab companies or his own two feet, when he could move any reasonable distance on crutches. His solution to this problem was simple. There was a small motel called The Pueblo, three blocks down from the office on Cerillos Road. On the 25th of January he changed motel addresses and moved in. He still used crutches, which made foot travel difficult, but he had the use of Manny's cabs, which gave him some independence. This was the way Quinn wanted it.

On most mornings Quinn could be seen using crutches and hobbling the three blocks to his office and back to his motel. The Pueblo was a one-story structure built out of adobe in the Spanish style, and Quinn's room opened up to the outdoors and the motel parking lot. So on this day he hobbled back and noticed a young lady peering into the trash cans at the far end of the motel. Quinn saw her carefully removing the metal lids to two cans and setting them gingerly on the ground. Then she began wading through the trash. She had short sandy blond hair, wore a red shirt with suspenders over and one strap broken, under a worn brown wool coat. She appeared slightly disheveled.

Normally, Quinn wouldn't have cared or paid her any attention. He had seen the hobos all around Albuquerque scrounging coal chips along the railroad tracks all throughout the Depression, and he couldn't help but have some empathy for their situation. But something about this lady drew his attention. Maybe it was the way she carefully removed the lids and seemed to surgically sift through the trash. As if she had done this so many times before.

"Hey…you there!" Quinn yelled out. "What are you doing?…You're trespassing!" he yelled as he moved towards her on his crutches.

The young girl pulled her hands out of the trash and looked up. "I was just pickin' through the trash, mister," she said back. "It's just stuff people are throwin' away anyway. I'm not hurting anything."

"Well," Quinn said as he walked over to her and tried to think of a good answer. She was a small woman, about five foot five. She had a thin face, blue eyes, and a chipped front tooth. Why Quinn continued to pursue a conversation with this girl he couldn't explain or answer, but he did. He just felt he should.

"What's your name?" said Quinn.

"Dixie," the young woman answered. "What's yours?"

"My name doesn't matter. Do you live around here?" he asked.

"No, sir," she stated. "I live down by the river. In the camp down there," she said.

"Camp by the river?" Quinn said quizzically.

"Yea, there's a whole group of us that lives there," she stated. "We get by as we can."

"What do you live in…a house?" asked Quinn.

"No…," she said laughing. "In whatever we can. I made myself a tent out of blankets for me and my daughter," she said. "Sometimes it gets cold, but we always can warm up by the fire."

Quinn stared at the thin young woman in her early 20s. She wore tattered leather slipper-like shoes. "Well, just be careful out there," he said.

"I will…I can take care of myself," said Dixie as she looked at Quinn and calmly smiled.

Quinn turned to move back down the sidewalk to his room, when he felt the coins in his right pocket jingle. He turned back towards the girl as she had resumed her search through the trash. Quinn grabbed the handful of coins out of his pocket. "Here," Quinn said as he reached out his hand and released the metal coins into Dixie's open hands. "I hope this helps some," he said.

"Thanks, mister! Thanks a lot!" she said as she replaced the trash can lids and turned to walk away.

"It's Quinn…my name's Quinn," he yelled to her.

"Thanks, Quinn!" she yelled back as she walked quickly away, disappearing over the small knoll behind the motel that led down to the road below.

Quinn watched the top of her head disappear as she walked away, and then he turned towards his new home…Room 12 at the Pueblo Inn. When he turned towards his room he immediately noticed another dark sedan parked in front of his room—with two men inside. As he approached on his crutches, the two men got out of their car and walked to him. One took out a badge from his trenchcoat and flashed it in front of Quinn.

"I'm Agent Ridnell," said the one with the badge.

"And I'm Agent Sauer of the Federal Bureau of Investigation," the smaller man said.

"Do you have a few minutes, Mr. Chase? I think it's important we talk," the taller one said. "Can we talk in your room briefly?"

Quinn opened his door and allowed the men in. His small room was very plain. Among the usual motel furniture pieces, there was a small table with pad and pen on it, along with several chairs. "Sit down, please," said Quinn in a near nervous tone as he motioned to the two chairs. "What can I do for you?" he asked.

The two men spent the next 40 minutes with Quinn. They began by asking about his accident. Did he have any idea who inflicted his injuries or who had a motive to do so. Eventually, their line of questioning moved from Quinn's injuries and activities to whether or not he knew of any secret government projects taking place around Santa Fe. Quinn denied any knowledge of such. "Mr. Chase, a word to the wise…don't play stupid with us!" the taller agent said. "We know you have contact with several individuals who may be foreign spies."

"One of them is a client of yours," said the other.

"You must have heard something about The Hill, otherwise known as Los Alamos?" the first agent said.

"What have you heard about The Hill, Mr. Chase?"

"Not much," said Quinn. "Only that they're making electric rocket engines, laser weapons, or something else fantastic up there," he said.

The two agents informed him that they suspected Laszlo Tibor of committing espionage and engaging in black-market smuggling and embezzlement. They also had a hunch that Joel Finebaum and his niece Katrina were up to wrongdoing, though they couldn't specify what yet. "Are you a loyal American citizen, Mr. Chase? Do you realize we have hundreds of thousands of men and women in uniform all over the world risking their lives for our country and the survival of humanity?"

"We know you wouldn't place their lives further in danger by concealing information you might have…would you, Mr. Chase?" said the taller man. "Because if so…then you're aiding our nation's enemies."

"No, gentlemen, not at all!" Quinn said. "My father fought in the First World War. I bleed red, white, and blue myself! I'm as loyal an American as they come! That doesn't change the fact that I don't know a thing about Los Alamos," Quinn said with a straight face. "And Laszlo Tibor is our client, but my partner Ethan Clark mostly deals with him…not me."

The agents shared a quick look between themselves.

"But, from everything I know about his case, Tibor is simply looking for some stolen Jewish art in Santa Fe. That's the reason he's here," Quinn stated.

"Well, Mr. Chase, we have yet to determine Mr. Tibor's real motives and purpose here. We don't even think Laszlo Tibor is his true name. We think he's a Russian spy. And we think his purpose is something other than art. And if it is, we'll catch him and he'll pay a heavy price!" said the smaller of the two agents.

"So, we want to ask you for a favor, Mr. Chase. Number one…forget you met us. We've never met, and you've never been contacted by the FBI," the taller agent said as he handed Quinn his card. The card was blank except for one phone number on it. "Your partner Ethan Clark is not to know of this visit and our discussion today. When and if we're ready to talk to him, we'll let you know ahead of time. We know you talk to the police and Lt. Huff. Even he is not to know you've spoken to us. But, if you hear anything out of the ordinary concerning the war effort or Los Alamos from anyone—your partner, Tibor, Huff, or anyone else—you call us immediately!" he said.

"We'll be in touch with you again in the future…just carry on with things like normal. We know there are foreign spies here in Santa Fe, and we think Laszlo Tibor is one of them. We can't tell you what's goin' on at Los Alamos…but let's just say it's crucial to the war effort," the other agent said.

The two agents walked to the door. Before opening it, the taller man said, "You don't have any short-term plans to leave Santa Fe do you, Mr. Chase?"

"No," Quinn answered. "I'll be staying in this room for a while. I have no plans to leave. I've lost my car in the accident and I can't replace it now. I'm on crutches as you can see so my ability to really go anywhere at the present time is limited."

"Good," said the smaller of the two agents. "We'll know where to find you."

Then they walked out of Quinn's hotel room that winter's day, shutting the door firmly behind them.

CHAPTER XLVI

It was 3:00 p.m. on a grey cloudy day during the first week of March, 1944. Quinn and Ethan went to see Laszlo Tibor at his suite at the La Fonda. The meeting was requested by Laszlo Tibor. "Gentlemen, it's good to see you again," said Laszlo, dressed in his usual afternoon parlor jacket, with a monocle over his left eye, as he sat back in the plush chair of his hotel suite. The balding and pudgy man actually appeared quite distinguished this day.

"May I offer you another Palinka?" Tibor asked as he reached for a small glass filled with the Hungarian Brandy on a silver tray. "I normally drink a small glass or two of my favorite Brandy in the afternoons and also enjoy a smoke." He pulled out an aromatic cigar from a box on the same tray, struck a match, and lit it. The delicious smoke began to fill the room. "I'm Catholic, gentlemen, and the Patron Saint of Labour, St. Joseph, employs us to work hard and conscientiously. I wholeheartedly agree, but I haven't read anywhere where it says we can't enjoy the benefits of our labor along the way! May I offer you a cigar, gentlemen?"

Ethan was quick to take him up on his offer, while Quinn respectfully declined. "Mr. Chase, your strange sense of duty and code of behavior amazes me. One cigar certainly will not affect or diminish your detective skills," said Lazlo.

"Mr. Tibor, I have to interrupt you for a moment," said Quinn. "Do you know several months ago a man who smuggled Degenerate Art into Santa Fe was arrested and held in City Jail…and was then shot dead execution-style right in the jail?" said Quinn.

"Yes, I heard about it and read about it too in the *New Mexican*," said Tibor. "While I have no firsthand knowledge of this incident, I've learned from other sources that the man named Goran Sebo was Croatian. As you may or may not know, gentlemen, Croatia has declared its support of Nazi Germany in this war, so it is not a complete surprise that a man from Croatia is found with stolen Nazi art. More likely than not, he was smuggling the art for the Nazis' benefit. But other than what I've learned from third parties, I have no connection or other knowledge about it, Mr. Chase. But if I hear anything else, I will be sure to let you know. Now getting back to my issues, gentlemen…," Laszlo said.

Ethan and Quinn shared a quick smile.

"Last week, I was walking along Canyon Road, on the top of the hill, east of the petrol station, when someone shot at me!" Laszlo said, barely containing a pent-up mixture of fear and indignation.

"Did you report this to the police?" asked Ethan.

"I don't need problems with your police or FBI," answered Laszlo. "I am convinced she is behind it," he continued. "I know her motives well. In essence, gentlemen, she and I are competitors here in the acquisition of art. But we go about our work differently. I am here looking for art taken from my clients back in Hungary. Marika Kraus is here spying for Germany and to profit personally at the same time! You should turn her in to your police or FBI immediately!" he said.

"Well, wait a minute, Laszlo…why would any foreign spies be here?" asked Quinn.

"You are an incredibly naïve man," said Laszlo staring at Quinn. "There's hordes of FBI agents crawling around town. It is well known that there is a top secret project being conducted near Santa Fe."

"I haven't heard of anything," stated Quinn, blatantly lying.

"What do you want us to do Mr. Tibor?" asked Ethan. "She hasn't done anything to us."

"I tell you…she is a spy for the Nazis!" Tibor raised his voice. "She is alluring and an attractive woman, so men are taken in by her. Don't make that mistake, gentlemen! She is as deadly as a poisonous snake. Turn her in now!"

"Why don't you report her?" asked Quinn. "You have the better claim as she seems to have shot at you, and not us."

"Because it's wartime and I'm a foreigner as well…and I might be suspected of something," he said.

After a brief moment where none could offer a solution, Tibor leaned forward with a gleam behind his monocle. "Here's what I will do…I will double your salary immediately if you investigate this woman," he stated. "Find out who her benefactor is, what she is doing in Santa Fe…anything that we can give to the authorities as proof for them to detain her or even deport her," he demanded.

Ethan wrote down some notes on his pad.

"I take my safety very seriously," Tibor stated. "If this woman wants me out of the way, for whatever reason, I will take measures to ensure my safety!" he said.

"Now, Laszlo, I don't know what you mean by measures," said Ethan. "I don't doubt you were shot at, but we have no evidence Marika Kraus was involved. Not yet, anyway. My partner and I can't get involved in shooting back and forth with someone else, and you should not resort to violence, either."

"Let me tell you, Mr. Clark, I have a right to defend myself. I'm sure if you investigate her, you will discover her shady past. She is a threat to your nation's security, I tell you! Turn her in now before it's too late!" he retorted with a raised voice.

It was all Quinn and Ethan could do to keep Laszlo Tibor calm that afternoon, soothing the man from his strange rants while exchanging puzzled looks at each other.

CHAPTER XLVII

Winter was slowly turning into Spring in early March 1944 in Santa Fe, New Mexico. But it was cold. The day when Quinn met Marika as planned was exceptionally brisk. They met at the corner of the Guadalupe St. Bridge that afternoon. Even in the cold weather she looked attractive, wearing a matching long-sleeved tiger-striped top and pant suit from a designer label of the day, a striped head-neck scarf, winter coat, and Willsonite sunglasses. All, modern fashions of the day.

She wanted to walk, and even though Quinn had trouble standing for any length of time and was recently released from the hospital, he took her arm and escorted her across the bridge. The sun was out, melting the ice and snow, making a stroll even more treacherous and unpleasant. Quinn had his cane, and they moved at a snail's pace, but they walked. Most of the streets around the plaza in Santa Fe were either cobblestone or dirt at that time, so they stuck to the sidewalks. They stopped at a bench adjacent to the road and sat down.

There was something on her mind, Quinn could tell. Finally she said, "I need your help. Recently I've acquired several originals. Paintings from…well let's just say they're from a renowned French artist. I've got them hidden. I may be leaving for Chicago soon, but if I can't go back for some reason…I will need help getting this art back home. They must be brought back to my gallery. The Volks Galleria, in Chicago. Once there we can begin to try and determine who the rightful owners are and at least protect these paintings. I don't want them ending up in South America in some Fascist's collection," she said.

"Okay," said Quinn. "We can talk about the paintings…but I have some questions for you first. Why is Laszlo Tibor convinced you're trying to kill him?"

"Because he's crazy," she said. Marika looked at Quinn with a puzzled look.

"Someone apparently shot at Tibor earlier this week, and he's convinced you're responsible."

"That old man really is crazy!" she said, laughing and shaking her head. "No, I don't own a gun, and I don't know a thing about any shooting!"

"How did you acquire these paintings, Marika?" asked Quinn.

"Don't be silly, my dear," she said. "If you're not interested in helping, just say so. You know I can't divulge details other than what I've told you. If you agree to help me, you will be paid well," she added. "You'll just have to bring them to Chicago and deliver them. That's all I'm asking you to do," she said.

"Well, the details do matter, Marika," Quinn said. "If this is Degenerate Art…and you are implying it is…then it's stolen from someone, probably some Jewish family in Europe. Stolen by the Nazis. So you're asking me to transport stolen art. Actually, art that was taken by force from the rightful owners by our enemies of war," said Quinn.

"Like I told you," she said, "this is a matter of trust. I am aware that these may have been stolen. But we don't have any idea who the original owners were. A private owner, or a museum, or maybe they were floating around the open art market and were stolen. I want to safeguard the paintings and try to find the rightful owners or at least ensure they end up in a museum here in America. I don't want them sold to the highest bidder on the black market somewhere else! So you'll have to have some trust in me!" said Marika.

Quinn took her delicate hand, and stroked the inside of her palm. She stood up holding his hand, indicating she was ready to walk again. He offered her his arm and led her again down the sidewalk, letting his cane pick their way forward.

"There are two keys you'll need," said Marika. "The paintings are in a storeroom above Dempsey's Drugstore on Cordova Street. The building used to be a bank, and the storeroom used to be a vault. The combination lock has been removed, but the room is very secure. There are two heavy-duty locks."

"So what am I supposed to do?" said Quinn.

"If for some reason I can't leave when I plan to, I want you to transport the paintings to my gallery, the Volks Galleria on Riverside Drive in Chicago," she said. "Inside the storeroom you'll find complete instructions with the paintings. Instructions on how to transport them and keep them safe. Instructions on how to open the safe. There's a safe with cash inside. This is to pay for your travel, expenses, and your compensation. Will you do this for me?" she asked again.

"I'll be in serious danger, won't I?" he asked. "The same bad guys will be chasing after me, or just as bad...," he added.

"You'll be completely safe. Here's the envelope with the keys. "Just like I'm asking you to trust me, I'm trusting that you'll only go into that room if I ask you to," she said.

"This all doesn't make much sense, but, okay, I agree to do it," said Quinn. She handed the envelope to him. They had walked about a hundred yards and weren't that far from where they started…by the bridge.

"You know I do have a conscience about the war and my role in it," she said.

He looked at her. "Before we go, let's talk about trust, Marika," said Quinn. "Where did you get that scarf you're wearing?" he asked.

"I'm not sure. I've had it many years as best I can remember," she said.

"The end of it seems torn, and I've never seen you wear torn clothes before," he said.

Marika remained silent.

"Let me see the torn end…maybe I can help." He held the torn end of her scarf in his left hand, and with his right hand took out the piece of clothing from his pocket he had been given by Velma Price several years earlier after the accident in Albuquerque. He took the small piece of torn clothing and put it up to the end of the scarf…the fabric pattern was the same. Quinn's small piece fit perfectly on the end of her scarf like the missing piece of a jigsaw puzzle.

"You were there that day, weren't you, Marika?"

She peered down at the ground. She didn't say a word, but her silence spoke volumes. Finally, she said, "Yes…I was there."

"Why didn't you tell me?" Quinn asked. "Now you want me to trust you? I nearly died in Albuquerque that day!" he said. "Why were you there? What really happened? If you want my help, tell me everything…everything, or take the envelope back!" Quinn said.

"I don't want to discuss this now," she said. "Meet me Saturday night at El Viajero at eight o'clock. Do you know where it is?"

Quinn nodded affirmatively and said, "It's a block off the Plaza."

"I'll tell you everything I know about it then. At the very least I owe you that. I'll see you in two days," she said. She threw her arms around him and kissed him on his cheek. And before he could get another word out… she was gone.

CHAPTER XLVIII

With all that was happening, Quinn wanted answers. *Marika says she'll tell me the truth in two days…but why has she kept this from me for so long? If I wouldn't have matched the cloth up with her scarf, would she be telling me at all?* he asked himself. He wasn't sure he could trust anyone now, including Joel and Katrina. *Are they spies too?*

The next night, Quinn decided he would stake out Joel's gallery. He didn't have a new car yet after his Buick Coupe was destroyed…but he had his friend Manny from "Manny's Cabs." So Quinn hired Manny as driver for the evening for thirty three dollars. Quinn decided he was getting a bargain at this price. At about eight o'clock, he saw Katrina leave the gallery in her uncle's truck, which was parked behind the building. He had no idea Katrina even knew how to drive…so, as surprised as he was, he had Manny follow her, keeping a safe distance behind. She drove her uncle's truck on the poorly paved two-lane roads north of Santa Fe. She drove through both the Tesuque and Pojoaque Indian Reservations to the base of the western Jemez Mountains, about 30 miles northwest. She never exceeded 35 miles per hour, so he had to keep his distance behind her as she went. He couldn't believe his eyes as she began to ascend the mountains on what seemed to be an old mining dirt road.

The dirt road eventually turned into a paved road again and Katrina passed a sign that read, "White Rock 2 mi." Quinn had heard of the village of White Rock before. He heard it was a small town about five miles from Los Alamos, and it had a gold mine. His interest was on high alert now, and he instructed Manny to continue to follow her. Katrina continued driving towards the town of White Rock.

It was about 10:15pm when the two cars entered the small village. Katrina's car pulled up to a brick building with no windows off of the main street. The building had the word "Laundry" painted on its side in large letters. There was a service loading dock on the far side of the building with a light on and a door that appeared to be open. Quinn, who could see well enough by moonlight, had Manny stay several blocks back and told Manny to cut the lights to his car. *What is she doing up here now, at this time of night?* he wondered.

Katrina cut the lights off on her uncle's truck and got out of the driver's side. She went to the back bed of the truck and climbed up on the back fender to look in the bed. She flipped open the retaining latch holding the rear door in place to the back of the truck and pulled out what appeared to be a large box. There was a carry handle that stuck through the cloth or sheet on top, so she lifted the box up by this handle and began walking towards the brick building. Quinn, totally puzzled, watched from afar. As she walked, the box swayed back and forth, and something fell out of the box from underneath the cloth that momentarily suspended itself in the night's air before twisting and gently floating to the ground. Feathers came out…birdfeathers! At least one bird was in the cage. Then Quinn remembered the first time he was in Joel's gallery, the strange noise coming from the ceiling and Katrina telling him her uncle raised pigeons.

She disappeared briefly with the cage inside the building. Quinn stared in absolute amazement. And after about 10 minutes, Katrina exited the building through the same door and walked back to her uncle's truck. She did not have the birdcage with her, so it was obvious she either gave it to someone inside or simply left it there. *What is going on?* Quinn asked himself again as he saw Katrina start her uncle's truck and back away from the building. He ordered Manny to follow her for the hour-long drive it took to get back to Santa Fe through two Indian reservations and up a steep climb on the bumpy and chopped-up two-lane road.

At last the lights to the City of Santa Fe appeared before them. It was almost midnight. He followed her back to her uncle's gallery, where she parked the truck in the back alley. The same alleyway where Berndt Kruger had been gunned down one year before. Quinn peered on from the far end of the alley as Katrina went into the back entrance of the Finebaum Gallery...her mission seemingly accomplished.

But what was she up to? What was the reason for her trip that night? he asked himself again.

CHAPTER XLIX

Professor Ariel Eisenbach drank his cognac in his casita at Los Alamos, otherwise referred to as "The Hill." The small structures at Los Alamos once housed the faculty and staff of the Los Alamos Ranch School for boys. Now these small houses, which were built around 1913, were home to the scientists working on the Manhattan Project there. Ariel Eisenbach had spent the day in lengthy discussion with Enrico Fermi and Niels Bohr, both preeminent Nobel Prize–winning scientists who had volunteered and were working at Los Alamos. The three professors and scientists filled up four blackboards with mathematical formulas attempting to prove one of Fermi's theories about plutonium being substituted for enriched uranium in order to create an atomic reaction. The three scientists were elated with their conclusion. If plutonium could be made and would work, then they wouldn't have to moderate an erratic atomic reaction using uranium that could get out of control. So Eisenbach sat on his small porch, drank his cognac, and watched as the sun slowly set behind the Jemez Mountains of northern New Mexico—pleased with himself and his accomplishments. After the sun fully set, he walked outside to a small storage shed behind his little house.

Ariel opened the door to the storage shed. There was a beating of wings and feathers floating in the air, drifting towards the ground. He heard the cooing of his 12 pigeons that he kept in the shed. He had become attached to some of them and had given them names. These were the pigeons that Katrina had brought up to White Rock, and then had been smuggled onto the Los Alamos grounds by Gross' Laundry who provided laundry service for most civilians and military personnel at the new Army camp on "The Hill" only a few miles away.

Sam Gross was Jewish, and worked with Joel Finebaum, whom he had met and collaborated with ever since the Finebaum Gallery had opened. Gross' instructions were to bring up only one or two pigeons at a time in small cardboard containers with breathing holes, concealed by laundry being returned to Professor Ariel Eisenbach. It was not difficult, quite frankly. The MPs at the front gate knew Sam Gross and never asked to search his laundry truck before Gross entered the compound. These were homing pigeons and would fly back to their location of origin upon being released. Eisenbach had two messages he wanted to get to Joel that night. The messages were encoded and placed in small plastic tubes with affixed tops and clips that would remain secure on the pigeons' legs. This was the first time Ariel had flown the pigeons out. He had great apprehension but great anticipation to see if they would actually make it to his brother Joel's attic in Santa Fe—their ultimate destination.

He grabbed the pigeons one after the other, tied the tubes to their legs, and released them into the night one at a time. The birds squawked and fluttered and seemed confused, but quickly disappeared into the starry night. The birds circled high above Eisenbach's little house and then got their bearings and flew high in the sky southward towards Santa Fe. The flight would take approximately 40 minutes for the birds, which generally flew at a fast rate of about 50 miles per hour. The homing pigeons had a natural compass and guidance capability that brought them back to their original home on the northeast corner of the Santa Fe Plaza right above the Finebaum Gallery. Joel had rigged the coop with an open chute above where the pigeons could enter from the outside, but they would be trapped inside once they arrived. The two pigeons sent by Eisenbach found their destination; they crawled into the coop and were safely inside, waiting for Joel when he opened the door to check on his birds.

Did Professor Ariel Eisenbach know he was committing treason? He did, and he also knew that the secrets he passed on concerning the Los Alamos National Laboratories would end up with Nazi scientists. But he also knew if he and his brother didn't cooperate with the Nazis, their entire family remaining in Germany would be sent to either Auschwitz or Buchenwald to be killed. Eisenbach was aware the Nazi's were trying to liquidate Europe's entire Jewish population. Over 50 members of Eisenbach's family were within the clutches of the Nazis. In order to have any hope of keeping them alive, he had to comply. So when he had to balance loyalty to his new country, the United States, versus the survival of his family, in Professor Ariel Eisenbach's mind the choice was clear. He would do whatever he could to keep his family alive.

CHAPTER L

Marika Kraus arrived on Saturday night, slightly before eight o'clock as planned. They took a small table in a corner near the fireplace. Quinn couldn't help but notice how sexy she looked. *To damn bad she's a spy for the other side…I still may have to turn her in.*

She took out and lit a cigarette. "Okay, now that I know you were there three years ago… please tell me what happened," he said.

"I said I would, and I will. But let me first say that I feel sorry for you, Quinn. Because something wrong happened back then," said Marika.

"Okay…tell me," asked Quinn.

"You thought you were transporting a scientist in your car that day. Maybe you still believe that. That wasn't Eisenbach in your car three years ago. I don't know who it was, but it wasn't the natural physics professor, Ariel Eisenbach from Germany. The man was a decoy. I have known Professor Eisenbach most of my life. I was first introduced to him when I was a teenager, when Werner Heisenberg won the Nobel Prize in 1932. That wasn't Ariel Eisenbach in your car, I tell you. I was sent there that day to acquire the professor. I wasn't sent there to kill him. We were going to smuggle him out and ship him to our contacts in Argentina. It seems like you were used in a scheme to trick us. We both were duped that day. The man we were both looking for was never there…they sent an imposter."

"You know who I am and generally why I'm here…I have no reason for perpetuating a lie now," Marika said. "I was sent to grab the professor… only he wasn't in your car. You were there guarding a decoy as part of a deception. I'm sorry you were hurt in the process, but I think you should blame your own government—not us," she said.

Quinn stared at her in disbelief.

"Since I'm bearing my soul to you, let me reveal something else. Do you really think you can trust the police here in Santa Fe? Haven't you wondered how some of the world's most valuable paintings have been able to pass through here time after time and our little operation hasn't been shut down yet?" Marika asked. "The police are in on it."

"You mean Huff and his detectives?" asked Quinn.

"Huff and his people? No, they're too low level," she said. "It goes much higher than Huff," she said. "High level government officials here in New Mexico and maybe even Washington are involved in this," she said.

Again, Quinn sat with a look of disbelief on his face as he listened to Marika Kraus. But deep inside he had always felt something was wrong with the mission to guard the professor three years ago. And deep down he also knew the Degenerate Art ring was corrupt, and had to have some level of complicity from the police, and maybe even the FBI.

She was just confirming what he had felt all along. "Okay, what else?" he said.

"You're in a place where most everyone is someone other than who they pretend to be," she said.

"Including you, Marika?"

"Oh, yes, me too…although I now realize the harm I have done by supporting this evil cause. Both my parents have passed away now, so they can't threaten me with their safety like before."

"There's also more going on here than just some smuggled stolen art, isn't there?" Quinn asked.

"Yes, I'm afraid there is. But I'm not involved with that. I only know a little about it," she said.

"So what is it, and who's involved?" he asked.

"I honestly don't know who," she told him. "But there is secret military work or research happening around Santa Fe. We think your military is building engines for electric missiles somewhere close by. That's about all I know, though. My mission is to report on these paintings as they are moved through Santa Fe to Los Angeles, and on to South America. Most of the paintings will be sold there, and the money will go back to Germany. My other mission is counterintelligence; to report on any Russians here and eliminate them if I am ordered to," she said.

"In Santa Fe?" Quinn mused. Just then a crashing noise was heard throughout the restaurant. The window just off to the side of Marika and Quinn exploded, shattering Quinn with glass and sending shards in every direction. Quinn's face was cut in several places and glass went in his eye. He was blinded momentarily and looked away. When he turned back to Marika, he saw blood on her collar, and he saw her collapsed body lying face down over her place setting on top of the small table. Another woman off to his left screamed at the top of her lungs, and a man rushed over to help. Quinn put his hand on Marika's shoulder. She didn't move. He gently raised her torso up from the table. Her head folded over, and her eyes rolled back. She was shot cleanly through her left temple. Marika Kraus had been assassinated.

Quinn yelled, "No!" and got up from his seat and ran outside to confront the shooter…but the street was empty. Whoever had pulled the trigger was gone. Marika Kraus' role in this crazy game of spies and smuggled art had come to a brutal end.

Quinn waited at the El Viajero for the authorities to arrive. He knew he was duty bound to stay there. He had found some shell casings outside that night, but for his own reasons would keep them to himself. He was the last person to have contact with her. So he waited…and finally the police arrived. Lt. Frank Huff was the first one through the door. Huff saw the body spread over the table. "What happened here?" Huff asked. "Who is this woman?"

"Her name is Marika Kraus…she's an art collector and dealer from Chicago," Quinn said.

"We'll have to check her for identification," Huff replied. "Were you here when she was shot, Chase? What's your involvement and connection to this woman?"

"She was a friend, detective, that's all. We were having dinner together. Right at this table."

"Are you carrying your handgun, Chase? Let me see it if you are."

"Lieutenant, you know my .32 wasn't used in this crime."

"I know what you're saying, but I'll be taking it into evidence just the same." He motioned for Quinn's handgun, and Quinn complied, handing it over to him.

Huff then said, "Mark this!" as he handed the gun to one of his assistants. "You should find bullet casings outside, lieutenant, from the shooter's weapon," Quinn said.

Huff then ordered his assistant to check outside the restaurant.

"Well, you were eating with her…what the hell happened?" Huff asked.

"We were drinking and talking when I looked away briefly. There was a thunderous popping noise, and I felt the shards of glass hit me from the window. When I looked back at Marika, she was lying face down on the table," Quinn said.

"You're just bad luck, Chase," Huff said. "The incident in Albuquerque and now this…I hope you don't have any plans on leaving the area anytime soon. You're now involved in my investigation into this. I just hope you don't lose your PI license over this Chase. What a shame that would be," Huff sarcastically said.

Quinn nearly exploded. He had tipped the police off, and that led to their biggest bust ever. Now the very detective Quinn helped to make into a local hero was mocking him. Huff saw Quinn's emotions on his face and that Quinn was losing control. The words from Quinn were just about ready to be hurled at Lt. Huff in the most offensive way.

Huff softened his demeanor, and then he said, "I'm sorry this happened to your friend, Chase. We'll do our best to solve the crime. The shooter was clearly outside the restaurant and shot in through the window. Of course we have no idea who the killer was, or any motive, so we will probably need to interview you again. Now I'm gonna process the crime scene and an ambulance should be here soon. If you want, you can stay here, but if you do, let us do the detective work here tonight, okay. If everything checks out, you can pick your handgun up in a day or two. Sorry again about your lady friend. I'll do everything I can to bring this killer to justice."

CHAPTER LI

Quinn couldn't sleep that night or the rest of the weekend and was in the office by 6:30 Monday morning. "You look like crap," said Ethan when he walked through the door. "It looks like you've been on a drinking binge for three days, old man."

"Marika Kraus was killed Saturday night, Ethan. Somebody shot her right through a window as she and I ate at El Viajero's. Actually, I have no way of knowing if the bullet that struck her wasn't really meant for me," Quinn said matter-of-factly.

"Tibor's nemesis? I know she was a friend of yours, Quinn, and I'm sorry," Ethan answered.

"She never did a thing to him. She considered him a misguided crazy old man. But Ethan, I know he's behind her shooting," said Quinn.

Quinn and Ethan went to see Laszlo Tibor at the La Fonda later in the day. Ethan gave the following warning to Quinn before they left the office. "I know you're highly upset about the shooting."

"Ethan, this was an assassination," Quinn said.

"Just make sure you keep your temper under control. He's an old man, and all you really have is your suspicion," said Ethan. Quinn acknowledged Ethan's warning and said he would keep his temper under control. At least that's what he said.

Laszlo Tibor cracked his suite door slightly and peered through when Ethan knocked. As soon as Quinn saw Laszlo's face he pushed the door and jarred it open. "You son of a bitch, you son of a bitch!" Quinn yelled. "I know you're responsible for her death! I'm gonna finish the job that she can't do now!" Quinn yelled.

"Chase! This man is our client!" Ethan exclaimed.

"Thank you, Mr. Clark," said Tibor, breathing heavily. "I'm glad someone in this room has kept their emotions under control and is displaying some common sense!"

"Bullshit! When does this charade and lying end, Tibor?" said Quinn.

"That's a matter of perspective, young man," said Tibor. "Most of it has been dreamt up in your head! I had nothing to do with Marika Kraus' death!" Tibor yelled out.

"If not you, then who the hell did? From the way you talked about her last, it seems like you had the perfect motive to kill her. You thought she shot at you and was trying to kill you!"

"That may be true, but I had nothing to do with her shooting! We've managed to coexist as rivals in the art world for years. We have kept one another informed in trying situations without even meaning to…and in a strange way we've balanced each other out. I wouldn't do this to her now. I have nothing to gain," Tibor said. "What's more, I have no idea who did, but it had to be someone involved with this art scam going on here."

"What the hell are you really doing here, anyway?" yelled Quinn.

Ethan interceded. "Laszlo, I apologize for the behavior of my partner. He's very upset about this woman's murder. Had I known he would behave like this —"

"Don't worry, Mr. Clark," replied Tibor. "At least he's passionate about something! He hasn't shown any enthusiasm about working on my case… I'm curious as well about what happened to the Nazi harlot."

With that, Quinn took a step forward, swung a roundhouse hook, and hit Laszlo Tibor hard across the jaw.

"Aagh!" Laszlo exclaimed as he fell to the ground.

Ethan yelled out, "Quinn! No…No!"

"I should kill you, you bastard! If you ever say anything like that again…!" Quinn screamed.

Laszlo didn't move for a few seconds and then grabbed his jaw with his right hand. "Aagh," he groaned. He was slow to get up. "You broke my jaw," he said with slurred speech.

"Laszlo, there's ice at the bar…let me get a towel and let's get some ice on that jaw quickly—it'll control the swelling," said Ethan.

"Quinn, get the hell out of here now before you get arrested or I shoot you!" Ethan yelled and motioned to Quinn.

"I'm so sorry.…We're sorry, Laszlo," said Ethan. "Forgive us, please…"

"I understand his feelings about Marika Kraus," Laszlo mumbled and slurred his words. "I will decide whether to terminate our professional relationship," he slurred again as he continued to hold his jaw.

The two private investigators left Tibor to deal with his pain on the third floor of the La Fonda Hotel, and got inside the rickety old elevator to ride down to the lobby.

"You goddamned idiot! What the hell were you doing? What's gotten into you, Quinn?" Ethan yelled as they walked out of the La Fonda on that Monday afternoon.

"Don't you see what's happening?" said Quinn. "Anyone and everyone connected with this Degenerate Art smuggling ring here is getting knocked off, or damn close to it. Including me! The question is, who's next? Not only that," said Quinn, "if there are stacks of this world-class precious artwork here in Santa Fe, then where the hell is it? "

"I know some strange shit has happened recently, and again I'm sorry about your friend," said Ethan.

"She was more than a friend, Ethan. She was also a trusted source of information. She was a goddamned spy, but believe me when I say, she was one of the few honest people I've met in this town," said Quinn. "And what's goin' on around here involves a lot more than just stolen artwork!"

"Listen, I know that, but Laszlo Tibor is our client. We've been paid to help this man, and right now we're failing in our job! We're going in the opposite direction. You just about put him in the hospital!"

"Ethan, the man's a goddamned Russian spy!" yelled Quinn.

"Don't go around saying that!" said Ethan. "We've both seen his documentation; his passport. I have no reason to doubt who he says he is…"

Quinn hung his head, acknowledging Ethan's measured and rational approach.

"And added to that, the man pays us very well and we have a duty to our clients! We both could end up losing our licenses over this—and I've got my life savings invested in this business. I'm sure it would make Huff's day if we both got our licenses yanked!" Ethan retorted.

CHAPTER LII

He could get as upset as he wanted, but Marika was gone...and there was nothing Quinn could do about it. His country was at war with Germany, yet he had a special connection to Marika. She was a spy...but also a lover and a friend. What was just as important to Quinn was that she had been honest with him while nobody else in this city had been. Quinn wasn't even sure now if he could trust his own business partner. The uncertainty and doubt that was consuming his life was becoming unbearable. He had to confide in someone. Marika had told him his own government and fellow members of the police department had set him up—maybe even tried to kill him. Finally, in Quinn's mind, he had to confront the possibility that this was true. He went to see Katrina. They took a walk and sat in one of the local parks.

"How long have you and your uncle been in America?" he asked.

"About ten years," she answered.

"And you've applied for your citizenship?" he asked again.

"Yes...but due to the war, all immigration decisions have been placed on hold. My uncle and I are still officially foreign refugees. It's extremely difficult for us here...not knowing what's happening with them. The stories we hear about life back there for my relatives makes me feel sick," she said.

"I wish there was something I could personally do," Quinn said.

"Just having someone who will listen at times helps a lot," she said. Quinn stared through the trees up into the sky.

They went to eat. During dinner, they just chatted. Small talk. Finally, Quinn said, "A good friend of mine died recently. She was killed Katrina. "

Katrina said, "I'm sorry to hear that…did they live here?"

"Yes, she did…you never knew Marika Kraus, did you?" he said.

"No, but the last name of Kraus is German, isn't it?"

"It is," said Quinn. "She was a very unusual woman. I wouldn't befriend just anyone," he said. "You get an odd feeling when a friend dies long before their time. It makes you kind of numb, and nothing seems like it was.… Nothing makes much sense anymore.…I just am very confused right now."

"I'm so sorry," she said.

"Thank you," he said to her. "At least I know you're sincere."

She laid her hand on top of his.

"Have you heard of any place locally referred to as The Hill?" he asked her.

"No, I haven't heard of anything like that around here," she said…blatantly lying to him.

"I'm not supposed to talk about it, but not long after I met you in Albuquerque when I was still a cop there several years ago, I was given the mission of guarding a scientist for a few days. His eventual destination, I think, was The Hill. It's some military research facility up in the Jemez Mountains that's top secret. Rumor has it they're making electric missile engines up there," Quinn said.

"I did hear something from my uncle some time ago," she said. "He said that there's some experimentation going on near here with laser beams and rays…and they melt whatever they hit. That would be a sure way to win the war…the Nazis don't have anything like that," Katrina said.

Quinn looked deep into her eyes, which shone a bright blue behind a surge of suppressed tears.

"But this war will probably end with both sides destroying one another," she said. "That would be so sad, because there is such natural beauty surrounding us," she said. "Look at these mountains, for instance."

After they finished their dinner, Quinn walked her back about a half mile to the gallery. He gave her a long hug and said goodnight. Although they smiled and kissed, Quinn had never felt so distant from her.

Before he walked off, Katrina said, "Come inside for a minute and see the new watercolors my uncle's painted. They're beautiful!" So Quinn went inside and began to inspect the 20 or so new watercolors Joel had displayed on easels throughout the front part of the gallery. They were mostly town scenes of Santa Fe; The Plaza, various hillside adobe homes and neighborhoods. He even painted the Cathedral of St. Francis. They were Modern works. He mixed form and shapes in a collage of colors. These were not Realist or Classical in style. The earthtones mixed in with the shades of orange, red, and yellow made the paintings stunning. Quinn became absorbed as he studied them. For a moment he became lost in the pictures before him.

"They are beautiful, Katrina…I've never seen anything like these before," he said.

"Which one do you like the best? You can take it. I'm gonna' convince my uncle to give it to you. You need something to cheer you up!" she said.

CHAPTER LIII

The days passed by quickly, almost merging one into another. Marika's death was published in the newspaper, but her body was transported out of town, paid for by some large mortgage company from back East. It was all hush-hush, and Quinn couldn't find out any further details from the police. Marika was simply gone—here yesterday and gone without a trace today. Quinn went to her small casita where she lived on the south end of Guadalupe Street, but within 24 hours the entire place had been emptied out. Quinn knew a part of him would always be empty. But as circumstances dictate, things were happening so fast in Santa Fe that Quinn didn't have time to focus on her passing for very long.

It was the middle of May, 1944. Due to increased criminal activity in Santa Fe, Quinn and Ethan were deputized by the county sheriff. Quinn found himself with less and less free time. Every day when he wasn't working, Quinn was in some sort of class at the police station or participating on a raid. He swore to himself his law enforcement days were over, but circumstances pulled him back in again. He even got his old crewcut that he had worn while he was on the force in Albuquerque. He still had the keys Marika had given him, but hadn't used them yet.

He reported to the police station at about 4:00 p.m.

"Here, take this vest," Lt. Huff stated as he handed Quinn a fairly heavy vest to put on. "These are bullet proof and will stop most bullets," he said. "If you are shot tonight," Huff said, "well, don't sue the department!"

There were now about 12 officers assembled in the basement of the Santa Fe Police Department. Lt. Huff addressed the group:

"Tonight's raid is important, based on what we suspect is being hidden in this warehouse," Huff said. "We believe, based on our informant, that a large amount of this Degenerate Art is still in Santa Fe. For those who don't know and never heard the term before, this is stolen artwork the Nazis have taken from museums and people in the countries they've occupied," Huff said. "We received a tip earlier in the day from our reliable source."

Quinn's ears perked up.

"We'll approach the warehouse from the street, and the various side entrances. You'll be briefed on this tonight. We expect the warehouse to be guarded if the artwork is in fact there. At the very least we expect guard dogs. But there may be guards as well, so you may have to use lethal force on this one," Lt. Huff said.

"We'll depart from here. The FBI is taking part in this, so you'll see some additional officers here tonight. Report back at 2100 hours. You'll be broken down into teams at that time. Once at the warehouse location, I will attempt to contact anyone inside, advise them of the warrant, and demand that they not interfere and allow us entrance. If we have no response at the warehouse, we will breach the front door and go in," he said.

"No one…and I mean no one, is authorized to draw their weapon unless given the alert signal. I will have an airhorn, and unless you hear the sound of this horn or come under direct contact where the use of your firearm is necessary for your personal safety or to enforce the law," Huff blew the loud horn to demonstrate, "you do not have authorization to use your weapons."

Everything Huff said was fairly standard. Quinn thought back to similar speeches for similar raids at the Albuquerque Police Department.

"You are dismissed, but roll call and final briefing is at 2100 tonight. Be on time!" Huff exclaimed.

CHAPTER LIV

At 9 p.m. that night the police team assembled at the police department. Quinn was there. Ethan was not there, even though he had been deputized also. There were several FBI agents, including the little agent and the tall agent who had talked with Quinn before—Sauer and Ridnell. They both introduced themselves to Quinn as if they had never laid eyes on or spoken to him before. The briefing pretty much followed what Lt. Huff had said earlier. The 16 or so people in attendance were broken down into four groups of three, four, or five officers. A large truck was going to be used as an entry-ramming vehicle if the entrances were blocked or barricaded. Huff did say this was supposed to be a surprise raid, but Santa Fe was a town of gossip and information leaks. If the bad guys inside the warehouse had been tipped off…it wouldn't have been a surprise to Quinn.

The warehouse was an old lumber and scrap metal depository that was supposed to be abandoned. It was located in the Railyard District. This was the area immediately adjacent to the Santa Fe Train Station. The group left the police station, about two miles away, and started moving towards the warehouse. Quinn rode in a standard police car with Lt. Huff and two of Huff's assistants. Huff reminded everyone in the vehicle about the restriction on using their firearms, glaring at Quinn as he issued the warning.

They reached the block just before the warehouse at about 9:45 that evening. The area was dark. This was the train track area around the station where most of the buildings were either abandoned or were businesses that supported the rail lines. There were no houses in this section of town, and no reason for anyone to be in this area at this time of day. Huff got out and used a flashlight to motion the rammer to move closer—about 75 yards from the front entrance of the warehouse. The four teams then split up and moved forward in groups. The plan was to surround the building, and then Huff would approach the front entrance, announcing his search warrant and demanding entry by megaphone. Then there would be a series of airhorn blasts that would signal the various teams what to do. The plan was, if they had to break the front entrance down, they would use the rammer, and the other teams would go in through the side and rear entrances, arresting anyone trying to flee the building.

As it turned out, they did end up using the rammer to smash through the large warehouse entrance doors, but the building was empty…at least empty of people inside. A guard dog tried to attack the first agent that came through the back door. They used a large spun net to subdue the dog and eventually tied the animal up in the net instead of killing it. They searched the entire warehouse but didn't find anything pertaining to the warrant. Then one of the officers discovered a trap door on the east side.

"Lt. Huff…you better get over here and check this out!" the officer yelled.

Huff, along with the two FBI agents, walked over.

"Somebody spent a lot of time trying to conceal this," Huff said. The door was a trap door built into the floor with two D-rings used for pulling, lifting, and opening it. A combination lock was set into the wood in the middle. "Get Haskins over here with the crowbar and other tools," said Huff. "We've gotta' break the lock here…we're goin' in," he said.

They used two sledgehammers, three crowbars, and a chain, which they fastened to one of the rings to finally open and lift the large door. They stared down a descending wooden staircase that disappeared into a dark basement below. Three of them had flashlights that shined down into the dark compartment below.

"Well, Lieutenant…we're here to search, so we might as well see what's down here," said Agent Sauer, the smaller FBI agent. "Wait," Lt. Huff answered. "The basement might be boobytrapped."

Quinn volunteered to check it out. He grabbed a flashlight and started to descend the staircase. The small FBI agent yelled out, "Don't go down there! It could be your life!"

"I'll take that risk," said Quinn. "I'm as curious as you all are…" Lt. Huff remained silent. So Quinn proceeded down the staircase about 10 feet. It led into two cellar rooms below the warehouse floor. In the first room there was a single bulb hanging from the ceiling. There was a switch built into the wall, and he flipped it, and the light turned on. Built against the wall was a wooden counter with three fairly large electrical-looking devices. Large black cables extended from these devices into wall sockets below. Two of the devices had dials and what looked like gauges with scales and needles. One of the devices appeared to be a short-wave radio, although Quinn hadn't seen anything like it before. There was writing on the devices, and it wasn't English. The writing was Russian. "Lieutenant Huff, you better get down here!" Quinn yelled out.

What they had discovered was a satellite Russian Intelligence station with a short-wave radio and encoder set up in typical configuration by

Russian Intelligence Services. There were file cabinets with many files inside. Eventually, all of the files would be scanned by Russian translators of the OSS. But what caught Quinn's attention was a portrait photograph lying on the counter next to the radio. He recognized the face immediately, although the picture was clearly taken years earlier, as Laszlo Tibor had jet-black hair and a much leaner face in the photo. Nevertheless, it was undoubtedly him. Quinn grabbed it and turned it over to the backside. There was Russian writing on the back, but Quinn focused on the sentence that read, "Vitali Chetkin, 1934, Sebastopol."

The bastard is a Russian agent, after all...Good Lord! Quinn said to himself.

The tall FBI agent then yelled out, "This is a National Security investigation now under the direction of the FBI! I want everyone out of this cellar now! You are not to touch or remove anything from this room as you leave…that would be a Federal crime and you will be prosecuted!"

Nobody noticed, but Quinn quickly stuffed Laszlo Tibor's photograph inside his coat before walking up the creaky wooden staircase into the large warehouse above.

CHAPTER LV

The next morning, Ethan and Quinn knocked on Laszlo Tibor's…
Vitali Chetkin's…door. He quickly answered. "We need to talk right now,"
said Ethan. Chetkin still held a hot compress up to his jaw where Quinn
had hit him.

"I know we've had our issues, but we're here in your best interest now,"
Quinn began. "I was with the FBI and the police last night when we raided
the warehouse in the railyard and found your transmitter, electronic equipment, and short-wave radio, Laszlo…Vitali…or whoever you really are.
They've got all the files—everything. My advice to you is to leave Santa
Fe as soon as you can or you'll be arrested, probably as early as tomorrow
morning. Here, this picture was near the radio transmitter. I picked it up
before anyone else saw it. They're gonna have all the files, and everything
else in those two rooms. It's probably only a matter of hours before they
come looking for you," Quinn said.

Vitali took the photo from Quinn while simultaneously pulling
matches from his pocket. He then said, "Excuse me," walked into the bath-
room, and lit the photographic portrait of himself on fire over the bath-
room sink. When finished burning his own portrait, he came back into the
main room.

"So, gentlemen, you know where I come from and who I work for. But you don't know what I am working on, and what my purpose here is," Vitali said. "Let me tell you…there's research going on around here that is revolutionary and will change the world!" he said. "You wouldn't believe me if I told you. I can't leave here!" he said. "They'd just catch me at an airport or train terminal. No…I wait for them instead."

"You could easily be hung or shot for what you've done," said Quinn.

"I accept whatever fate has in store for me, Mr. Chase. But my mission here was just beginning. The Soviet Union and United States are allies in this war. My government will not turn its back on me. Something will be worked out."

"What about the paintings? Is there a large cache in Santa Fe?" asked Quinn.

"At any given time, there may be 30 or so stolen paintings hidden for a time in Santa Fe, before they are moved out to the West Coast and eventually smuggled by ship to South America," Vitali said. "It has been going on for some time and will continue as long as the police here look the other way," he said. "There are many people in this town involved in the underground trade of the art. The list would surprise you, Mr. Chase."

"Do you know who killed Marika Kraus?" asked Quinn.

"No, honestly I don't, but I have my suspicions, Mr. Chase. However, I won't suggest a name without more proof. I swear to you though I had nothing to do with her killing. Like I told you, she and I balanced each other out in our clandestine world," he said.

"Tell me about this research up on The Hill you mentioned earlier," Quinn demanded. "They're not making electric missiles up there, are they?"

Tibor displayed a sarcastic smile. "It's a new form of science, Mr. Chase. It's something so fantastic the normal person wouldn't even be able to comprehend or imagine it. This new science eventually will transform the world! There are scientists from all over the world involved! But most people speaking German up there are the Jewish scientists the Nazis expelled. Dumb of them, wasn't it?"

Just then there was a banging on Laszlo Tibor's suite door. "Open up! This is the police. We have a warrant!"

Tibor complied and opened the door. Standing in the hallway with guns drawn were FBI Agents Sauer and Ridnell with five police officers. "Vitali Chetkin?" asked the smaller and more vocal FBI agent.

"Yes, that is my real name," said Tibor.

"You are under arrest for violating the Foreign Espionage Act of 1917, Title 50, US Code. Turn around, with your hands behind your back, now!" said Agent Sauer.

Chetkin looked at Quinn in the eye just before being ushered out and said, "Did I play my role well? If so, then applause, because the comedy is finished! Those were the last words uttered by Roman Emperor Augustus. Goodbye Mr. Chase!"

And then Vitali Chetkin was ushered out and was gone, never to return to America or be seen by Ethan Clark or Quinn Chase again.

CHAPTER LVI

Quinn once again realized how much he needed to rely on Katrina. He managed to see Katrina once or twice a week, despite Joel Finebaum's efforts to keep him away. It seemed like the more they were supposed to stay away from one another, the more fate brought them closer. Their typical date night was dinner out at one of Santa Fe's more simple restaurants, and then a long walk, culminating in romantic interludes at Fort Marcy Park. The physical attraction between the pair was obvious. Emotionally, they appeared to be on the same level too. But in life, many factors can influence one's romantic destiny. It remained to be seen what if any obstacles would stand in the way of Quinn and Katrina's deepening affection.

It was a Thursday night, and Quinn was set to be at the Finebaum Gallery at 6:00 p.m. to pick Katrina up for their date. Before leaving his motel, Quinn walked outside and saw Dixie sifting through the trash at the far end of the building. This time, Dixie had her small daughter with her, standing off to the side. The little girl couldn't have been more than four years old. Quinn watched for a minute or two and then limped towards them cautiously.

"So, you're back again," he said.

Dixie turned her head towards him and smiled as she continued peering into the large trash can. The little girl looked up too. She was small in height and had reddish hair with freckles and appeared slightly disheveled. "Are you gonna' tell on me and get me in trouble, mister?" Dixie sarcastically asked and brandished a smile. "I'm really not doin' any harm."

Quinn came closer. "I see you've got someone taggin' along today," he said. The little girl smiled and looked up at Quinn.

"This is my little girl, Haley," Dixie said.

"Hello, Haley, my name's Quinn," he said as he smiled at the little girl about one-fourth his size.

"Hello" was all the little girl said as she ran to her mother's side and grabbed onto Dixie's pantleg, looking back at Quinn. Haley then coughed several times.

"Thanks again for the coins," said Dixie. "I bought Haley clothes and shoes at Salvation Army, and we ate good all week long," she said.

"Good. I'm glad," Quinn stated. "How old is she?" asked Quinn as the little girl stared up at him.

"She just turned four years old," said Dixie.

"Well, she looks like her mother," Quinn stated.

"She's got my personality too. Fiesty and stubborn! Nothin' gets by her!" said Dixie.

Quinn laughed. "I can sense that!"

The little girl coughed loudly several more times.

"Well, thanks for the money, and it's been good talkin' with you again, mister," said Dixie, "but we've got to be on our way."

"Where are you going from here?" asked Quinn. "You should have someone—a nurse or doctor—look at your daughter's cough."

"Oh, she'll be alright…she has a little cold, that's all."

"I can call a cab for you," Quinn said.

"Thanks, but that's okay. We like to walk. We have several more places to check out, anyway. Come on, Haley," Dixie said as she took the little girl's hand. "Say goodbye to this nice man."

"It's Quinn…Call me Quinn."

The little girl waved goodbye with her free hand as she and her mother began to walk away in the opposite direction.

"Be safe out there and stay warm!" Quinn yelled.

Dixie turned around and waved. Quinn stood and watched the mother and her small daughter walk up and over the knoll behind the Pueblo Inn motel and disappear over the small hill.

He called Manny and got a lift to pick up Katrina at the gallery. On this night they went to Lou's Diner. Lou's was a local diner in the 1940s sense. A narrow building made to resemble the dining car of a train, with an eating counter and a few booths. Lou Gibson, the owner himself, was the cook, and he had two waitresses who helped him out. The food was simple at Lou's, but good.

"I've missed seeing you the last week," Quinn said to Katrina.

"Me too," she said. "It's been a long week, and my Uncle Joel can be demanding."

"It seems like he doesn't want me around," said Quinn.

"Well, business has been slow and that nosey police detective with the long coat has been coming around lately," she said. "Since everything that happened in Germany and New York, my uncle doesn't trust many people. Especially the police, because they remind him of the Gestapo, the Nazi secret police."

"Katrina, I understand if you never want to talk about your time in Germany," said Quinn.

"It was a terrible and very fearful time for us," she said.

"But your life is different now, and you should try to forget about that past and look forward to the future life you want here," said Quinn.

"I try, but it's not that easy to forget such horrible things," she said. "In some ways it will always remain with me."

It was now about 7:00 in the evening. The sun was beginning to disappear over the horizon. "Sometimes I try and make sense of what happened, and what is going on in Germany," she said. "It's so different over there. Now I can sit in this peaceful park and look up at the clouds in the sky with no worries or concerns," she said. "I couldn't do that over there. We were worried something would happen to us whenever we went out in public. My father was an apothecary in our village near Darmstadt, and had his own shop. I had a wonderful childhood and life with my friends in our village…going to school and summers and holidays. But things changed for us in 1930, and things changed so fast."

Katrina continued…"It started for me at school. Our teacher started talking about what it meant to be a loyal German citizen. She made me sit in the back of my class. Then rocks were thrown through the front window of our shop, wrapped in poster paper that called us names and with threats of what they would do to us! My mother was walking down the street, and the town brownshirts threw stones at her. She wasn't hurt that day, but she never left our house alone after that. It got worse right up to the time we left."

"Forget those things! Try to forget them at least," said Quinn as he put his arms around her. "You're safe here with me now…It's still a beautiful world, Katrina! Nobody wants to harm you here," he said.

"Look at those clouds up in the sky." "They look like deer or antelope galloping across the sky, don't they? Maybe that's exactly what they're doing," said Quinn. "Maybe they're galloping across the sky looking for a home…like all of us are."

She looked up too. They stared for a minute before their eyes met each other's….Seconds later their lips touched and locked in what would last for several minutes of sweet bliss. "I don't want you to be afraid, Katrina. No one will hurt you here… I promise," he whispered in her ear.

CHAPTER LVII

In the early 1940's, Werner Karl Heisenberg, the man credited for developing quantum mechanics for which he won the Nobel Prize in Physics in 1932, gave a lecture regarding nuclear fission at the Harnack Haus in Berlin, Germany. This was at the famous Max Planck Physics Institute which was considered the "Oxford" of Germany at the time. Although he and his researchers were physicists and professors, they worked for and were funded by the German Army. In attendance that day, along with other professors, were high-ranking German Army generals. Like most military organizations and projects in Nazi Germany, Heisenberg's Kaiser Wilhelm Institute for Physics (KWIP) was run in a decentralized manner to create competition between it and Kurt Diebner's larger, more political organization, the Heereswaffenamt, (HWA). The Nazi brass and Hitler were paranoid, and did not trust any single military or governmental agency becoming too powerful. Hitler saw this as a way to prevent any serious internal threat to his power, as these organizations would always have to compete against one another for his favor.

During this lecture, Heisenberg explained that the nuclear fission process would take years of research and development. Their efforts were slowed down by the lack of heavy water now being delivered from the Norsk Hydro Plant in Norway, which was essential for even moderate nuclear reactions. Heisenberg stated that energy obtained from splitting uranium atoms would best be used for civilian pursuits like providing energy for German cities, but the military officers assembled on this date were interested in the military applications of atomic energy.

"Can this physics be used to construct a bomb?" one general asked.

"It is feasible on paper and in the research laboratory," Heisenberg answered. "But we are still in the early stages of research," he cautioned. "We would need to first develop an atomic reactor and conduct a lot of testing. We would need more resources and money unfortunately before we could begin constructing a weapon of any type."

He tried to convince the generals that the development of atomic energy would have to be a national effort, combining research at several labs and testing facilities in Germany where they worked in sync and under a centralized command. Maybe even operating in different countries but with one definite chain of command. He mentioned the assistance of scientists from other countries that the Reich would need to rely on. Heisenberg even credited several Jewish scientists for their contributions to German research. When he made these comments, he could see the frowns and scowls on many of the generals' faces.

"Why should we spend time and money on this form of energy, Professor Heisenberg?" one of the general's questioned.

"What will be the benefit to the war effort?" another general asked.

"That is not an easy question to answer," said Heisenberg. "But, a small amount of enriched uranium undergoing the right reaction could create an explosion equal to, say, 10 kilotons of TNT. Thus, small quantities that undergo the proper reaction can yield incredible bursts of energy."

The murmurs among the crowd raised the volume level considerably. "Aaagh!" were the gasps of surprise from the impeccably uniformed and groomed group of senior Nazi officers. Then another general in attendance asked Heisenberg, "Professor, if such a weapon could be constructed, what size bomb would it take to say…destroy a city the size of Paris?"

Heisenberg sighed before answering the question. "That is a difficult hypothetical question, General. Many factors would need to be considered, and all based on our current research and progress. But, if such a weapon with this type of energy were developed, it probably wouldn't take a large bomb to destroy a city like Paris. A bomb roughly the size of a pineapple might be sufficient."

Again, there was an overwhelming gasp from the crowd assembled, and then the officer who asked the question stood up and began to applaud. Before Heisenberg could say another word, all 100 senior Army officers present were on their feet applauding. For this revelation about the potential of atomic energy, Werner Heisenberg received a four-minute standing ovation.

CHAPTER LVIII

"You know what it is we need, Finebaum," said Franz Dietrich, the new Nazi spy and courier.

"You can't come here again, Dietrich," said Joel Finebaum. "We're probably being watched right now. You know Berndt Kruger was suspiciously murdered in the alley right behind us not too long ago."

"Have someone drop off the pictures with a canvas cover. I'll pick them up and be gone. I'll be out of Santa Fe within a few hours," said Dietrich.

"Okay, since we won't be doing this again for quite some time, my niece will drop them off on the expected date and time," Joel said. "For this, what assurances do I have that my family in Germany will remain safe?"

"Here are some recent photographs of your family in Theresienstadt. Joel…Joel, you are an asset to the Reich. Your contribution is valued, and appreciated," said Dietrich. "Of course your family is well cared for and happy in Germany! Germany is a happy place! We are not villains and animals! We do what we must for the protection of our people from others who want to harm us. Just look at these pictures. This is a mutually beneficial relationship. Have her drop the watercolors off at the far end of the Guadalupe St. Bridge this Friday at 10:25 p.m. when there are fewer pedestrians out. Have her lay the watercolors on the ground and leaning against the cement base of bridge on Don Gaspar Avenue. I'll be close by to pick them up," Dietrich said.

Joel Finebaum nodded in affirmation that he understood.

"Remember, 10:25, Friday evening, sharp." Dietrich then turned and walked out the back door and into the dark night.

"Katrina, you know what you must do this Friday for me…and for our family. You will drop off the package at the Guadalupe St. Bridge. You must do this correctly."

"Yes, Uncle, but I did have a date that night," Katrina said.

"Not with Mr. Chase, Katrina!" Katrina nodded affirmatively. "I told you not to see that man, Katrina! He's a former policeman and an investigator. Our future and that of our family depend on secrecy and us carrying out our mission here! That man has no understanding of what we've been through…or how serious the stakes are for our family. I made a big mistake by telling him you were here! You cannot continue to see him!"

"Don't worry, Uncle. He's a friend to me, that's all. I won't discuss anything about the art gallery or any of our family matters. I don't even talk about myself that much with him. I can't lock myself in my room," she said.

"Yes, I know, and I want you to have friends here, Katrina. But the less this man knows about us, the better! You must break your date with him on Friday. Tell him you're not feeling well. Do not tell him that you have something else to do that evening. I don't doubt that he spies on us," said Joel. "That's what detectives in this country do. They're just like the Gestapo!"

Katrina had her instructions. She broke her date off with Quinn. At 10:00 p.m. on the night in question, she departed with the watercolors individually wrapped in parchment paper and the entire bundle of five watercolors was wrapped in a burlap sack and tied. She easily carried them under her arm as she walked. It was late summertime, so there were a fair amount of people out that evening, but she didn't see anyone she knew as she walked the eight blocks to her destination.

She knew what she had to do. She was to surveil the area of the bridge herself, and if everything appeared clear, leave the package leaning alongside the cement support of the bridge at one end. At the prescribed time, she approached the far side, which was the north side of the bridge. She didn't hesitate. She laid the bundle up against the inside of the thick cement support of the bridge crossing, according to her instructions, and—not losing a single step—she proceeded to walk down the opposite side of the street where she turned and started her walk home.

Within 45 seconds of the drop, Franz Dietrich had picked up the bundle left by Katrina and was moving away from the area. Nobody noticed him, and no one was the wiser. The drop and pickup went smoothly. Everything in this little operation went off without a hitch.

The watercolors Katrina had dropped off and the secret information hidden within each watercolor would alert the German government of the atomic research being conducted at Project Y, otherwise known as The Hill. To Werner Heisenberg, Kurt Diebner, and other German physicists, this information would be more valuable than pure gold. To J. Robert Oppenheimer and the other scientists working at Los Alamos on research and atomic development efforts, this betrayal and transfer of information to our most dangerous and ruthless enemy was a major breach of security that was hard to measure.

CHAPTER LIX

By the summer of 1944, it was obvious to most Generals of the German high command that winning the war in Europe was hopeless. On June 6,1944, Operation Overlord, otherwise known as the D-Day landings at Normandy, France, began. This would be a second front opened against an already beleaguered and exhausted German military.

On June 17, 1944, Hitler spoke to Field Marshall Erwin Rommel, one of his top generals at Hitler's headquarters in Berchtesgaden, Germany. Rommel began, "My Fuhrer, we don't have the manpower and equipment to contain the British and Americans in Normandy. They're bringing in thousands of new troops and tons of new supplies every day. It won't be long before they break out of our defenses around St. Lo and head north into Belgium and eventually into Germany itself," said Rommel.

"You, you! You are projecting the invasion of our own Fatherland, Field Marshall?" said Hitler. "I should consider this talk as treasonous! The war is far from over! Our scientists and physicists are developing super-weapons of such destruction that will turn the course of this so-called invasion and make the British and Americans tremble in fear before us! Field Marshall, how dare you suggest that the war is lost for our nation! I don't think I have to remind you of your duty as an Officer of the Reich to fight our enemy with every ounce of strength and purpose you have! What I need from you is to provide our nation with a little more time. I will release 10 tank divisions from the 5th Panzer Corps for you to counterattack with in the Normandy sector. Drive these British and American bastards back into the sea, General Rommel. Just give me a little more time! I will show you military might and weapons never before contemplated on this planet, and with such devastation, that they will bring decisive victory to the Reich! Our nation just asks you to delay and contain the enemy in France. Give us more time…we must have more time!"

Germany however wouldn't get the time it desperately needed. World War II in Europe was over one year later, in early June 1945. While there is some evidence the Nazis conducted atomic tests several times before war's end in the eastern province of Thuringia, they were never able to develop and field a functional weapon. Erwin Rommel, widely regarded as one of Germany's greatest generals ever, was accused of treason against the Reich due to his implicit support of the famous July 20, 1944 assassination attempt on Adolf Hitler. Erwin Rommel took his own life in October of 1944 rather than face trial in a Nazi court and risk the safety of his own family. Hitler himself committed suicide on April 30th of 1945 in Berlin, which was under siege by two Soviet Army groups totaling approximately 2,500,000 soldiers. In early May 1945, Berlin lay in total ruin. The entire German military unconditionally surrendered to the Allies on May 7, 1945. The war with Germany was over.

CHAPTER LX

Three people stared at one another in the main room of the Finebaum art gallery later that same night across the Atlantic and more than 3,000 miles away. It was a warm night, but a cloudy haze set in, partially smothering the lights of the Santa Fe Plaza. The effect of the haze created an eerie glow all around. Joel, Katrina, and Quinn just stared at one another for about a minute with no one saying a word. "I like you both…in a strange way you're like family to me," said Quinn. "But eventually I will have to report the espionage to our authorities, Joel. I won't have a choice. This nation is still at war, and you've committed a serious crime of treason by passing secret information to our enemy. And you say you want to become an American citizen?" Quinn mused sarcastically.

"They held over 50 members of my family for over seven years," Joel said in rebuttal. "Lord only knows what has become of them now. If we hadn't done this, they would have all been killed immediately!"

"Even if you had done everything those brutal fanatics asked of you, Joel, sooner or later your relatives would have suffered the ultimate fate at their hands! You and Katrina are most likely on the list for assassination right now for what you know," said Quinn. "The Nazis are the biggest group of deranged psychopaths the world has ever seen. I'm sorry, Joel, but your relatives' fates were decided long before you agreed to help the Nazis out. Look, I don't know what they're planning or constructing up on The Hill, but whatever it is…it's for the war effort and I can't let you give more information to our enemies again," Quinn said.

Just then another voice was heard from the back of the gallery. "One of your biggest faults, Quinn, is that you always overestimate your own capabilities! What makes you think you have any control over what happens around here?" It was a voice Quinn had heard almost every day for the past several years, so he recognized it immediately. Ethan Clark stepped out from behind a gallery wall, pointing his Luger 1900 carbine directly at him.

Quinn stared down at the barrel of the pistol and at Ethan. "Don't you see what's happening here, Ethan?"

"My dear partner, the more urgent question is what's going to happen to you?" replied Ethan. "You're about to be eliminated!" said Ethan calmly.

"What made you flip, Ethan? You were a loyal police detective…and we're at war," Quinn asked.

"Without providing an exhaustive explanation…let's just say it has to do with an awful lot of money partner. And as you know, that's something I've always wanted and desperately needed Quinn…" Ethan replied.

"But this is your country and your government!" said Quinn.

"My government? The government could care less about me, and believe me, it cares even less about you! The government set us up, knowing both of us could easily be killed protecting their decoy who played the role of a professor! Maybe that was their plan four years ago. We were expendable and nobody's to them. And our boss, Captain Brock Garrett… he was in on it from the start. He knew the whole thing was a farce. He probably told you it was just professional babysitting. I don't think he ever cared whether we made it through alive or not. Probably hoped we'd die so there wouldn't be witnesses to their little scam. Don't talk to me about my government! Our government kept my mother and father down and in poverty throughout the 20s and 30s when my father couldn't find work. We handwashed our clothes my mother had made for us, stitch by stitch. We couldn't afford to buy shoes, so in the summertime my little brother and sister went barefoot. In the wintertime we scoured the railroad tracks hoping to find chips and slivers of coal to heat our apartment because we couldn't pay our heating bill. Our government hasn't shown a shred of loyalty to me, my dear friend!" replied Ethan in a raised voice.

"Are you involved in the Degenerate Art scam too? You are The Merchant aren't you?" asked Quinn.

"What's happening here Quinn is a carefully conceived and executed logistical plan, partner. I wouldn't refer to it as a scam," Ethan replied. "I'm a cog in the wheel with regards to this artwork, and it's a very real trade. I didn't create the title of The Merchant! It was given to me. If it wasn't me ensuring the art was kept safe and secure while it's in Santa Fe, somebody else would have provided the service. Your friend Marika Kraus tried to interfere."

"So you're responsible for everything that's happened…you? The hourglass shell casings I found in the alleyway and outside El Viajero were from your gun, weren't they?"

"I did what I had to do," replied Ethan. "The point had been reached to where Marika Kraus wasn't useful to us anymore. Then she tried to cut in on my action. That was a big mistake on her part. She became a liability. Also, we couldn't take a chance on her hooking up with the British Foreign Service, or OSS…excuse the pun," said Ethan. "And Goran Sebo-it was you who killed him!" Exclaimed Quinn.

"And my little headfirst spill over the mountainside?" asked Quinn.

Ethan pointed his finger at Quinn. "You turned out to be too good a detective for your own good, Quinn! We couldn't take the chance you'd break the case. The Albuquerque PD made a big mistake. They never should have let you go!"

"Ethan you lecherous traitor!...You're nothing but a pathetic coward and murderer! You'll hang or spend the rest of your life behind bars for this!" said Quinn.

"You know, Quinn, I have always liked you. But now you're getting on my nerves. And now, you're a liability."

Ethan pointed his finger at Joel, "Search him. He normally carries a gun in his left breast pocket," said Ethan.

Joel furtively patted Quinn's outer jacket, looking for a gun, while Katrina remained off to the side. "I should shoot you right here, but I think we'll do this in a more civil way," said Ethan.

"Take his gun," he ordered Joel. Joel obeyed and found Quinn's .32 caliber in his breast pocket. Joel reached in and pulled it out.

"Throw the gun off to the side."

"I'm sorry, Mr. Chase," Joel said as he tossed the pistol into the corner of the gallery 20 feet away.

"Let's take a walk out to the truck in the back alley, Quinn!" Ethan said with a sarcastic smile. "Then we'll take a little ride....Move!"

As Quinn began to walk, Ethan kept his Luger trained at the small of Quinn's back. Suddenly the lights in the gallery went out...all was dark! Katrina had found the main junction switch and flipped it, cutting out all light to the building. Quinn fell to the ground and crawled on his stomach to the far side wall.

"Quinn, you bastard…where the hell are you?" yelled Ethan.

Quinn didn't say a word, but carefully reached down to his left ankle where his Derringer was holstered. He undid the safety strap and silently pulled the small Derringer out. Joel had now located the electric junction box and flipped the switch back on again. Quinn found cover behind a desk in the corner. He was armed now, but with a small gun that only had two loaded shots.

Ethan couldn't see Quinn but pointed the Luger in Quinn's direction.

"Quinn, run!" yelled Katrina. She rushed at Ethan, grabbing his extended shooting arm. A round went off and almost hit Quinn.

"Bitch!" Ethan yelled as he stumbled. Then he backhanded Katrina hard across her face with his pistol. She cried out and fell to the ground, blood streaming from her mouth. Quinn then emerged from behind the large picture and pointed the loaded Derringer at Ethan. The two men faced off 10 feet away from each other in the large gallery room.

"Drop it! It's over," yelled Quinn.

Ethan raised his gun again, pointing the loaded 9mm German Luger at Quinn. "It's just beginning!" yelled Ethan as he pulled the trigger and shot Quinn in his right shoulder. Quinn winced with pain and fell to the ground while squeezing off a round. The small Derringer came loose from his hand and bounced several times across the gallery floor out of Quinn's reach.

But the .32 caliber bullet from the Derringer struck Ethan below his left knee. Ethan fell to the ground, gripping his knee in pain. "You son-of-a-bitch!" Ethan yelled, obviously in pain. Katrina screamed.

In what seemed like only a second or two, Ethan recovered and stood up on his feet with a pained look on his face; the Luger dangling from his right hand…he pointed the pistol again at Quinn who was still on the ground. "You know, Quinn, you're so inadequate a foe this almost seems unfair. Well, you didn't suspect me, so I guess I should show some gratitude. I'll kill you here instead of making you suffer. Been fun knowing you, rummy!" said Ethan as he started to pull the trigger.

Then a popping noise was heard and Ethan's facial expression quickly changed. He took on a look of sudden surprise, and his firing arm lowered as he turned slowly to his right. When Ethan had almost completely turned to look behind him, he saw Joel holding Quinn's .32 caliber; smoke oozing out from the barrel.

Katrina screamed again as she saw a large red blotch expanding on the back of Ethan's shirt where Joel had shot him. Ethan mumbled something…but he couldn't get the words out. His body fell forward like a statue tipped from the top. He had a blank expression as he fell to the ground face forward. Ethan Clark took his last breath well before his body hit the ground. The man who was The Merchant, who had controlled this art scam from nearly the start and had eliminated just about everyone who got in his way, had met a similar end.

Now Joel, Katrina, and Quinn just stared at one another in the lobby of the gallery. Quinn spoke first. "You two have to get the hell out of here now…the police will be here soon! I'll make a story up…I'll tell them I came upon him trying to steal your art and he pulled a gun on me. He shot me, and then I shot him in self-defense. I'll deal with the consequences. As to the espionage, Joel," said Quinn, "both of you must leave Santa Fe. I can wait a few days…maybe a week or so before I have to tell the authorities… but eventually I'll have to talk."

"What about us, Quinn?" asked Katrina. "I want to be with you!" she said.

Quinn looked at the ground, and then back at the precious, fragile girl he had come to love. "Katrina you'll always have a special place in my heart. And we'll see each other again someday, I promise you that. But you deserve better than to be tied down to a guy like me. I would only cause you problems here. And you can't stay here now…these people won't understand and sympathize with you and your uncle. Once they find out, you'll be arrested…and even though you did it for a good reason—to save your family—you'll be put in jail for the rest of your lives, shot, or hung. Get on that train headed to the west coast, get on a ship or plane to South America…go anywhere else you'll be safe. Just live! You can't do that here now. And your relative up on The Hill…take him with you. Just go!"

"Katrina, he's right. We must leave now!" Joel said. "How can I ever thank you?" Joel asked, as the tears poured down Katrina's cheeks.

"You just saved my life," said Quinn to the frail looking smaller man. "That's thanks enough. Now there's very little time. Gather up the belongings and paintings you want. You won't be able to ever return here! Hurry!" said Quinn.

"There is one thing," said Joel. "I want you to keep this as a token of our association over the last several years. It's a token of my gratitude," said Joel. "I was going to take this and sell it, Mr. Chase. But as someone who appreciates fine art…I can't. People gave up their lives for this…I know you'll appreciate it and take care of it," he said.

With that, Joel walked over to a large armoire against one of the gallery walls and pressed a hidden button on the side of the furniture. A drawer at the bottom of the armoire popped open. Joel took out what appeared to be a print wrapped in parchment paper and walked over to Quinn. "Open this," Joel said as he handed the package to Quinn.

Quinn took the 3 by 3, covered canvas and slowly removed the parchment paper. Underneath was a bluish-grey pastel of five young ballerinas moving as they performed their dance at various points of their performance. The painting was a beautiful blend of style, color, grace, and motion. The last name of the artist, "Degas" appeared in the bottom right corner of the painting. "My God!" said Quinn as he stared at the painting. "It's the *Five Dancing Women,* by Edgar Degas. What a remarkable piece of artwork. You've had it all along!"

CHAPTER LXI

There was a lengthy investigation into what happened at the Finebaum Gallery that night; and the "un-American" activities of nearly everyone involved. Quinn was placed on suspension for several months and underwent thorough questioning again from Lt. Frank Huff and the FBI. Joel and Katrina escaped after being smuggled as "cargo" onto an ocean liner out of Los Angeles to South America. They made it to the Chilean port of Valparaiso and eventually made their way to the Island of Barbados, off the coast of Venezuela.

Any and all paintings that were smuggled into Santa Fe as Degenerate Art in public buildings, including those still at the Finebaum Gallery and at City Hall, were confiscated by the FBI. But they had no knowledge about the painting Quinn had acquired from Joel; or about those he was about to acquire, care of Marika Kraus.

Following Joel's request, Quinn held onto *Five Dancing Women*. In the end, Quinn was exonerated from any wrongdoing and was not charged with the shooting of Ethan Clark. He walked out of the police department, after all was said and done, a free man. Although free in the legal sense, Quinn's conscience would not let him rest. Quinn knew he had several tasks ahead of him to make things right. He started by going to Marika's hideaway vault above Dempsey's drugstore. Quinn found the letter she had prepared for him and opened the small safe there. In that room, he found the two small paintings by Jean Metzinger which were an example of the Cubist method. He now had all three works of art that Laszlo Tibor had hired him to find.

"Laszlo," or Vitali, was now safely back in Russia where he was returned as the result of a secret "spy for spy" exchange, with our ally The Soviet Union. Quinn however had more work to do. He carefully read the instructions Marika left for him. He took the money in the envelope from her safe and found with the paintings, and he purchased a train ticket to Chicago.

While the war with Germany was finished in early May, and marked by V-E Day and raucous celebrations on May 8, 1945, most of Europe was destroyed and would require the next 30 to 40 years to rebuild. The war took its toll on the people and cities of Europe, but also caused an incredible impact on the soldiers and citizens of the USA. President Franklin D. Roosevelt didn't live to witness the unconditional surrender of Germany or Japan. He had served in office as President and as Commander in Chief for a record four terms, beginning in 1933. Although he was perhaps the most important leader of WWII, his health had been in decline for some time, and he died unexpectedly while still in office on April 12, 1945…only a few short weeks before Germany surrendered.

It was not lost on President Roosevelt before his untimely death that much of Europe's priceless art had either been stolen, hidden, or destroyed during the war. As the war in Europe was winding down, Roosevelt approved the actual creation of an actual military unit, nicknamed the "Monuments Men." This specialized small group of mostly art historians, were handpicked to travel throughout Germany and other occupied countries in Europe in an attempt to search and locate art that had been stolen by the Nazis. At the end of the war in Europe, many priceless works of art were recovered in caves, abandoned buildings, and salt mines by The Monuments Men.

The Allies had defeated Nazi Germany without the need of an atomic bomb, but as it turned out, even though they were defeated in practical terms, the Japanese refused to surrender and continued to fight on. In Europe though, following the surrender of Germany the difficult and complex job of reconstruction began. One of the first tasks of the Allies was bringing those who had committed war crimes and crimes against humanity - to justice. The Nuremberg Trials became known as the main public trials where the most serious Nazi criminals faced justice for their actions during the war.

Werner Heisenberg and 10 of the top German scientists were not put on trial for their scientific work for Nazi Germany. However, they were captured by the British Special Operations "T-Force," and were sent to a special prison in England, near Cambridge, named Farm Hall. Here, they were kept by the British in detention, but not in prison cells. They lived in a large estate home and they were allowed to freely associate with one another. The rationale behind this was the British wanted to find out how advanced the Nazi atomic research was at the end of the war. Most interaction and discussion between the German scientists was secretly recorded. Of most concern to the Allies was…How close did the Nazi's actually come to building an atomic weapon?

"Werner, have you seen the newspaper today?" Otto Hahn, a German chemist and scientist also interred at Farm Hall, asked Heisenberg on August 6, 1945, "This article says the Allies have dropped an atomic bomb on Japan."

"Hiroshima, Japan!" exclaimed Otto Hahn. "I don't believe it," said Heisenberg.

"Good Lord, Werner!" said another captured German physicist, Carl Friedrich von Weizsacker. "It looks like building an atomic weapon was possible after all."

"Let me see the newspaper," said Heisenberg. "It's just not possible, Carl! The Americans weren't that far ahead of us in research and development! They had the same problems with an atomic reaction that we had... the processing of enriched uranium. The British are playing a trick on us... they're playing with our minds. This can't be true!" said Heisenberg.

"What if it is true Werner? What if these reports are true? How do you feel about the Americans developing this technology, when we couldn't?" proffered Hahn.

"I try not to think about such things, Hahn, and if such thoughts do enter my mind...certainly I do not wish to openly discuss them. My objective was to produce atomic energy for civil use and peaceful purposes. I'm glad we never built a bomb or other device to be used for destruction. But these news articles are not true, I tell you! It would take thousands of people working every hour of every day for years...and an incredible amount of money to build a reactor to even conduct a test for such a reaction. This is nonsense, Hahn. Pure fantasy!" said Heisenberg.

CHAPTER LXII

It took him 10 days in all and two long-distance, otherwise dull, train rides…but he brought the three works of art back to the Volks Galleria on Chicago's Northside. Quinn knew these paintings would fetch an untold amount of money…probably in South America or maybe even Asia. But he owed it to Marika as well as the victims who had their artwork stolen right before their eyes, losing their personal property, homes, and most likely their lives in some Nazi concentration camp. He simply smiled and handed the pastel and paintings over to the curator with the letter Marika had written. The curator, Ms. Harper, nearly fell over when she saw the artwork. A few seconds later she broke down in tears when she read the letter. "Mr. Chase, the major museums of Europe and Metropolitan Art Societies of Chicago and New York will pay you a reward for these paintings. It will take some time, but you're entitled to a reward for returning these priceless paintings. I promise you you'll get it…I won't rest until you do. It will be substantial too," she said.

"That's not why I brought these here," Quinn replied.

Quinn spent the night in Chicago, attending a show at the famous Conga Room, and then he boarded the train for the long ride back to Albuquerque in the morning. As the train left the station bound for the West, Quinn thought, *I've honored the wishes of a Nazi spy. She was an enemy of my country…but all in all she was one of the most honest people I've ever known, dammit!*

When Quinn returned from Chicago, he was lost, and found himself spending more and more time in Albuquerque, and at his old hangout, The 9:15. Despite the herculean efforts he had made for others and his country, he was basically right where he was four years ago—middle-aged, depressed, and alone. The two woman he had emotional connections with were gone for good. So now, as far as Quinn was concerned the first order of business for him was simply to …drink more bourbon.

The police department in Santa Fe had made an offer to him to start work again as a detective. Amazingly it was Lt. Frank Huff who was the driving force who pushed to have Quinn's badge reinstated. Huff even said, "I have to admit Chase, you're one hell of a detective! I'd be honored to work with you!" So at least there was some bright spot on the horizon. But before Quinn could even consider joining any police force again – he knew he still had several tasks to perform. If his plan worked he might actually find peace in his life, and things might get back to normal. But if he failed…Quinn probably wouldn't ever have much of a life or a future and he knew it.

CHAPTER LXIII

Quinn went to his former office on Cerillos Road to clean his desk out and get his personal effects. He had an odd feeling walking into the building where he and Ethan had spent so much time together, when in the end it turned out he didn't really know his partner at all. He put all of his belongings and the pictures on the walls in two boxes and brought them out to his new Buick placing them in the backseat. The weather was strange for a day in the month of November—the sun shined brightly. Quinn had received a sizable reward for returning the three paintings by Metzinger and Degas; a $6,500 certified check.. This was an enormous sum of money in 1945. *Hell, I don't have any retirement from the police department*, Quinn thought. *This could be my retirement!* Then he thought again, *No, it wouldn't be right.*

He was preparing to move back to Albuquerque, so he thought he'd take a sentimental drive around Santa Fe. With all that had gone down the last few months, Quinn knew he needed time and space to think things through.

First, he drove to the Plaza. The streets surrounding the plaza were mainly cobblestone. He parked and walked to the east side facing the empty storefront that used to be Joel and Katrina's art gallery. *I wonder where they are now? I hope they're safe. Maybe I'll get a letter from her someday.*

The overhead sign had been removed. The place was now empty, and masking tape crisscrossed the front window. He walked over and faced the large Cathedral of St. Francis of Assisi on the east side. The imposing Catholic church was constructed in the late 1800s with the large sand stones from a nearby quarry. It was an incredible monument to see, even to Quinn who wasn't particularly religious. He wasn't sure when he'd be back again. He knew he would miss the quaint adobe architecture and the unique people of this small city. He also knew there were a couple of things he had to do before getting on the road back home—Albuquerque.

It was about one in the afternoon. He drove up Cordova Street to the community center where most days Skitts Jones could be found card-sharkin'. He parked in the lot outside and walked in. It was quiet…a few people sitting around in the front room listening to the various programs on the radio. Today they featured Edgar Bergen the ventriloquist with sidekick Charlie McCarthy. This was a comedy act and the act was popular at the time. Then there was slow, ballad-type music for a lazy day at the center. Quinn could hear a few loud voices emanating from the back card room however, when he walked in. It seemed like the card games were just getting started. He walked into the backroom where the card tables were set up, and there, in the far left corner, was the unmistakable Fedora and noticeable laugh of Skitts Jones. "You boys can try your best today…but I got a feelin'!" laughed Skitts as he shuffled the deck and started to deal.

Quinn approached the table from the side while drawing looks from other players in the room. "Hey, I hear that Skitts Jones is a real sucker for somebody who knows how to bluff!" Quinn said with a raised voice.

Skitts' eyebrows shot up. "Well, I hear that Detective Chase puts his money where his mouth is. And he's gonna' sit right down here and give us all a lesson on the finer points of poker!" laughed Skitts. "What's goin' on detective?"

"Life's been interesting, Skitts. I was just wonderin' if you had a few minutes. I won't take your whole afternoon up."

"I wouldn't disrupt my activities for just anyone, but for you, detective…I think I can spare some time," he said while laughing again.

They left the center and walked to Clifton Park where they had talked before. "So what do I owe the honor of this visit to?" Skitts asked.

"I just wanted to say thanks for all your information and help," said Quinn. "Remember you tipped me off about The Merchant?"

"Oh, yeah, he was supposedly the dude running the art smuggling around here," replied Skitts.

"You're not gonna believe this…it turns out The Merchant was my former partner at our PI firm. He was workin' for the Nazis the entire time. It didn't end well for him," said Quinn.

"Boy, I bet those paintings are worth lots of money," said Skitts.

"Yeah…but they're contraband," said Quinn. "What's more, the art was taken from Jewish families overseas who probably made the ultimate sacrifice themselves in the end. The government and everybody and his brother is tryin' to track these paintings down. Well, I went to Chicago and turned over a couple of paintings I had. It was the right thing to do, and they gave me a reward. I think it's only right I share some of it with you," said Quinn.

"Detective your always full of surprises, but Skitts definitely believes in the concept of sharing!"

"Thanks for your helpful tips during the case," Quinn said as he placed three $100 bills in Skitt's shirt pocket. "I'm leavin' town soon, and I think

I'm gonna try another line of work," said Quinn. "This type of work wears on you…know what I mean?"

"I can imagine," said Skitts.

The two men talked for a few more minutes while walking back to Quinn's car. Skitts thanked Quinn, and the two shook hands and said their goodbyes. Quinn's parting words were, "If you come back to Albuquerque, you'll find me at The 9:15. Stop in some time, and we'll have a few. I'll be sitting at the south end. It'll be my treat."

"Detective, you know I owe you one, or two! You take care of yourself!" said Skitts as he turned to walk back into the building. Quinn got into his newly acquired car and drove out knowing he had one more thing to do before he could leave Santa Fe.

He drove south down several streets hoping to find Dixie and Haley. He figured maybe he'd drive down to the river area and look for them. He was headed south down St. Francis Drive when he saw Dixie off on the left side of the street. She was looking through some odds and ends that had been dumped in a vacant lot there. Haley was standing off to the side. Quinn pulled over to the side of the road, got out, and approached the two.

"Hi, Quinn," Dixie finally said, looking up with a smile. Haley smiled and waved to him.

"I was hoping to find you two. How about joining me for a little ride? There's something I want to show you," Quinn said.

"What is it?" she asked.

"Well, I'll show you. Come on…we won't be that long. You two sit in the back. I'll bring you right back here when we're done."

The mother and daughter both had a worn-down and disheveled look about them as though they'd been out in the elements for some time.

Haley asked, "Are we gonna ride in that car, mommy?"

Dixie nodded and guided her daughter to the back door of Quinn's new 1945 Buick. The two of them got in the backseat. They started out and drove for about three miles towards the west side of town. The paved road turned to a dirt road. The area was just open land with no buildings of any kind in sight. Finally, they saw a sign on the right side of the road that read Country Estates.

"What's this?" asked Dixie.

"New homes being built for the returning soldiers and their families," Quinn answered. The dirt street they drove down had small lots on both sides with construction equipment and piles of stacked wood. Construction on many homes had already started. There was one small four-room house on one of the lots that was almost complete. Quinn drove down the street almost to the very end, then stopped his car in front of one of the barren dirt lots. There were some 2x4's stacked up in the center and a cement mixer on the lot.

Quinn turned around and looked at both of them in his back seat. "Well, what do you think?" he asked.

Dixie had a perplexed look. "Think about what?"

"This is gonna' be the site of your new home, Dixie. It's for both of you. You're gonna' have a house to live in. Move here from the river and start a new life. You're gonna' sleep in your own beds at night…that have sheets! I came into some money recently and worked a deal out with Mr. Harris, the developer of these homes, and Santa Fe Savings and Loan. I want you two to live here and own it. You deserve a new start.

It was as if Dixie had been placed in sudden shock. She and Haley both stared out the window of Quinn's car at the basic framework of the small home before them. For over a minute Dixie didn't say a word and barely even blinked. Then, tears welled up in Dixie's eyes and began to stream down her face.

CHAPTER LXIV

Unlike Santa Fe, Albuquerque had a barren and cold look in November of 1945. But by all reasonable expectations, Quinn should have still been riding a positive wave of emotion. World War II was over, and the Allies had won two great victories on different sides of the world. Hundreds of thousands of war veterans were coming home after sacrificing nearly everything in their hard-fought victories over Germany and Japan. Quinn had nearly singlehandedly solved the Degenerate Art ring in Santa Fe and became a hero in the process. The Santa Fe Police Department had made an employment offer to Quinn to work again as a detective. Quinn was finally recognized for his accomplishments. And he had just separated himself from his personal savings by performing a selfless act for two people he barely knew. And yet he wasn't done yet. He had one more thing to do before he could ever work on any police force again.

Quinn went to The 9:15 just after noon that day. He ordered two Old Fashioned's each with double shots of bourbon. He knew he was ready as he borrowed some mouthwash to cover the scent of the booze. At about 2:00 p.m. he left the bar and drove to the Albuquerque Police Department, about two miles away. There was virtually no one in the lobby. He knew where he was going, so he walked up the staircase to the third floor. He headed for the office of Police Chief, Brock Garrett.

"Hello, my name is Quinn Chase…I'm a former detective and I used to be on the APD. I'm an old friend of Chief Garrett," Quinn said to the new secretary. "I just thought I'd stop in and say hello…I'm sure he'll be interested in seeing me."

"It depends if he has the time. Otherwise you'll have to make an appointment and come back!" said the secretary. She walked into Garrett's office and closed the door.

After being informed Quinn Chase was outside, Garrett replied, "Quinn Chase…he's still around?" About two minutes later after deciding what to do, the door to the chief's office opened and Garrett walked out smiling. "Well, I'll be damned! If it isn't one of my favorite detectives, Quinn Chase! Damnya's, Quinn! What the hell have you been up to the last four years?" Garrett said with a broad grin while extending his hand. "We've been worried about you and Ethan Clark! We've been hoping we'd hear something sometime!"

Quinn displayed a wry smile as he shook Garrett's hand, but offered only a short answer. "I've been on a real journey, chief!"

"Hell, it's great to see you!" said Garrett. "Come on in here, have some coffee, or a belt of whiskey! Fill me in on your adventures!"

"Thanks, chief, I was hoping you would have a few minutes," Quinn said as he walked from the visitor's couch in the outer office. "I've got so much to share with you!" said Quinn.

They both looked at one another and laughed as Quinn displayed the widest smile he could muster. He walked into the chief's office, a folder under his left arm in which Quinn carried a typed confession for the chief to sign. It was about the events from four years ago. The document essentially read that Brock Garrett, along with high-ranking members of the

US Army, sent Quinn and Ethan Clark on a fraudulent, near–suicide mission without informing either man or gaining either man's consent. Once signed, the confession would probably end Garrett's career as Chief of Police and might even put him behind bars. At the very least this injustice would be exposed. Concealed in Quinn's pocket was his small Derringer. The small handgun was fully loaded with two .32 caliber bullets; one in each chamber. The way Quinn viewed the situation was that for the good of the police force, and for the country, he had to act. If Garrett wouldn't sign the confession, Quinn would never have a better opportunity to set things straight than now. If Garrett wouldn't sign the confession, Quinn knew instead of beginning a new job and new life – he'd be going to jail. But in Quinn's mind the act would be justified and he would have done the right thing. He would meet and sort the details out with God at a later time, and figured he would be forgiven. It would be a fitting conclusion to this tragic chapter of his life. And in the overall scheme of things on that day in the life of a true detective…that's all that mattered to Quinn.

EPILOGUE

In 2010…nearly 70 years after the end of WWII and during a routine border check and crossing between Switzerland and Germany, an interesting event took place. An elderly man in his late 70s was crossing the border from Switzerland into Germany by train. Customs officers checking passports and other documents later described the man as particularly nervous when they inspected his passport and credentials. This caused the customs officers to become suspicious. They searched the man and found about 5,000 Euros (equivalent of $9,000) in cash. Most of the man's cash was crisp new bills, which made the customs officials even more suspicious. Upon further inspection they found that the man was sort of a mystery himself as they could not find his name in any government database. The man had never held a documented job. He had never paid taxes. Even stranger, he was not registered in the German national healthcare database. His name did not appear in the phone book, and he had no working phone. It was later discovered that he did not even own a television set. The man turned out to be a recluse with no personal or cultural associations with any clubs, churches, or other organizations. The man was Cornelius Gurlitt. And he was the son of the famous WWII art dealer made mention of in this story—Hildebrand Gurlitt.

His identified profession was Art Collector. He had purchased an apartment in Munich, paid for in cash where he had lived alone since the 1960s. He had also purchased a home in Salzburg, Austria.

Following the "Border Incident," in 2012 local officials in Munich insisted on searching Cornelius Gurlitts' apartment. They were completely shocked to find 112 framed works of art and over 1,100 unframed watercolors, sketches, and oil paintings mostly from the 18th and 19th centuries inside. These works of art were painted by some of the most well-known artists. Cornelius Gurlitt had paintings by Henri Matisse, Marc Chagall, Pablo Picasso, Renoir, Gauguin, Van Gogh, and Gustav Klimt, Gustave Courbet, and Emil Nolde. The estimated value of Gurlitt's collection found in his Munich apartment was one billion Euros (approximately $2 billion USD). Gurlitt maintained these near-priceless paintings since his father Hildebrand died in the 1950s and passed the collection on to him. He referred to the artwork in his apartment as "his friends." More information came to light about this mysterious man. Though strange, Cornelius Gurlitt proved to be honest and straightforward. When questioned by the police or reporters, he didn't conceal a thing. It seemed that his only close contact or relationship during his adult life was with his sister Renate. She passed away in 2012. In the only interview he gave following the confiscation of his art treasure trove given to him by his father, Cornelius Gurlitt claimed that the last time he had watched TV was in 1963 and the last time he had seen a movie at a cinema was 1967. The interview was with *Der Spiegel* magazine in 2012.

The paintings were initially seized by local government authorities in Munich, but Germany's laws dealing with looted Nazi art from WWII were, and are still, complicated. Even if artwork is identified and proven to be "stolen" and taken during the Nazi era (commonly recognized from 1933 to 1945), the modern-day German law does not require immediate return of the artwork to the original owners unless they had made a claim within the 30-year statute of limitations, which expired in the mid-1970s. Since the majority of victims alive today related to the Holocaust were children in the early 1940s, it is highly unlikely they were knowledgeable enough about their parents' private collections looted during the Holocaust, or about German law to make claims later. So most WWII survivors and descendants did not make claims during the statute of limitations period; and so now they must initiate complex and expensive civil lawsuits to attempt to reclaim their families' stolen artwork from a different era.

Cornelius Gurlitt had heart surgery in 2012 and passed away in May of 2014. He did make out a will where he directed various works of art in his possession to be returned to their original owners. The bitter irony of it all is that the oil paintings, sketches, and watercolors found in Gurlitt's Munich apartment and home in Salzburg, Austria, have not been dispersed to date according to his will, which has been contested. The artwork he kept for so many years is currently held in a warehouse outside Munich, to undergo cleaning and restoration. The eventual fate of the pieces remains undetermined. The man who was given these masterpieces by his father after WWII told *Der Spiegel,* "I had no part in taking them [artwork], only in maintaining them." Cornelius Gurlitt also claimed during his interview that losing the paintings "was a greater loss to me than losing my parents or sister." An insight into one man's bizarre life, and a partial answer as to what happened to some of the world's great works of art - resulting from the human tragedy we collectively name *The Holocaust.*

AUTHOR'S NOTE

Although most of the historical accounts in this story are accurate, the story is fictional. During the Second World War, great security efforts were made to conceal all activity at the site of America's atomic research, "The Hill" (later to officially be named Los Alamos National Laboratories) at Los Alamos, New Mexico. Although it is well accepted that foreign espionage activity was conducted by the Soviet Union (our ally during WWII) and that information the Soviets obtained from Klaus Fuchs, Ted Hall, and Harry Gold greatly assisted the Soviets with their nuclear development program, no tangible evidence exists of espionage activity by Nazi Germany or Japan at Los Alamos. To this author's best knowledge, there is no evidence that local civilians attempted to assist Nazi Germany with espionage at Los Alamos.

Although both Japan and Germany had research facilities, as described in this story, their programs were inferior and ineffective with regards to the actual development of an atomic weapon. Also, the foreign intelligence (spy) programs of Germany and Japan, if even attempted, were ineffective in piercing the security of Los Alamos. Any references or statements in this story with regards to Nazi Germany actually obtaining nuclear "secrets" from Los Alamos specifically or any other source in New Mexico are untrue and fictional. This author in no way attempts to disparage the security efforts made by military intelligence and those of law enforcement during this time.

Some further explanation regarding the portrait which is an important part of this story is necessary. Around 1875, Edgar Degas, the French Impressionist painter, created his pastel, *Five Dancing Women… (Ballerinas)*. The work of art had several owners, the last documented owner being Baron Mór Lipót Herzog of Hungary prior to the Second World War, who was an art collector and owner of the famous Herzog Art Collection. In this story, this pastel painting was smuggled to and hidden in Santa Fe, New Mexico. In reality however, the *Five Dancing Women… (Ballerinas)* by Degas has not been seen and remains unaccounted for since the Nazis confiscated most of the Herzog Collection from Hungary in 1944. This pastel is widely considered among the *Top 10 Most Wanted Missing Art Works from WWII*. While there have been alleged sightings of the painting since 1944, the actual whereabouts of *Five Dancing Women… (Ballerinas)* by Edgar Degas is unknown to this day. It remains an unsolved mystery from the Second World War.

ABOUT THE AUTHOR

Efren O'brien has had a keen interest in US history and the history of WWII since he was in grade school. O'brien's father was a WWII veteran who was actively involved in the European Theatre in 1944 and 1945. Also as an admirer of modern art, a resident of New Mexico and a visitor to Los Alamos National Laboratories, O'brien gained the familiarity and inspiration for this story. This is Efren O'brien's second historical fiction novel. His first published novel is *The Deserving*.